Terry Taylor was born in Lancashire in 1950 and attended both primary and grammar schools in Blackpool. He has a degree in engineering and has spent most of his working life on the Continent involved in the aerospace industry. He is currently based in Munich but makes frequent visits to Lancashire and London. *Kicking Around* is his first novel.

KICKING AROUND

Terry Taylor

BLACK SWAN

KICKING AROUND
A BLACK SWAN BOOK : 0 552 99809 5

First publication in Great Britain

PRINTING HISTORY
Black Swan edition published 1999

Set in 10½pt Melior by
County Typesetters, Margate, Kent

Black Swan Books are published by Transworld Publishers Ltd,
61–63 Uxbridge Road, London W5 5SA,
in Australia by Transworld Publishers (Australia) Pty Ltd,
15–25 Helles Avenue, Moorebank, NSW 2170,
and in New Zealand by Transworld Publishers (NZ) Ltd,
3 William Pickering Drive, Albany, Auckland.

Reproduced, printed and bound in Great Britain by
Cox & Wyman Ltd, Reading, Berks.

To Ellen and Bill,
each for different reasons.

CONTENTS

PART 1

The Rise and Fall of a Right-Footed Outside Left

1

The first time you see human blood in any quantity, it leaves an impression on you. This impression gains real depth and permanence, if the stuff in question happens to be your own.

I tottered down the pathway towards the door of number fourteen, George Avenue, my clothes ripped, my elbows and knees grazed and my nose pumping gore. I might have been staggering away from a particularly hotly contested corner of Stalingrad. Wailing like an air-raid siren, I was even supplying my own sound effects. But more as precaution really, because deep down I was surprised and interested to note that it didn't hurt at all. Shock, I suppose.

Tibby was sitting by the door in front of three empty milk bottles, arranged exactly like a set of wickets. He was sideways on with his head erect and his paws at middle and leg, as if he expected me to deliver him an off-break. All the way down the path he stared at me with what I took to be real concern, but was in fact just feline intensity. As I drew level, he concluded I wasn't going to stroke him, torment him, or get him something to eat, so promptly lost interest. It was a revealing moment. Until then, I had thought of Tibby as an only slightly junior partner in a very significant relationship – the sort that their respective owners shared with Flicka, Rin Tin Tin and Lassie. Lassie would have leapt over the gate, cantered off down George Avenue and returned minutes later with a paediatric surgeon clamped between her teeth by the seat of the pants. Tibby narrowed his eyes, lifted his left foot and began to lick his paw as if it were made of best butter. The heartless nonchalance of it set me bawling with renewed vigour.

Which seemed to crank some internal pump. Blood meandered in little parallel tributaries down my face and soaked into my shirt. It dripped onto my grey woolly socks, concertinaed in wrinkles around my ankles, and left huge crimson blobs on my scuffed and battered shoes. It smeared over the door knocker and stained-glass, heavy-leaded window as if I had been up-ended and squirted at my own home. How long could I sustain this sort of leakage?

I heard feet thumping down the narrow stairs, and the door opened to reveal my elder brother Jim, running a comb through lavishly Brylcreemed hair. He was evidently annoyed at being disturbed. Judging by his expression and former location, probably from what Father Ryan called self-abuse. At thirteen, it was currently his most consuming hobby. He was always taunting me to try it, then hooting derisively because my little worm wouldn't stand up.

At the sight of war-torn me, the irritation drained from his face with the colour. The latter ended up a sort of olive hue, and the former took on the lines of someone who suspects the anaesthetic is beginning to wear off in the middle of his vasectomy.

'Tim. Oh my God . . .' he croaked.

Up until then, I had held out vague hopes that someone would tell me again to stop being a baby, it was only a scratch. Shortly after my nose had collided with the kerb of George Avenue, I had registered the look of gaping horror in Tesser Hallam's NH-bespectacled eyes, or rather eye, he being one of the legion of children at that time condemned to wearing glasses with one lens blanked off by sticking-plaster. It would never have occurred to any of us to ask why. I'm not sure I know now.

'It's only a scratch, Tim,' had been Tesser's chummy

exhortation. Then, after a few seconds of unchecked artery-sluicing, giving away the enormity of it with a feeble, lip-trembling protest. 'It weren't me.'

'What'll Dad say?' Jim asked now, real fear in his voice.

When it came to parental authority, we were living in a period which was decidedly Old Testament. Our household frequently reverberated to my father's thunderous commands. 'Don't slouch!' 'Fetch my cuff-links!' 'Don't gulp your food!' 'Stop licking your bollocks!' Fortunately this latter was invariably aimed at Tibby, who would pause briefly, narrow his eyes warily, then throw his leg back over his shoulder and continue with long, loving strokes of his head.

I began to feel faint.

'Mum and Dad are out,' he whimpered, as if I were a dustman after his Christmas tip. 'So's Nonnie,' he added miserably. This was my sister, whose real name was Yvonne. He was trying desperately to tear his eyes away from my nose but not quite succeeding. 'So's John!' His voice rose woefully as he descended through the family hierarchy.

For one wild moment, I thought he was going to slam the door, so avoiding any risk of incrimination. But after a second's thought he led me into what we would never in a million years have dreamt of calling the lounge, but rather the front room. Through a slowly intensifying crimson film, I surveyed the walnut writing-bureau that no-one ever wrote at, the mahogany dining-table that nobody dined at, the three-piece suite with black vinyl trim and splayed wooden metal-tipped legs that very rarely got sat on, and the china cabinet displaying decades of family porcelain, there being no silver, that nobody ever ate off. God alone knew what had possessed him to bring me in here. Possibly, since it was used so rarely, some lunatic sense of 'occasion'.

We stared at each other, Jim panting, eyes wide. I continued to drip on faithfully. Some of the great blobs managed to miss me, my clothes and my shoes, and pat resoundingly onto the carpet that never got trodden on. Gaudy and florid, it contained every shade of every colour in creation except blood red.

'Oh, no!' Jim shrieked, nearing hysteria now. 'What'll Mum say!'

He whimpered and tried to manoeuvre me so that I bled over a dark patch. Then he desperately cupped his hands and made to catch the drops as they fell. Looking around for somewhere to dispose of my life's blood, and seeing nothing of which even the legitimate use didn't entail desecration, he put his bloody hands to his lips and licked vigorously. I became aware he wasn't handling this well.

Perhaps seeing my accusing look, his panic subsided slightly. He thrust back my head so that most of the blood trickled down inside my shirt and out of harm's way, then ushered me into the bathroom. In our pre-war house, this was thoughtfully positioned downstairs next to the kitchen-dining-room. He laid me down on the floor, my head on a bath mat, drenched a towel in warm water at the wash-basin and placed it over my nose. In only a slightly shaky voice, he asked me what had happened.

'I was goadkeeper,' I told him, 'Tesser Haddam toog a benaldy. The gerb banged by dose.' The passive voice was instinctive, intended to establish my complete innocence from the outset whilst cunningly throwing suspicion on the kerb.

Epic sporting clashes were of course nothing foreign to George Avenue. The printed warnings headed POLICE NOTICE pasted on all prominent expanses of brickwork – along with a chalked set of goalposts – reminded you that according to clause such and such, paragraph whatever of the Road Traffic Act of sometime or other, the pursuance of sporting activities and ball games on the public highway was STRICTLY PROHIBITED. But the Road Traffic Act was enforced by an occasional solitary bobby on a bike. As yet, only the Hardmans at thirty-seven, and the Hatches at forty-four had cars, which left quite a sizeable, if irregular-shaped expanse of playing area. And a couple of cast-iron green lampposts made an ideal set of goals. Only the playing surface was somewhat unforgiving of human frailty.

'Am I going do die?' I asked him, gazing upwards into features which, if you took away the half-jar of Brylcreem and the beginnings of an Elvis Presley quiff, and added a lot of freckles, could have been my own.

'Yes,' he said at length. 'Unless I can get help, you'll bleed to death.'

'The Domsons at dwendy-doo have a delephone!' I blurted, suddenly motivated to innovative thought. 'Dial dine, dine, dine!'

He considered, then nodded, tight-lipped. As he rose to go I bawled, 'Don't leave be!'

He came back and crouched again, looking down, with mild horror, not at me but at the blood-soaked mat. He grabbed the back of my head and swung me round through a half-circle, releasing my skull with a clunk onto the lino beneath the washbasin.

'Think of something else,' he said, then, with sudden inspiration, 'think of your Easter egg.

'Just a minute,' he added brightly, then left me and returned seconds later with the Easter egg under his arm. Flipping down the lid of the lavatory, he perched the egg on top, where I could see it clearly, if I just tilted my head back agonizingly and risked choking on my own blood. This I did.

He paused at the door and waved. I moved my eyes, but not my head. Then he was gone.

I was horribly alone. The cistern cupboard began emitting the sinister gurgles and belches, *Quatermass and the Pit*-like, which made me give it a wide berth unless accompanied. For the same reason, I always insisted on having the bathroom door open when sitting on the loo. Yes, even at mealtimes. *Especially* at mealtimes, since the rest of them were the ones who insisted on watching *Quatermass* anyway.

Shock began to fade and pain set in. This was it. I was dying, just like Jim had said. Panic stampeded a herd of frenzied thoughts through my mind.

I imagined my father's face with eyes narrowed and tongue sideways protruding between tight lips. This was the pose he struck when wildly administering flathanders, sometimes so indiscriminately that even my mother ducked. I thought of Eddie Hopkinson, now left to soldier on keeping goal for England for another decade, my plans to succeed him cruelly thwarted by Tesser Hallam's perfectly placed penalty. I contemplated life without a nose – the nicknames at school! My fallback career – to become a brilliant dancing comic and musician – now in ruins. 'Britain's answer to Danny Kaye,' I had told them. My dad had said he knew Britain's answer to Max Bygraves. 'Eh?' we had gabbled, 'Max Bygraves *is* British.' My dad had laughed darkly then farted (loudly), a real zipper, something the rest of us got clouted for. 'Oh Robert,' mum had said, 'how could you?' Prissy, but not quite keeping the tremolo out of her voice. 'Can you think of a better answer to Max Bygraves?' he had asked, face all innocence.

I was tormented by the splashes from a week's supply of long johns dripping heavily from the pulley over the bath. The towel went cold and congealed on my face. I could have sworn the cistern cupboard doors were slowly creaking open. My Easter egg began to seem just a piece of spheroid chocolate confectionery.

Suddenly, I was being lifted onto a canvas stretcher by two ambulance men, huge and incongruous in the tiny bathroom.

'It'll need a local,' one mused, lifting up the towelling and peering into my face. I shivered and prepared to face the music. This could only be something involving my father.

I remembered afterwards the resigned way in which he blew through his ginger moustache when I clamoured for the egg to be placed in my arms before being borne away to the ambulance; the rattling ride across town to the infirmary, in the background the earnest, exclusively quantitative enquiries from Jim about how much an ambulance could do, how many patients had died on the way to hospital, how many pints of blood did they think I'd lost; the pretty cadet nurse who pinched my nostrils with cotton wool as she tenderly brushed my fringe from my eyes, and the stern one with grey hair who pinched her own as she peeled off my shoes and socks and sampled the cheesy aroma of the grime between my toes. Only as the irritated young Asian in the white coat, having punctured my nose with a hypodermic the size of a portable refracting telescope, proceeded to push an evidently blunt needle and thread through it, did I falter. The idea that people could be darned like socks had never occurred to me. As he drew it through for the first time with a determined jerk, my eyes crossed stupidly in an attempt to focus in disbelief on the end of my own nose, and I lapsed into blissful unconsciousness.

2

'You'll be all right Armstrong, don't 'edd anything.'

Mr Adam's words echoed through my mind as I splashed into Lake Superior after Patsie Hunieghan and Edmundo Denato Pecchio. For a moment I lost them in the cascade of dirty foam thrown up by their boots, but Lake Superior was small for the time of year. After a dozen or so soggy strides I was through it and my feet were sucking and squelching their way into St Wilfred's penalty area.

Not that I really needed any encouragement to follow his bidding. I had anticipated making my début for the school team as goalkeeper, not outside left, and I don't think I had ever successfully headed a football in my life.

As I huddled into the little knot of figures gathering stickily in the goal-mouth, I glanced back down the length of the pitch. Flanked by two narrow parallel strips of sickly yellow grass, a great morass of bubbling black sludge stretched back to the minute and isolated figure of Frank Macnally in our goal. Frank was minute, principally because he was crouched down with his arms stretched out in front of him. This was how he had been given to understand goalkeepers stood when not otherwise engaged. Also, he was isolated because everyone else on the pitch formed a mob orbiting erratically within ten yards of the ball. The game as we played it was characterized by a sort of mobile scrummage which moved around the pitch pretty much the way that the cup moves around an Ouija board.

'Foul! Free kick St John's,' Mr Adam bellowed in *basso profundo* Lancastrian. He had one of those booming voices that people develop when they spend their lives shouting from touch-lines. He was our manager and coach, and for home games like this one our referee as well. During the week he doubled as my class teacher.

'Haw! Haw! Haw!' This came from Mr Thompson, coach for the opposition. He stood frustrated on the sidelines, one of a total crowd of three, and was attempting to laugh sarcastically at the top of his voice, no simple task. A couple of crows barked in emulation from the row of winter-stripped elms which lined one side of the pitch, leafless greasy black talons, clawing a cold blue sky.

'Michael Atherton, get over here and take this,' Mr Adam shouted.

A rotund figure, less muddied and a head taller than the rest, wobbled lazily towards him. Atherton was in the team for his momentum, or at least that percentage of it which he could transfer to a stationary football via a ponderous ten-yard charge and a wild swing of his boot.

'Just get it up in the air Atherton,' Mr Adam encouraged. 'Toe-end it if you have to.'

'THA'S REFEREE, NOT COACH JOHN ADAM,' bawled Mr Thompson, in a voice which might have issued forth from behind the clouds.

The ball arced through the air towards the goal-mouth. I say 'ball', but use the term in historical context. We were playing with what was colloquially known as a 'cassey', a vaguely spherical object of stitched leather sporting a huge scar of lacing down one side which, impacting at speed, could inflict wounds more devastating than shrapnel. In the mud and rain predominant on the Fylde coast, a cassey could gain up to six pounds in weight during the game, thereby taking on the power and proportions of a medieval siege weapon. Panic-stricken defenders and attackers fled alike in all directions.

All save one. Patsie Hunieghan strode forward majestically and rose to meet it like a man with a vision. It was a vision of about fifteen years hence actually, when footballs would be waterproofed by a coating of something polyunpronounceable, and a flighted ball into the centre could be met by an agile centre forward rising gracefully to snake it home with a gentle flick of head and shoulders.

A sickening squelchy thud ensued and Patsie dropped as if shot. There were gasps of concern from all sides.

Seconds later, he was propped between Edmundo and myself, knees bent, shoulders slumped, eyeballs slowly spiralling upwards towards the roof of his head. There was a perfect black circle on his forehead as if someone had blown a hole in it.

'Aye, well we'll call it half-time anyway,' Mr Adam said, taking a cursory look at him. He raised his whistle to his lips and his cheeks filled out. There was a sound like someone rattling a marble in a plastic cup and blowing on it at the same time. He looked at his whistle quizzically and said something brief and Icelandic to it, then called, 'Gather round St John's. Over here.'

'Over to me St Wilfred's, to me!' Something in Mr Thompson's tone managed to convey the impression that he was offering sanctuary from gross injustices.

The St John of the Cross under-eleven team rallied to its mentor, whose appearance as our referee differed in only one detail from his appearance as our teacher. The thick-soled suede brogues which in the classroom would complete his outfit of check sports jacket strategically patched with leather, thick brown cardigan over grey shirt and nondescript tie worn together with generously cut grey flannels, were replaced in the former case by an ancient pair of football boots, and his flannels were protected from the mud, not entirely successfully, by a pair of bicycle-clips. In both roles, as in any role, he carried under his arm a bicycle-pump, like a field marshal of the working classes, reflecting either a curious sense of values or a naturally distrustful nature.

He looked down on us through heavily-framed tortoiseshell glasses which almost obscured the craggy upper half of his face, and scratched in irritation at his blue sandpapery chops. Then, I would have guessed his age at marginally post-Cretaceous. He was probably about thirty-five.

'Nil–nil,' he growled. 'You lot look as much like scoring as . . . as that lot do and that's saying summat. Peachyo, will you stop fairying about wi' t'ball and hoof it.'

Mr Adam's philosophy of the game could be condensed into a few easily-remembered homilies. 'If in doubt, kick it out', 'Don't muck around, kick for ground' and the like, all aimed at encouraging frontal assault. He repeated one now to Edmundo.

'Only babies dribble!'

There were one or two titters. Edmundo was our ace exponent of the continental game. Beneath a muddy mask, his brown Latin eyes narrowed darkly.

We were joined by the other two spectators. Andy Malloy's presence wasn't strictly speaking voluntary since he was our reserve, but Miss Cocker, despite having a choice, never missed a game. She was the needlework and handicraft teacher and obviously these bracing Saturday excursions into the inclement Lancashire elements provided her life with a splash of – of what?

Colour? Then she must have been fond of combinations in shades of silage and chlorine. Anyway here she was, as always her generous motherly curves concealed in a grey gabardine buttoned to the neck, and wearing a headscarf in the style popularized by fleeing Polish refugees during the Second World War. On her feet were a pair of wellingtons big enough for her to go for a walk in without actually leaving the spot.

'Sir! I think Patsie's got concoshing.' This came anxiously from Charles Vart. The witticisms that name inspired!

All heads turned towards Patsie. His eyes had stopped revolving but his expression was decidedly vacant. Still swaying slightly, he sought brief solace by resting his poor aching head on Miss Cocker's ample bosom. Smiling to reveal the chipped tooth which was her most striking feature, she placed a solicitous arm around him and stroked his cheek, but it was no good. Even in front of the whole team, Patsie couldn't prevent the tears from welling up in his eyes. Wordlessly, he staggered off on a very indirect course towards the changing-room, one hand at his damaged bonce, the other vaguely massaging the air in front of him. After a few yards, a faint ululation came back to us on the wind.

Mr Adam tutted. These were the days before substitution. He raised his cap and ran a hand through leathery, greying hair.

'Malloy,' he said, warily glancing towards the opposition camp, 'go with him. If he's not coming back, get his kit off him and sneak back on.'

'Aye all right sir,' said Andy Malloy conspiratorially, turning to depart.

'Make sure you put—' Mr Adam waved Malloy back and lowered his voice. 'Make sure you put some mud on your face. Dirty yourself up. Don't let Thompson notice.'

'Yes sir.' He was gone.

Miss Cocker's head shook almost imperceptibly and her lips tightened to a horizontal line.

'John Adam, I don't know,' she said quietly. 'I really don't know.'

A running commentary on the second-half proceedings would have a great deal in common with a blow-by-blow account of a pinball session when the player was on a good run. 'The ball appeared to be going right, was deflected from an obstacle and went left, zigzagged for a time in a confined enclosure consisting of four objects each immediately countering the impulse provided by its predecessor, was suddenly violently propelled westward and then equally savagely despatched on a reciprocal . . .' All this to the accompaniment of excited seagull-like squeals, which were now and again brutally eclipsed by the deafening report of one of Mr Thompson's rhetorical demands. 'What's 'ee givin' now? Can you BELIEVE IT! WHAT'S 'E GIVIN' NOW!'

A goalless draw didn't simply threaten, it began to sound klaxons. Minutes remained. Something momentous needed to happen. It did.

Momentarily exhausted, I found myself trailing the pack by a few yards, then pausing briefly to make a judgement on its general drift in an attempt to head it off, and finally, face contorted and chest heaving, giving up the hunt altogether and taking a breather, hands on hips. Mr Adam's newsletter 'Soccer News' in the parish magazine the following Sunday described it thus: *'Emulating his idol, Johnny Haynes, Armstrong found space before goal and hovered expectantly, awaiting the ghost of a half-chance.'*

Suddenly, something narrowly missed my head and landed with a flat plop a few yards in front of me in the direction of St Wilfred's goal. *'A well-timed pass from Atherton was neatly headed on by Pecchio directly into Armstrong's path.'*

I ran at the ball and hit it with all the power and muscle at my knobbly, slim-limbed disposal. It rolled over once. I gave it a left. Then a right. It flopped a couple of times like a largish fish stranded on a sandbank.

'*Armstrong guided the ball with easy strides towards the opposition's goal.*'

This was going to take eternity. The glistening quagmire spread out in front of me, an impassable ocean of ooze with the goalkeeper a distant figure, lost on a wide shiny sea. '*From then on, the outcome was never in doubt.*'

The cassey trundled lazily forward, gathering a coating of ponderous mud with every agonizing stab of my toe. '*The ball flashed across the turf.*'

It was hopeless. Feeble from exhaustion, I slowed to await reinforcements. I was aware of a pair of muddy grey flannels crimped in bicycle-clips falling in beside me, accommodating their pace with mine. From just above my right ear a voice growled, 'You cock this oop you little boogar and I'll drop-kick you into t' middle o' next week.' Suddenly I found reserves of strength I didn't know I had.

'*Urged on by the yells of encouragement from his team-mates, Armstrong approached St Wilfred's goal-mouth.*'

The goalkeeper advanced to meet me, blue from cold and inactivity despite his woolly roll-neck jumper, hands rigid and outstretched as if to ward off a spectre. 'To his left you daft little . . . to his left,' Mr Adam urged between clenched teeth.

Both my feet cleared the ground for an instant as I pointed myself at the right-hand goalpost and launched a violent assault, foot first, on the amorphous mass in front of me. It jumped reluctantly into the air with a dull spongy thud, sped over the goalkeeper's right shoulder, landed behind him with a splat and slid to a halt six inches in front of the goal-line. '*With a cracking right-foot drive which arched the roof of the net.*'

'Goal!' Mr Adam roared, speeding past the goalkeeper and, whilst appearing painstakingly to confirm the validity of his premature jubilation, providing with his right toecap the minutest prod of assistance which the ball needed to complete those last critical inches. 'Goal!

Brilliant, Armstrong! Well played!'

The pack arrived. I was surrounded by smiling, cheering team-mates. My back was slapped. I was hugged. I gloried in cries of 'Fantastic!' 'Brilliant!' 'Smasher, Tim!'

I looked at Mr Adam. He tussled my hair, pointed towards the centre spot and put his whistle to his mouth. It rattled. 'Didn't you . . . I thought . . .'

'Took my pass just right Tim,' Edmundo said. 'Ace.' The team captain placed his arm around my shoulder and patted in congratulation.

Fair enough.

I modestly spread my arms like an aeroplane and set off on a wide-sweeping triumphal arc back to our half, taking pains to provide Miss Cocker with a fly-past on the way.

3

Monday-morning assembly at St John of the Cross Primary School took place in a hall which had once been a church, was now a gymnasium, and resembled neither.

In the early days of the parish, before the church was completed, mass had been said here every Sunday. The only relics of that were two statues mounted on small marble ledges on the wall which faced the door. One was of Our Lady or 'Vurgin Murry' as we affectionately called her, hands joined devoutly and dressed in white, and the other was of Our Lord as the Sacred Heart.

The trappings of a meagre gymnasium – heavy straw mats, wooden skittles, hoops, medicine balls – were heaped in one corner. These apart, the hall was an ordinary place of assembly built *circa* 1935. An ill-fitting parquet floor was starting to break up like crazy paving; the walls were green to the window-ledges and cream from there up – the colours of institutional England in the 1950s.

They were also the colours of the St John's uniform,

though a lot of illegal but tolerated grey crept in on things like white shirts. The overall impression was shabbily paramilitary as the entire school stood in rows by class, each next to their teacher, from the five-year-olds at the front who were called 'the babies' and were allowed to sit cross-legged, to the eleven-plus year at the back which was us. Me.

From where Father Ryan had once said, '*Domine non sum dignus*,' the headmaster, Mr Mason-Jones, now said, 'And I'll bally well wallop the backside of anyone who doesn't clearly understand that.'

The silence was total. Mr Mason-Jones was a figure of Olympian authority in our lives. He wore a suit with a waistcoat, came from Tunbridge Wells and was one of only two people in my narrow world who spoke what my father called officerese. The other was Dr Bond.

'That announcement over,' he went on, sweeping his right hand across his perfectly circular bald spot and tickling the neatly trimmed fringe of hair somewhere below his left ear – a complicated idiosyncrasy he had when agitated, 'we'll move on to more pleasant things.' There was a sort of collective sigh throughout the gathering and throats were cleared here and there. At his side Miss Hodge, the deputy head, allowed a sheepish smile to tug at the corners of her mouth as if her backside were as much on the line as anyone else's.

This was it. Mr Adam had tipped us off. Edmundo and I fidgeted, glanced at each other and simultaneously fought hard to suppress grins.

'Badges,' said Mr Mason-Jones.

Six badges were awarded each week among the entire school. Two were for courtesy, two for good conduct and two for merit. You got to wear them from Monday morning until you went home on Friday afternoon, and they carried an aura and distinction which it is difficult to overstate and hard to comprehend outside a competitive if-my-mum-could-see-me-now community. Wearing one of these badges, you were holy.

Once in my entire career at St John's, I had been awarded a merit badge. Just once. It had ended in calamity.

I looked across at Miss Hodge, erect and forbidding. She had a great billowing mane of grey hair and a pink face, scored with lines at her eyes and mouth. Close up, she had whiskers like Tibby. Under any circumstances, she was enough to strike fear into the heart of a ten-year-old. But, added to that, I couldn't look at her without remembering my merit badge.

I had received it for raising the fire alarm when I saw smoke coming from the caretaker's window. It was a genuine fire – nothing very spectacular, and the source was ultimately traced to a smouldering wellie – but raising the alarm was a plucky enough thing for a six-year-old to do. Somewhat ill-advised on the part of authority mind you, because my award stimulated a rash of false fire alarms which had Mr Mason-Jones contorted in self-imposed half nelsons of rage before the assembly, and actually culminated in attempted arson. That said, you might begin to appreciate the social status conveyed by one of these badges.

I had vaunted mine as if it were the Congressional Medal of Honor. For a full hour after assembly, as Miss Hodge took the rest of the class through the mundane particulars of the three times table, I basked in my triumph, chest thrust outward, head never still, smile as fixed as if painted. Then what happens to everyone at some stage in their earlier school career happened to me. It must have been the excitement. Perhaps the over-sugared porridge I had eaten for breakfast. At any rate, my sudden frozen stare, clenched teeth and rigid grip on the desktop were not, as Miss Hodge assumed, the outward manifestations of a young mind struggling to reconcile the exigencies of solving three times seven. I felt the sudden capitulation of desperately constricted muscle, the downward displacement of a troubling weight in the gut and then my buttocks were being warmly massaged by something bulbous yet yielding. Too late, I thought of asking to be excused. It was all over in seconds.

At a stroke, I was shrunken, defeated, miserable. I could have hurled the bloody badge across the classroom. But I managed to conceal the immediate consequences and gradually began to accommodate myself to sitting in the stuff. I began wondering if locomotion were feasible. Perhaps if I adopted a nothing-too-hasty, shuffling sort of gait? At least, I resolved to stick it out until lunch-time. Imagine my horror, nay naked terror, when Miss Hodge, in the middle of the whole class chanting the 'three-times' back at her, began wrinkling her nostrils enquiringly, then brought them all up with an indignant bellow of, '*Who* has let Polly out of prison?'

The silence was deathly. Everyone adopted an expression of saintly innocence. There was even a prim, exonerating sniff or two. All was not lost, I told myself. I could bluff this one out. Sweat began prickling my forehead, but I remained calm. No-one was going to own up to *that*, least of all me. She'd just have to go and jump for an answer.

But I hadn't reckoned with her tenacity. She waited a few seconds, marched to one of the rear corners of the class, bent down and began wandering along the back row. I shall never forget my feeling of astonished dismay. The blasted woman was SNIFFING BUMS! Just what sort of a person did I have to deal with here!

A few seconds of it was all I could take. Before she homed in on me like a snuffling beagle, I leapt to my feet, exploded into tears and made the most difficult admission of my life.

This time it would be different.

'There are no awards for good conduct,' Mr Mason-Jones announced, his voice heavy with meaning. Feet shuffled in a brief resumption of tension. The coke-throwing affair would claim victims yet. 'However,' he went on, his tone brightening, 'I'm pleased to say we do have two merit awards.

'Most of you will be aware that after a poor start to the season, our soccer team has recently been going from strength to strength. This is of course in no small measure due to the unflagging efforts of the team's trainer, Mr Adam!'

Heads turned to find Mr Adam adjusting the line of his tie and running hasty fingers through dishevelled hair. A stablehand suddenly called to court. He smiled and nodded in acknowledgement.

'On Saturday the lads took on St Wilfred's, last season's champions and current Southpool Minor League leaders, and pulled off a one–nil victory. It was St Wilfred's first defeat of the season, and moves the team into second place in the league, if I'm not mistaken Mr Adam? I think congratulations are in order.'

'Aye, that's right,' Mr Adam said, stifling a brief smattering of applause by raising both hands. 'And if you don't mind, Mr Mason-Jones, I'd like to express the team's thanks for the considerable support we've had from another quarter as well.'

'Oh, that's really very kind,' began the headmaster modestly.

'No, not you,' Mr Adam said genuinely, if somewhat ill-advisedly, 'Miss Cocker.'

This time heads swivelled to the opposite wall where Miss Cocker's face immediately assumed an alarming shade of magenta. Edmundo and I exchanged puzzled glances, then looked at Mr Adam. There was an odd look in his eye. I'd seen it somewhere before, but couldn't quite place it. Fawning yet aggressive. Proprietary yet subservient. It was rum.

'Yes, ehm.' Mr Mason-Jones recovered his composure with a brief stroke of his crown. When he continued, it was with a let's-get-this-over-with strain to his voice. 'The merit awards for this week go to the soccer team captain, Edmundo Denato Pecchio, and Saturday's scorer, Timothy Armstrong.'

At last. We marched forward to applause which was a

trickle at the rear ranks but became a torrent as we approached the front. The babies were going wild, like an American TV studio audience. They hadn't a clue what was going on but they sure loved a spot of unchecked hullabaloo.

'Well done skipper,' said Mr Mason-Jones to Edmundo, handing him a badge. Then to me, 'Mr Adam said your goal nearly gave him a heart attack.'

'Oh, he only had to tap it in,' I answered distractedly. Judging by his reaction not the response he expected, but I was nervously eyeing Miss Hodge. She looked on, a stern effigy in pink and grey, very straight with her fingers interlocked before her, as formidable as ever. I knew what she was thinking. Worse still, her expression said, 'I know you know what I'm thinking.'

I hurried past her, head down.

As we resumed our places, the applause fizzled out, and, at a nod from Mr Mason-Jones, Miss Hodge began to read the scripture passage. Not bad for a début, I reflected. I may have bled for soccer, but in no time at all it had repaid me tenfold. I registered the glances of admiration and envy from my classmates, a freckle-covered smile from Charles Vart, a friendly wink from a fully recovered Patsie Hunieghan. Mr Adam beamed down on us benevolently. I was experiencing something not quickly forgotten. For the first time, I had tasted that heady cocktail made up of the adulation of one's contemporaries, and the unreserved approval of one's betters. All because of a demonstration of marginal prowess with a spherical object full of air. In such moments are implanted the seeds of an infatuation.

The rapid monotone of Miss Hodge's reading was grinding down to the conclusive 'Amen amen I say unto you' bit that winds up most scripture passages. Her voice double-declutched.

'For what doth it profiteth a man,' she intoned piously, 'if he gaineth the whole worldeth . . .'

Even to me there seemed to be a holy lisp too many there. She noticed it too and paused in brief embarrassment. Mr Adam snorted, throwing her completely.

'. . . But thuffer the loth of his own thoul.'

There was an involuntary titter or two amongst the teachers, but Mr Adam threw back his head and roared. Watching him, I laughed too. Because I was happy. Because Mr Adam was laughing. Because I had a merit badge. Because it was Miss Hodge. Unfortunately, he clapped a hand over his mouth and stopped abruptly, several seconds before I did. I tripped on for a while, gaily solo. Suddenly, I became aware that I was something of a centre of attention.

If Mr Mason-Jones was looking daggers at me, Miss Hodge's eyes were two-handed Viking broadswords . . .

4

But it was Mr Adam's expression as he contemplated Miss Cocker that stuck in my mind. It was like a silk ribbon on a pug dog. Yet strangely familiar. It reappeared to me several times during the day, persisting like an itch in the small of the back.

Moreover, I had seen him wearing it before. The previous Saturday, I had left the pitch to some quite enjoyable acclaim including one or two highly repeatable tributes from Mr Adam. I sought him out as I was leaving, just in case he might want to enlarge on any of them before I took home the final versions for quoting. I found him loading his bicycle into the back of Miss Cocker's van. I half registered that as an unusual thing to be doing.

'I'm just off then sir,' I informed him.

Turning away from Miss Cocker, he had removed exactly that same expression from his face in order to grimace at me. 'Well thank you Armstrong. I'm so glad you dropped by to let me know. I was just wondering how

I was going to get through t' weekend without seeing you again.'

On the strength of my merit badge, I collared Maureen Keene at morning playtime and told her to tell Linda Miller, 'Tim Armstrong says Cliff's latest.' She chose the dinner queue as Edmundo and I chatted loftily to a couple of temporarily deferential classmates to convey the piercing and tactless response, 'Linda says tell Tim Armstrong Eden Kane.'

Pretending not to hear, I spun round to come face to face with Mrs Miggs the dinner lady, a scoop in each hand, poised over tubs of mashed veg as though they contained anmunition. She hit me with a dollop of potato from the right and followed up with carrot from the left, setting my plate rolling and pitching precariously. I hoped the others didn't understand.

'It's called "Get Lost",' Edmundo explained helpfully.

Declarations, affirmations and propositions were quite usually made via intermediaries carrying snippets of pop songs. Linda Miller later pointed out to me that the second line of Eden Kane's hit would invite me to lose myself in her arms. Unfortunately, it was seventeen years later, by which time she had a husband and two children, so it did little to allay the feeling of shock and embarrassment with which I faced Mrs Miggs.

Still, a sexual conquest would have been icing on the cake. I was contented enough to be enjoying the spoils of countenance without suffering the soils of incontinence. That evening, as we headed towards the gap in the wall where the school gate should have been, Edmundo and I still trailed a small entourage. Gap in the wall, because the gate, like all wrought-iron gates, had been requisitioned during the war and not yet replaced. 'To make aeroplanes' Jim had assured me when I asked, and for years afterwards I remained convinced that our technical edge in wrought-iron bombers had been instrumental in bringing Nazi Germany to its knees.

Our entourage consisted of Patsie HuniegKhan whose

fatal header had meanwhile become a brave near miss of legendary proportions, Michael Atherton, who I now noticed in addition to being voluminous and abnormally tall was also pigeon-toed, Frank Macnally, suitably enough for a goalkeeper clutching a plastic football in gloved hands, and Kevin Lowe, the Catarrh Kid, whose nostrils were inverted thimbles full of pea soup which occasionally threatened to brim over, but which would implode at the critical moment with a sound like drains being cleared, causing the seething green mass to recede a half-millimetre, but never disappear.

As we filed through the gap in the wall, we were joined by Charles Vart. In addition to suffering agonies of torment over wordplay witticism on his surname, Charles was frequently ridiculed for his carroty hair and nebulae of freckles. Patsie said he had been standing too close when the shit hit the fan.

Michael Atherton began kicking a stone along the pavement and declared an intention to kick it all the way home without once letting it run onto the road. Bets were taken, none of them involving stakes which were remotely redeemable. Kevin took a red exercise book and pencil from his pocket, folded back the close-lined pages and revealed a long list of car-registration numbers in uncertain capitals. No model, no colour, just the numbers. He followed a green Hillman intently as it passed down Albert Street, read off its number from the rear, and studiously added HFX 435 to the list. As a childhood collecting craze this wasn't so much a hobby as a neurosis. It was destined to be short-lived.

I proposed a game of 'goalies'.

'What's that?' Edmundo asked. No-one else knew either. This wasn't surprising since I had invented it, and it was known to only a small circle of confidants in and around George Avenue.

'Well, say I start. I have to think of a goalkeeper. I tell you his name, club and country and make a save with the ball. Then you each have to think of one from the same country and do it too. For each one who can't, I get a point. Then it's someone else's go.'

They shrugged.

'OK,' Edmundo said. The others nodded. I took the ball from Frank.

'Albert Dunlop of Everton and England,' I announced, with a voice which was a cross between a TV chat-show host presenting his star guest and a ten-year-old reading meticulously from the back of a bubble-gum card. I threw the ball in the air, leapt like an electrocuted ballet-dancer and clawed it around an imaginary post, exhaling loudly in simulation of ecstatic crowd noises. Then I tossed the ball to Edmundo.

He thought for a while and plumped for Eddie Hopkinson. This was the easy round, of course.

The advantage of 'goalies' was that it didn't stifle conversation and could be played on the move. Anyway, the outcome was a foregone conclusion. What the rest of them didn't know was that, in 1959, I knew the name, club and nationality of every goalkeeper in the entire world.

'Hey,' Patsie said as he was handed the ball, 'Mr Adam when Miss Hodge mixed up at prayers.' He did a fair parody. We all laughed.

'Susan Hopcroft says Miss Hodge didn't half give him what for at playtime,' Frank chipped in. 'Made him say sorry.'

'Honest?'

'Yeah. Three times, 'course.'

There was another chorus of laughter. This was an unconcealed jibe at Miss Hodge's antiquated teaching methods. Central among them were frequent instructions to the whole class to chant three times any fact or conclusion which she considered worthy of particular emphasis, whilst she beat time with a ruler. Primitive. Divorced of any concept or hope of success. I had heard it described thus by Miss Cocker in an aside to another teacher. As the word 'divorce' had left her lips, an orchestration of young voices somewhere at the back of my mind had brayed, 'What God hath joined together, let no man put asunder. What God hath joined together let no man put asunder. What God hath . . .' Miss Hodge took us for religion too.

'Harry Gregg. Manchester United and Ireland,' Patsie said, leaning forward to smother a low drive by cradling the ball to his chest.

'Well Pop Adam can talk,' Edmundo complained. 'He's no-one to crow about saying things right.' He flicked back a thick mop of auburn hair from coffee-coloured skin not yet bleached by England's winters, and looked wounded.

'How d'you mean, Eddie?' I asked.

'My name. It's not Eddie, it's Edmundo. And it's Pecchio.' He hadn't the trace of an Italian accent, but his voice rolled exotically as he said his name. 'Kkk. Pecchio. It's important. Pop Adam calls me Peachyo. That means . . .'

We waited expectantly.

'In Italian, it means prick.'

We were silent. Michael said he didn't know any Irish goalkeepers. He kicked his stone spitefully, then ducked and froze as it bounced along the pavement and pinged off a parked car, luckily unoccupied.

'My dad's called Willy,' Charlie Vart offered, as if in compensation. 'Mine's called Dick,' Kevin added.

'My brother's John Thomas,' I said, putting my arm across Edmundo's shoulder. He held the pout for a few seconds then laughed.

As we turned into Wharley Street, Edmundo attempted to put some pressure on with a round of Italian goalkeepers. I deliberately chose Tony Marcedo of Fulham to see if anyone knew he had taken out English naturalization papers. No-one did. I decided it was time to put some distance between me and the opposition.

'Igor Groscics. Ferenzvaros Budapest and Hungary,' I said evenly, with a minimum gesture at a save. I was aware of five gasps of admiration and a gurgle smothered in mucus.

Edmundo tried 'Lev Jashin' in a tone which was much more question than statement. I answered half apologetically, 'Spartack Moscow and Russia.'

There was a long pause.

'Can we have same country twice?' Frank asked.

'Aye. But not same goalkeeper.'

They began another round of Englishmen.

Wharley Street was much wider and carried more traffic. Kevin began writing feverishly in his exercise book and Michael side-footed his pebble carefully a few feet at a time.

'Any rate, Pop Adam got you a badge,' I pointed out to Edmundo.

'Blimey. Talk of the devil,' he answered.

A few yards further down the street, Miss Cocker's van was parked with the rear doors open. Mr Adam was unloading his bicycle from the back. We ran forward to him, Michael bringing up the rear at a slow dribble.

There was a discordant chorus of Hiyasirs.

Mr Adam was taken unawares, as though the last possible thing he expected to meet half a mile from St John of the Cross Primary School was a group of St John of the Cross Primary School pupils.

'You lot,' was all he said at first. He leaned on his handlebars and seemed to recover some composure. 'Do your tie up Armstrong,' he said to me, straightening his cap.

The engine had been running. It stopped and Miss Cocker got out and closed the van doors.

'Hello you lads,' she said. She patted Edmundo on the head and smiled to reveal that chipped front tooth. Close up, I noticed it was browning at the edge. Even so, she was pretty in a snuggly sort of way. She smiled a lot. She touched your cheek sometimes lightly with the back of her fingers, as if you were special, or put her arm around your shoulder as you walked by her side. There was something soft and giving and comforting about her. Like your mother but different in a way you couldn't define, intrinsically, inexplicably mixed up with what Jim laughed at me for not being able to do. As if Miss Cocker could have anything to do with that.

She looked across at me.

'Well done, you two. I'm so pleased about your merit badges.'

'Thanks, Miss. Are you coming on Saturday?'

She was. We chatted briskly about the relative strengths and weaknesses of Tewkes Endowed. She said we seemed to be taking our time getting home.

'Aye. Get a move on,' Mr Adam said bluntly, mounting his bike. 'And watch yourselves. 'Night Alice.'

With a cursory glance over his shoulder he injected himself into the traffic, right arm extended, wobbling as he got up speed. Miss Cocker's gaze followed him for a long time after he was obscured by a double-decker. She turned to us as if suddenly remembering we were there.

'Don't dawdle you boys or your mothers will worry. Good night.'

She got back into the van with a wave and drove off.

Edmundo snorted. Patsie drew back his top lip, pushed his front tooth forward and assumed a hooting voice. 'Would you like me to be your girlfriend, Mr Adam?'

He said this to Edmundo, who pulled his school cap down over his eyes and growled. 'Aye Alice. I'll put my bike in your van any time.'

The others laughed. I laughed too, if less lustily.

The traffic noises swelled and became enriched by the hum and rattle of trams. Kevin rolled up his exercise book and slipped it into his inside pocket. I wrapped up the game of 'goalies' with Jose Maria Ramillies of Independiente Quito and Ecuador. This was the sole piece of intelligence I possessed about that far-off country, but I could tell the rest of them had never heard of the place, which made a knowledge of its goalkeeping fraternity less than likely.

We approached the row of shops leading up to Lindley Square, set back from the road behind a largish forecourt. Frank automatically dropped the ball and we began shunting it between us, as we moved past the shops.

Nick Butler's was the barber Jim and I were sent to every month. He gave you a complete haircut without once removing the fag from his mouth. Unknown to us, he was under strict instructions to ignore any request we made and ensure we came away with a British Army short-back-and-sides, creamed and parted centre-left. Allan was the butcher who sang 'Ma, he's making eyes at me' as he threw dollops of liver in greaseproof onto the scales, or hacked at ribs on his scarred wooden table. We had stopped going to him because he was suspected of adding cheap cuts when you asked for a pound of best steak, minced. Rita's was the second-hand clothes shop which had done very nicely indeed thank you after the war, but was coming on hard times as Fifties austerity gave way to – well, less austerity. Then came the post office from which I had four half-crown savings stamps in a book at home. I hated going there to pick up the family allowance of seven and sixpence. The woman behind the counter was coldly beautiful, as superior and distant as a goddess. Her hair and perfume made me feel unwashed. When she looked at me with those intelligent eyes I felt unspeakably artless. The way she stamped the book told me I belonged to a family of foul-smelling uneducated oiks who were begging charity off the Government. Then came Oliver's, the grocer's, which we didn't use because we always shopped at the Co-op, where you received checks to the value of everything you bought and once a year drew the divvy, a real godsend just before Christmas. Then came the fish and chip shop which we shunned because my parents would rather starve than eat such rubbish. Or tinned vegetables. Or sliced bread. The launderette we didn't need because my mother washed everything in the bath, ran it through a hand mangle in the back garden, dried it on the pulley if the weather wasn't fine and ironed every Monday night in front of the fire. The off-licence was a concept my father didn't agree with although he drank four pints of bitter every night of his life. At Christmas he and John would pick up two dozen Double Diamonds, a bottle of QC sherry and a Johnny Walker, which would be displayed hospitably on the front-room table, but, that apart, there was never alcohol in the house. At the very end of the row was Marsden's the newsagents, which my parents still called Turner's although old Mr Turner had died before I was born. Mr Marsden was a joyless Scot with a club foot and a bad-tempered ageing Labrador called Judy, who was so huge she severely hampered freedom of movement in what was already a limited space.

By a sort of common unexpressed understanding, we moved the ball in the direction of Marsden's. Of course, in addition to newspapers and magazines he sold sweets, although he managed somehow to purge any pleasure from the act of procuring them. You never got away without some complaint or reproval. You were buying too little; you were taking away his change; you were gabbling; couldn't you make your mind up *what* you wanted. The previous morning after mass, determined to relieve the mind-numbing boredom of a Sunday which yawned before me – *Forces Favourites*, the lingering reek of boiled cabbage, steamed-up windows from so many simmering saucepans, the endless dreary rigmarole of Sunday dinner (or 'lonsh' as my dad now insisted we called it, in playful mockery of Jim's newly acquired grammar-school vocabulary) the sluggish hours spent awkwardly in Sunday best – I resolved to blow sixpence of my 'spends' and brighten the day. Two ounces of Jap Dessert, two ounces of salted peanuts and two ounces of Creamy Bon Bons. That lot ought to see me through until *Sunday Night at the London Palladium*.

'Now ye. Ye'd no be having me scamper round after scrapings o' this and ha'penny's worth o' that wid ye?' had been his respectful welcome to the prospective customer as I contemplated the shelves of toffee jars. Judy had risen, slowly moved around behind me and growled, like a bouncer called to a troublesome client. I had decided to stick with just the Jap Dessert.

But now I was buoyed by numbers. Michael stayed outside with his pebble, but the rest of us hit Marsden's counter like a shock wave which had Judy backing into the birthday-card display.

'Penny chew please.'

'Penny bubbly please.'

'Penny Spanish please.'

Marsden was rearranging his magazines. He contented himself with a tut and shuffled round to the sweets and confectionery counter. He wasn't slowed down just by his foot but carried the additional handicap to manoeuvrability imposed by three layers of pullovers and a duffle coat, because he hated to have his shop heated.

'Now ye,' he said as he dropped a bubble gum in front of me, 'ye'll tell your mam and dad there's six weeks papers owing. That's more 'n ten shillin'.'

'Right Mr Marsden.'

As if on cue the evening papers arrived. To a throaty snarl from Judy, two men in dirty yellow jackets deposited several hundred copies of the *Southpool Sentinel* on top of his magazine counter. Two of his paper-boys followed them in, bags over shoulders, and Marsden began counting out their 'round' to them. Patsie, whose father was chairman of the Knights of St Columba and whose brother had recently been despatched to a seminary, took advantage of the confusion to help himself to a Milky Bar from the front of the display.

As we left the shop, the tram for the town centre glided noisily into Lindley Square. Edmundo, Kevin, Charlie, Frank and Patsie set off at a run towards it. Patsie booted Michael's precious stone into the middle of Whalley Street and knocked his cap off his head as they passed. As he jumped onto the tram, he broke off half the stolen Milky Bar and handed it to Edmundo, then called to me.

'Hey, Tim Armstrong. Guess who plays goalkeeper for China. Tim No Dong.'

I just had time to see the conductor fetch him one before the doors closed and the tram pulled out.

'See you Athers,' I said to Michael, and set off at a run. I ran everywhere when not actively restrained, because getting there was just the nothing between two somethings, wasn't it. But tonight I didn't want to miss seeing *Children's Hour* which was *Zoo Time* with Dr Desmond Morris at five, followed by *Ivanhoe* at twenty-five past. Before then, my mum would want me to run to the Co-op. I knew this with the same certainty that I knew *Ivanhoe* would end in a sword fight. There was no time to lose. All the same, I avoided Phillip Street, the direct route, because it was guarded by a huge, unpredictable Alsatian which squatted like the Sphinx outside number eight. Sometimes it would let me jog by, serenely observing, other times it made me tearfully beg leave to be allowed home against a savage cacophony of barks and growls. It had no idea of the influence it was having on my life. Or perhaps it did. Perhaps it was sitting there now, panting in anticipation, thinking doggily, 'The little bugger'll be along any minute now. Shall I have him tonight? Dominant species on the planet. Arf. Arf.'

'Mam, I won a merit badge. Mr Mason-Jones said it were a brilliant goal. Everyone in t' team wants to be my friend. Maureen Keene asked if she can be my girl. I think Pop Adam and Miss Cocker are goin' to get married.'

She was in the kitchen, having a quiet moment at the table with a cuppa and a cigarette, amid the warm, appetizing smell of tonight's tea. She listened to my rapid-fire summary of the day's events and as always made her comment on the last item.

'Well, I should imagine Mary Adam will have something to say about that.'

'Who's she?'

'The woman he's married to already.'

She poured milk and sliced Battenberg.

'Have I to go to t' Co-op?'

'Aye, if you will.'

'I'll have that when I get back then. With telly. Can I?'

She handed me the Co-op book. 'We s'll see. Off you go then. Ask Clare to put me six custard slices by for tomorrow.'

I scampered off.

'Tim!'

I scurried back.

'Shopping bag.'

I darted away.

I wondered why parents always said, 'We s'll see.' Never 'Yes.' Never 'No.'

5

'Spaghetti!' My father spat out the word as though it were an indignity he had been made to suffer. 'Spaghetti. Pff.'

I contemplated his back, clothed in a thick woollen vest with his braces peeled down to his waist. He sat, not quite *in* the fire, but with one boot planted firmly either side of it in the hearth. To say my father liked a nice fire would be like saying Aleric the Bold, who laid waste to all Christendom, was partial to a spot of vandalism. In summer, his modest demands on the home-comfort front were usually limited to a medium-sized conflagration, but, in winter, every evening around six thirty, the living-room of fourteen George Avenue went supernova. Shortly before we sat down to eat, my mother would throw on a shovel of coal and add a couple of the enormous logs which my father chopped specifically for the purpose at weekends. He would come in from his meal to face a blazing beacon which was throwing off gigawatts at the same rate as the surface of the sun, pull up his chair, slap his hands together and sigh in contentment. Only Tibby could hang in with him. The cat would sit between my father's legs, eyes closed, chest thrust out proudly. Any other living creature would have needed an asbestos suit. If Dad read the paper it quite often achieved spontaneous combustion. The logs would hiss menacingly, then, with a violent crack, despatch a glowing red tracer over his shoulder, sending the rest of us diving for cover as it ricocheted off the lampshade, or a spark would sing with a firework whine between his body and arm, trailing smoke like a downed Spitfire. They never seemed to harm him. Once in a while, Tibby would widen his eyes at one of the more apocalyptic bangs and retire discreetly, mere fractions of a degree from flashpoint.

Of course, in pre-central-heating days, you sensed something of a contrast if you strayed to other parts of the house. In fact, being despatched upstairs to fetch his cuff-links was rather like leaving the mother ship for a space walk. So the rest of us sweated it out in different parts of the living-room. Mum on the couch with Nonnie who was reading *Marilyn*. John in the easy chair with a manual on fuel injection open on his lap. Jim at the table, scratching away at his grammar-school homework.

All of this was normal. The most conspicuous sign that things were radically amiss, apart from my father's monosyllabic invective against the flagship of Italian cuisine, was that the television was switched off. Not only that it was off, but that at that very moment *Rawhide* was showing on ITV. The sound of lowing longhorns carried through the wall from next door's front room. With the noted exception of my father, the members of my family would no sooner miss an episode of *Rawhide* than Sunday mass, and failure to attend the latter entailed damnation and eternal torment. But the television was most definitely 'off' on my father's say-so. And everyone except him knew I was to blame.

My mother's knitting needles clicked industriously.

It had to be end of part one. Faintly jingling through from next door's, in tones of perky American harmony we were told we'd wonder where the yellow went, if we brushed our teeth with Pepsodent.

'Spaghetti,' he said again in disgust. My mother looked at me sternly from the couch and shook her head almost inperceptibly in silent reproach.

It had happened as follows.

I had sprinted back to Lindley Square where the Co-op stood, an imposing edifice in dappled-marble and white-tiled frontage, built to last, solid evocation of a durable empire. Inside there was a wall clock that would have graced Waterloo station, and the ornately carved and lavishly varnished oak counters wouldn't have looked out of place in a church. The walls were lined with glass-doored cupboards as if the goods were for display only, like in a museum. Clare was in the back, grinding coffee. The shop was rich with the aroma.

'Evening, young man,' said Mr Aden with his hand out. Mr Aden was the manager. His white coat was spotless and his not inconsiderable bulk was held as if he were a military man, which possibly he had been. He had a moustache which looked as if he measured the length and width to a precise number of hairs and he was bald in a way which was actually imposing, probably because he not only made no attempt to hide the fact, but seemed to suppress hair growth to a minimum as if it were something slovenly.

He took the book from me, opened it, whipped a needle-sharp yellow pencil from behind his ear and began ticking off and pricing the goods as he fetched them. Flicking tissue paper round a large plain loaf, he looked around the shop to make sure no-one was within earshot, and said in a low firm voice, 'Tell your mum and dad I'd like to see something paid off the balance this weekend would you? It's going up not down.'

'Yes Mr Aden, I will.' I could feel myself going red, though God knows, and he did, there was little reason. Finance in our house, like millions of others, was like one of those plate-spinning acts you see at the circus. To keep one set humming, others slowed down, sometimes precariously, but rarely crashed to disaster. A new school uniform meant the Co-op waited a week or two. When the rates came due, the TV licence marked time. They worried, argued, even cried over it, but always got by. If the worst came to the worst, the annual fortnight in Blackpool sometimes became a week of day trips. Trough-of-Bowland. Bolton Abbey. Trentham Gardens. Glasson Dock. Windermere. The plates kept spinning.

He winked at me. 'Fetch your beans while I get the onions.'

I turned towards the pile of tins. 'From the top,' I heard him call as he went to the back.

And there was Mr Adam. Not the real Mr Adam, of course. It was a cardboard cut-out. Life-size. He'd been there for weeks pointing to a stack of Heinz baked beans with a big balloon coming out of his mouth which said 'Get stuck in. It'll do you good!' Come to think of it, he didn't actually look much like Mr Adam. He had the same glasses and greying hair, but the face was much softer. No, it was that expression. It was identical. The same goofy optimism I kept seeing inappropriately on Mr Adam's rugged mug. Instead of a plate of beans, sausage, bacon and eggs, he could have been clutching Miss Cocker. As I picked up two tins I couldn't tear my eyes away from his. 'Get stuck in. It'll do you good.' How on earth could Mr Adam see Miss Cocker as a Sunday fry-up?

And how was I to know they had moved him to help push the new line in spaghetti?

My father was meanwhile contenting himself with a series of nonverbal, though no less penetrating expressions of discontent. 'Tut. Pfff. Ssh.' Just when you thought he'd got over it, he'd add 'Ugh!' or something.

The distant sound of mooing returned from beyond the wall. My mother looked across at me and shook her head again, mutely vexed. With a sickly sinking feeling, I realized I'd forgotten about the six custard slices as well.

6

Tewkes Endowed proved truculent in defence but totally devoid of an attacking concept. After the match Mr Adam, again referee, informed us we had won eleven–nil. This created some puzzlement since, adding up the goals claimed by individual scorers, my three among them, we arrived at only seven. Edmundo tackled him about it.

'It's important sir. For our goal-scoring statistics.'

'Statistics is it Peachyo,' Mr Adam replied scornfully. 'Do you know lad, statistics show that one in every four people in t' world is a Chinese. If I managed this team on statistics, I'd have three Chinks instead of an Eyetie and two Poles in it wouldn't I?'

Edmundo looked thoughtful, then confused, then resentful.

But three goals from me, you notice. Within a few weeks, I had forgotten my dreams of goalkeeping and decided to become the first right-footed outside left to play for England. I scored in each of the following two games, a claim which has to be tempered by the admission that so did everyone else except the goalkeepers, since the scores were seventeen–fourteen and nineteen–sixteen respectively. Goals seemed to be like avalanches – they either didn't happen at all or everybody got smothered in them.

But our growing success couldn't be denied. After five straight wins we slipped into first place ahead of St Wilfred's, and, to our hushed astonishment, saw for the first time Mr Mason-Jones appear on the touch-line next to Miss Cocker.

After the game, he gathered a few of us together and delivered a stentorian discourse, part accolade part exhortation, full of punchy gestures with his right fist, sometimes into the air, sometimes into his own left palm, hopping from foot to foot on the netball pitch outside the changing-room.

We stood dutifully in a half-circle around him, caked in mud.

'No hanging back in the tackle' – smack – 'give it all you've bally well' – smack – 'got. Hello! Why is Mr Adam putting his bicycle into the back of Miss Cocker's van?' (– smack, absently).

He gazed over our heads, then looked down at us.

There was silence. For the moment, he had forgotten that he was talking to Catholic children whose germinal intellect was being nurtured on the Resurrection, the Immaculate Conception, transubstantiation and having three persons in one God.

'It's a mystery, sir,' Charles Vart told him. 'A divine mystery.'

Mr Mason-Jones stared at Charlie for a long time.

7

'Mum,' I said, joining her at the kitchen sink and looking up with what I hoped was an angelic smile, like something from a washing-up-liquid advertisement, 'can I have a pair of continentals?'

She brushed back a curl of hair with the crook of her wrist, dexterously denuded a potato in one continuous movement before plunging it into the water, and then tossed it to the pan on her right like a gutted fish.

She looked down.

'And what might continentals be?' she asked, no more than dutiful curiosity in her voice.

'Boots,' I said. 'Footy boots.'

'And what's wrong wi' them you've got now?'

Her peeling and plunging went on unabated.

'They're old.'

'Aye. So will you be one day. So's yer grand-dad. That doesn't mean you want a new one does it?'

'That's different,' I said, and quite rightly. 'Everyone

wears continentals now. Nylon studs. Low ankles. White stripes down t' side.'

'Oh white stripes must be vital to kickin' right,' she scoffed. I felt momentarily frustrated at debating skills more practised than my own.

'It's not just that. It's toecap. Ones I'm wearing now were bought for John. And Jim wore 'em. Things were different then. Styles and that. They look like—' I drew breath for effect – '"skwawddies' hawbnails".'

This brought her up sharply. She paused and turned towards me, showing real interest for the first time.

'And what might you know about squaddies' hobnails?' she asked, genuinely curious.

I could see I had her hooked.

'It's what Mr Mason-Jones said on Saturday after t' match.'

'Oh aye?'

'Aye.' I paused and frowned in concentration at the effort of attempting BBC English and at the same time taking on the resonant tones of adult authority.

'"Armstrong," he said, "you hower best plair. Hyule nevah get to plare like Paylay wearing skwawddies' hawbnails."'

She considered, unamused, then after a time asked, 'Who's Paylay?'

'That's just how he says it,' I told her. 'He's really called Pelly. He won t' World Cup for Brazil.'

She appeared to be thinking furiously. After a while she resumed her potato-peeling, from time to time raising her head to gaze out of the kitchen window. Her mind was grappling with the intricate complexities of introducing thirteen and eleven for a pair of football boots into a huge equation which was already over-complicated by terms including a two pounds ten down payment on the rates, the first of fifteen ten-bob instalments on a blue pinstripe made-to-measure at John Colliers, and various imponderables the full magnitude of which would only become apparent once the old man got his time sheets done.

'Did he really say that about you being best player?' she asked at length.

Might there be a bit of pride in her voice? I suddenly began to feel excited.

'He did Mum, honest. Cross my heart and hope to die.' I did so.

'Don't *do* that,' she said, irritated, then resumed her thinking. For a while there was silence except for a subdued splashing and scraping accompanied by the rumble of freshly peeled spuds scuttling into the pan.

'So can I have some continentals?' I ventured after a couple of minutes.

She sighed and shook her head slightly, then uttered the words which I knew would be the best I could expect.

'We s'll see.'

8

There was the faintest of tinkles, and a perfect silver spider's web appeared on the bottom left-hand pane of glass of Mr Mason-Jones' office window. The ball bounced innocently back into play but proceedings were suspended whilst everyone awaited retribution. It was a fairly frequent practice-evening occurrence, but usually the headmaster's office, being sideways-on to the playground, was spared any mutilation. Unfortunately, over on the right, Terry Welsh the wizard winger had attempted a left-foot cross which had skimmed off the outside of his foot, screwed diagonally across the direction of play, seemed to gain speed as it bounced, and then whirred window-wards as if fitted with a homing device.

'I warned you!' roared Mr Adam, his voice full of portent. He strode purposefully across the playground with his hand perfectly poised to impart a considerable amount of topspin to the back of Terry Welsh's head. At the critical moment, Mr Mason-Jones appeared from his office. He was in shirtsleeves and waistcoat and chuckling like Santa.

'Well, well, well, Welsh,' he called, not without some alliterative difficulty, 'looks like that one packed a bit of punch.'

He fingered the cracked pane almost admiringly and sauntered towards Mr Adam. Most of the figures who were scattered about the yard converged warily in a loose cluster around the two of them.

'No, no,' he said, pursing his lips. Mr Adam had hold of Terry Welsh by the collar so that his feet were dangling just clear of the ground as if he were suspended from a meathook. He let him drop unceremoniously.

'Accidents will of course happen,' Mr Mason-Jones went on, placing his hands in his pockets nonchalantly and rocking on his heels. 'As a matter of fact I have been sort of wondering why you choose to play Tim Armstrong,' he pointed at me, 'who's right-footed, on the left wing, and Terry Welsh,' heads swivelled, 'who's left-footed, on the,' he paused with delicacy, 'on the er, right.'

Mr Adam's nostrils widened just perceptibly. His lips disappeared and his mouth formed a flat line. He worked his bicycle-pump in and out a few times whilst we waited expectantly, then said what I took to be 'Noel's odd' under his breath.

I pondered and cocked an eyebrow at the wizard winger. Now he came to mention it.

Mr Adam had the barely concealed air of one whose patience is being tried.

'Because, Mr Mason-Jones,' he said very lucidly, 'the result of your average eleven-year-old, when going at full kelter, attempting to forcefully hoof a cassey at right angles to his direction of travel, is usually a swipe at clean air, a triple pirouette, and a short sharp period spent shooting along on his backside as if greased, smiling inanely in the direction he's just come from.'

Mr Mason-Jones nodded seriously a few times. It was

trench-hardened platoon sergeant to nosy staff officer; the parallels were inescapable.

'If, however, he is made to stop, turn, and put the ball onto his best foot . . .' He left the sentence deliberately unfinished, smiling smugly.

The headmaster showed not the slightest sign of just having been put in his place. On the contrary, he beamed.

'Of course, of course. I should have known better than to question the expert. Results speak for themselves.' He clapped his hands and made to be off with, 'I'll leave you to it. Keep up the good work.'

At the last moment he turned with an afterthought, index finger raised.

'I must say, I couldn't help noticing,' he began with his voice much lowered, 'that we don't supply our young chaps with football stockings to go with their kit. The result seems to be a bit of a mixture. Oh, I accept the lads will have their allegiances, but I must have recognized everything from Manchester to Mönchengladbach.'

Few could catch his words now as his voice became almost confidential, but I was right next to Mr Adam.

'The overall impact is a bit ragtag. Patsie Hunieghan's have been dyed bright pink in the wash,' he commented, without malevolence. 'Anyway, the point is, I've seen Canon Creaney, and it appears we can stretch to a dozen pairs in claret and blue to match the jerseys.'

Mr Adam was clearly floored. 'Oh. Well. That's er, very—'

The headmaster touched him on the arm affably.

'And a referee's kit in regulation black and white for yourself.'

The effect could hardly have been more conspicuous if he'd offered to play centre forward. Mr Adam's eyes widened in real amazement. He tucked the bicycle-pump smartly under one arm and seemed on the verge of a salute.

'Not at all,' Mr Mason-Jones said soothingly. 'It was long overdue. Credit where it's due.'

He lifted his head and called brief encouragement to the team at large before setting off back to his office.

Mr Adam watched him go with an expression that was as much puzzlement as gratification. He clawed briefly at his blue sandpaper cheek, then resettled his thick tortoiseshells.

'Well, young Armstrong,' he murmured, looking down at me, 'we seem to be making our number with Mr Penalty Spot.'

It took me some time to work out that this was an unkind reference to Mr Mason-Jones' balding crown, now receding in the direction of the office.

9

'Class dismissed,' grunted Mr Adam a few days later. 'Everyone can clear – STOP BANGING THOSE DESK LIDS – out except Armstrong.'

I felt unease replace confusion. The unease was to be recurrent throughout the seventeen years of my educational career and arise whenever the announcement of my name singled me out from my fellows; it rarely spells anything good in academia. The confusion was at Mr Adam's just-completed science class. It had been on the subject of something he referred to as 'Err Pressure'. Like all of his lessons, it had included a short experiment illustrating the fundamentals of the topic in question. Invariably, these experiments were accomplished using a simple apparatus consisting of a Bunsen burner, a ruler, a beaker of water, a spring balance, and a bag of nails. No matter what the hypothesis, no matter how intricate the principle or how tentative the theory, Mr Adam interpreted its validation in terms of this modest bit of kit. If asked to demonstrate that matter and energy were interchangeable via Einstein's constant and the square of the speed of light, Mr Adam would begin assembling Bunsen burner, ruler, beaker of water, spring balance and nails . . .

After the room had emptied, I stood beside him whilst he continued writing at his desk. For a time, he ignored me. Every once in a while the corners of his mouth would flick upward into a cynical smile, as if at some very private spot of black humour.

I cast my eyes around at the rows of heavy dark-varnished desks with their wrought-iron frames and porcelain inkwells. That reminded me that I was ink monitor at the next class, which was Miss Hodge taking us for 'real writing'. A mental image of her pinkly leonine visage was enough to have me wishing Mr Adam would hurry up.

Mr Adam wrote on, chuckling darkly and ignoring me. I looked idly around. Following the walls of the classroom, almost blocking out the light from two windows, was a huge strip of black cartridge paper over which was pinned a piece of card inscribed 'The Pageant of History'. It was divided into centuries and the idea was that any little illustrative artefact, picture or bit of text would be gummed to its relevant patch in the march of time. It wasn't going well, to be frank. The offerings had been too sporadic. Not to mention subjective. The only thing BC was a picture of Stonehenge. There was a reproduction of Dürer's *Knight Death and the Devil* about where the Great Plague should have been, and, in the middle of a huge vacant expanse representing hundreds of years of inactivity, a drawing of a cannon simply labelled 'Cressy'. Towards more modern times, brought in by a Forces child recently returned from Germany, was a very tenuously appropriate picture of Adolf Hitler accepting half the contents of a flower shop from a little Alpine angel over the huge inscription '*Blümen für Unseren Führer*'.

Across the entire remainder of the twentieth century, obliterating postwar world history and even edging into the next millennium, was the banner headline 'POOL WIN CUP! LAST-MINUTE THRILLER! MORTY AND MATTHEWS MAGIC!' I had a Cavalier and a Roundhead in my desk but knew only that they should precede Adolf.

Mr Adam's gruff demand brought me back to the matter in hand.

'Here, Armstrong. Take a gander at this.'

I read 'Primary School Appoints Physical Education Instructor'.

'No, not that,' he growled, momentarily irritated. 'That!'

He stabbed a finger at the lower half of the paper he had given me, on which he had scrawled several lines of text around a blank square, obviously intended to hold a photograph.

'This Sunday's contribution to the parish magazine,' he informed me.

'School Team Tops League,' it ran. 'Profile of Top Scorer – Timothy Armstrong.'

I recovered my surprise enough to stare at him, more than a little disconcerted. He smiled encouragement and nodded. I read on slowly, in some difficulty without my bookmark to give me a straight edge.

'Until recently, Tim Armstrong of 3A, pictured right, thought he was a goalkeeper. Despite an unparalleled background knowledge of the craft, he was hampered not only by his diminutive size but also by a total and complete lack of any aptitude for the position. As a result, he languished many a month as the team's third choice.

'On the advice of the trainer, Mr J. Adam, he switched to outside left recently and what a transformation! The result? Twenty-six goals in six matches (nine of them in a twenty-two–nil drumming of Poppy Acre) and more dizzy right backs in the Southpool Minor League than in the average nuthouse.

'This is not the first time Tim has risen "head and shoulders" above the crowd at St John's. Two years ago he won third prize in the Spring Bulb competition (Narcissus/Daffodil) and was presented with a book entitled *Chaplains in Action*.

'Off the pitch too, Tim's life has not remained unchanged. Gaining in confidence and influence with each game, he has changed from being counted amongst the school's diffident but regular little chocolate soldiers, to becoming one of those insufferable little Mussos whom all the kids strive to impress, and plead to number amongst their friends.

'His performances improve with each match. Recently, Tim has incorporated several essential elements of the popular continental game into his style, and is frequently to be observed wearing his jersey outside his shorts, standing around with his hands on his hips and spitting profusely.'

I gazed at him in astonishment.

'Well?' he asked, evidently pleased with himself. 'Professional research job as we journalists say, eh?'

I hadn't understood all the words, but more than enough to immediately launch breathless protest.

'Sir – I'm not sure—' I began.

'Oh the last bit's only a joke,' he chided, as if to someone lacking a sense of fun. 'I'm only pulling your leg. I suppose it needs a bit of a rewrite.'

My racing heart began to calm and my gulp-rate subsided slightly. In a minute I might be able to breathe.

'You mean . . . ?'

'Yes Armstrong, when it goes in you won't have anything to worry about.'

'You're writing a bit . . . about me, though? Really? In the parish magazine?'

'Correct,' he said with finality. 'And it would hardly be in either of our best interests to phrase it in anything other than glowing terms.'

He had the air of one pandering to someone's vanity, although I wasn't at all sure whose. All the same, I began to feel a lot easier.

'When they read what I write on Sunday my lad, people will be asking you for your autograph.'

From feeling easier, I started to like the idea. Then I began to feel the faintest batsqueak of excitement.

'After all,' he said amiably, 'not everyone can say

they've torn apart the Holy Family one week, and put a hat trick past Christ the King the next.'

He laughed in a curiously cynical, grown-up sort of way, but I could tell he was pleased.

'Hello Alice!' I heard him say. His voice became baritone attempting the soprano bit.

I turned round to see Miss Cocker entering the room. She was carrying a huge photograph of a currant cake cut from *Woman's Realm*. After a lesson on Alfred the Great, this was Susan Hopcroft's contribution to 'the Pageant' for the entire eighth century. It would have to be trimmed drastically to prevent it from blotting out the Renaissance.

'OK you – out,' Mr Adam hissed, suddenly very tense.

I started to leave, still dazed but now vaguely pleased. As I passed Miss Cocker, she brushed a hand over my hair, smoothing back my fringe. Something mighty within me stirred, sighed, then slumbered again.

At the door, I looked back. They were both staring at me, waiting for me to leave, obviously keen to get on with gumming Susan Hopcroft's cake to the Historical Pageant.

10

I was in a building which might have been a multi-storey car park.

At least, it had rudimentary cement floors and plain walls, and was windowless with wide gaps open to the elements at regular intervals. I was high up as well, a dozen floors at least. The nearest opening let onto a broad vista of central Lancashire. An industrial town, tall chimneys belching smoke and neat geometric rows of back-to-backs spiked with television aerials, was cradled in a fold of low blue hills, bleak and windswept in the distance, which could only be the Pennines.

But it wasn't a car park. There were no cars for one thing. It was totally empty. The room I was in, more an enclosure of bare brick walls really, had many entrances, but none was much wider than a slit hardly big enough to admit a person. Also I could see these opened on to narrow corridors or other similar chamber-like enclosures of greater or smaller size, seemingly haphazard in arrangement.

I was dressed in my football kit – the complete St John's claret and blue rig-out, down to my new continentals with nylon studs which rolled and growled on the concrete when I moved.

There was a scudding and scraping sound and a boy my age entered from the far end. He stood out, incongruously colourful in red and white stripes, and he was dribbling a cassey. With the territorial instinct of a protective animal, I went for him. There was a brief tussle and I dispossessed him. I kicked the ball into one of the narrow corridors and gave chase, all the time struggling against his restraining arms and elbows, and slipping unsteadily on the unfamiliar surface.

'Tim!' a voice called urgently.

Edmundo waited at a corner, his hand extended towards me as if we were in a relay race. His voice was anxious. 'Tim! To me!'

Before I could pass, the red-and-white-shirted adversary interposed a boot which struck the ball hard against the wall with an echoing slap. He trapped the return expertly under his right foot, spun on the spot and disappeared through another entrance. I followed, but he had a team-mate in there who took a long pass and slipped out with the ball via another slit about a dozen yards or so distant.

Something told me I shouldn't follow. There was an overall strategy based on positional discipline. I made back to my original chamber, noting on the way that Edmundo had vanished, and waited there. Occasionally I would hear the sound of nearby scuffles and bounces, and once in a while claret-and-blue- or red-shirted figures would dash fleetingly past one of the openings. But no-one entered. Just once, far in the distance, muffled and indeterminate, I heard shouts and a faint cheer.

A more complicated game than I had thought, I told myself.

I waited. No-one came. Gradually the intermittent noises ceased. The place became so quiet I could hear myself breathe. I even fancied it seemed to be breathing with me. Two faint and distant organ notes, one rising, the other falling.

I went on waiting, tinged with unease, it seemed for a long time.

Presently Miss Cocker appeared at one of the slit-like openings. She was dressed in something like an elaborate toga and wore leather sandals on her feet. Her costume was off the shoulder and billowed wide from her body, falling in many folds and with much loose material collected over her arm, which she held elegantly extended as she walked towards me. The fabric was stiff crinoline, and held its form like frozen ripples of meringue, except where it was agitated by the movement of her lower legs as she walked.

'Tim,' she said in a tone of gentle surprise, 'the game's over.'

I said nothing, just stared at her. It wasn't a wedding dress, but it was designed to feminize and accentuate. I followed the line of her smooth bare shoulders, marvelling at the whiteness and roundness of them. She followed my gaze.

Smiling fondly, with the air of one offering a small treat which she knew would be welcomed, she asked, 'Would you like to kiss me, here?'

With a simple, two-handed movement, she removed the entire clothing from her upper body. Her breasts were full and ponderous, with huge nipples crowning copper-coloured saucers. She looked down at them, proudly possessive, then back at me.

I nodded. She widened her smile in invitation.

I placed my lips against the fleshy softness. First one,

ɹen the other. She smelled of sugar puffs.

She brushed my hair and let her hand linger at my neck, then lowered her head towards me. Her voice, when she spoke again, was full of understanding, as if I had been creating tortuous complications over something which was really very simple.

'Would you like to see between my legs?'

My breathing quickened. How could she possibly know? This was The Great Mystery. I hardly trusted myself to speak. When I did, it was in an awed whisper.

'Yes.'

Stepping back, she made another simple adjustment to her clothing. The costume cascaded in white clouds to her knees.

Sprouting from between her legs was something like a piggy's tail, but much longer. At its root as thick as the stem of a stout bush, it quickly tapered and curled, until after a couple of coils it came to a fine point like the tip of a carrot. It had the colour and look of a plucked bird, but the skin was coarse and flaked with dandruff, and the whole was covered with fine whitish hair.

'It is called a twat,' she said lucidly.

I threw her a fixed stare. I knew what it was called – Patsie had told me about his sister's – I just hadn't seen one before. I was determined not to draw back, even though the sight of it scared me a bit, like something you weren't sure was dangerous, a different type of spider, say, or a coiled-up snake. For one terrible moment I feared she was about to ask me to touch it. Since everyone else seemed to find these things so desirable I couldn't shirk it, but shuddered at the prospect. Thankfully she just continued to smile, a little amused by my fixed, expressionless stare.

When I returned my gaze to her eyes they had a knowing glint, and her amusement seemed to intensify. She knew my thoughts more clearly than I did.

'And would you like to look at my bottom?'

I couldn't avoid a catch in my breathing and an audible

gulp as if I were trying to swallow a pebble. She had known this was what I wanted all the time, the tone in her voice said that. I nodded, but she was going to make me ask. I had to take in a couple of lungfuls of air which came in gasps. I could hear my own heart beating. The distant organ wheezed its two notes with swelling volume.

'Would you?' she said again.

When I spoke, my voice was a croak.

'Yes please, Miss.'

Smiling all the time, she turned her back, but continued to look at me askance, her chin resting on her right shoulder. She placed her weight on one foot which accentuated the curve of her hip. The gathered material at her feet gave the impression of a peeled, exposed white fruit. Her bottom was large but smooth and taut. Snowy hillocks plunged into valleys of mysterious pleasure. She continued to regard me from over her shoulder with that look of amused power, languidly blinking occasionally.

The organ notes intensified, threatening to overwhelm.

'And would you like to stroke it, Tim? Squeeze it? Smack it?'

I felt as if I was being strangled.

'Urgh-argh!'

I awoke to blackness and a still and complete silence broken only by the sound of my lungs clutching air and the muted thuds of my own heart. A yard from me was the indistinct outline of Jim's sleeping figure, rising and falling gently.

I lay for a moment whilst my racing pulse slowed and my breathing quietened. After a few seconds, I moved back a fold of the covers to allow cool air to my sweating face and chest. As I returned it, my hand touched something warm and wet in the bed beside me.

I groaned. I hadn't wet the bed for years. This would bring down an inquisition of epic proportions. The humiliation!

But no, it wasn't water. There wasn't much of it and it

was curiously tacky. Like spittle? No, heavier. Blood? I feverishly explored the little patch with my fingertips. I imagined something like my dying uncle Frank might cough up there in the bed beside me.

In the darkness, my sweat cooled. I shivered and prayed for sleep.

11

Much amended, Mr Adam's piece about me appeared the following Sunday in the parish magazine, which was on sale after mass, priced three pence.

It was customary to hang around in the church car park for a while after each service. There was no graveyard, the church was new and modern and looked like the Department of Health and Social Security with a steeple. The men would huddle in huge heavy overcoats which fell to their ankles like curtains, sporting Anthony Eden hats, and ask each other mysterious, clipped questions like 'Hast tha sorted that bit o' business for me Andy?' to which the answer would be a curt nod and something along the lines of 'Asull see thee down at club.' The women would parade in coats with lapels the size of car doors and hats which threw off twenty-inch feathers tangentially at alarming and dangerous angles, saying things like '. . . and by t' time she passed on, it were t' size of an orange.' Father Ryan and Canon Creaney would move amongst them in clerical black, giving information on social evenings, reminders about jumble sales, planning beetle drives, announcing whist drives, dispensing Park Drives.

When the parish magazine appeared, I was an instant celebrity. I had tried to tell the family beforehand, but when faced with a vociferous, overexcited ten-year-old, my parents would either hush it, humour it, feed it or fetch it one, in escalating order of tactical response. As a farmer's son, my father's sporting interests were limited to trout-fishing and killing things, but he looked down at me fondly enough now, stooped and ruined my parting, then gave me a bob pocket money instead of the usual ninepence. I didn't tell him he'd paid out once already.

My uncle Tom gave me a tanner. Mrs Malloy called me her little bobby-dazzler. Twenty-seven people asked me which team I was going to play for when I grew up. My mother dug me out from the folds of her coat where I had fled, red-faced and contorted with embarrassment, to warn me not to let it make me conceited.

Only Jim put a damper on the proceedings. Having spent the entire time watching silently from the sidelines, he moved in when the fuss had died down.

'Well, our nip,' he warned, 'looks like you'll be failing your eleven plus.'

He flipped my tie out of my jacket dexterously with one finger.

I was horrified.

'Why should I?' I gasped, fumbling with the tie.

'Well, if you pass, you'll be going to t' grammar school and playing,' he raised his nose, 'raggah.'

'Well you go to grammar school and you don't play rugby,' I retorted.

But he simply stared intently into my eyes, lifted an index finger and placed it along the side of his nose, saying nothing.

On the Thursday afternoon after what Jim insisted on calling my academic epitaph, games were cancelled because it was raining more than usual. The boys were herded into one classroom to watch a slide show on football technique given by Mr Adam, and the girls into another where, there being either no slide show or no technique to netball and rounders, Miss Hodge would read them a story.

At the front of the class, Mr Adam slowly assembled a highly unstable contraption made from grey metal plate which was draped at the sides with black curtain. It resembled a sort of funereal Punch and Judy booth, though there was a flat white screen where the puppets should appear. He plugged in a wire and the screen glowed. Every now and then he would poke his head behind the curtain and slot in a plate about the size of a flagstone, which then flashed up miraculously as a black and white still on the small screen. In just discernible shades of grey would be Stanley Matthews kicking a ball; Billy Wright chesting one; Jackie Blanchflower heading clear. Mr Adam would tell us what they were doing wrong, and occasionally right.

'Here's Eddie Hopkinson rising to a corner. Notice how he's picking the ball out of the err.'

'As opposed to picking it out of the back of the net like he usually does,' Edmundo quipped.

'Peachyo,' Mr Adam barked through the laughter. 'One more peep out o' you and you'll be feeling the flat of my hand. Alice.' Kettledrums became tinkling cymbals in the space of a syllable.

There was a general rustling and clanging of benches as the entire class rose to deliver the customary caterwauling *en masse.*

'Good-aft-ernoon-Miss-Cock-err.'

Mr Adam was momentarily out of his stride. He went to switch off the machine but didn't, inserted his head into the curtain and caught it painfully on the metal frame, made to put down his slide then carried it with him as he moved towards her.

'Just talk quietly amongst yourselves for a while lads,' he requested, nervously and unwisely. It was tantamount to inviting an alcoholic to take a nip. Background buzz quickly took on more cogency.

Edmundo and I turned at a thump from Charles Vart.

'Heh. Did you know that there's a prison in London called the Bloody Tower.'

I sniggered.

'Garn,' Edmundo said.

''Strue.'

'That reminds me then,' Patsie Hunieghan said, 'that

there's a brothel in Liverpool called the Fucking Palace.'

This time the laughter was intermingled with gasps at his daring. Fucking meant nothing to me at all and I had only the vaguest notion of what a brothel was. I had an idea it was something to do with aftershave lotion. My dad had once told a story about his days in the army out east when an officer had stopped him and his mate as they set off for a night out with, 'Armstrong, my wife would say you smell like a brothel,' to which my dad had replied, 'Really sir? My wife wouldn't know what a brothel smells like.' My dad always used Old Spice.

I searched my mind for something relevant to say.

'My sister thought there was a church in Paris called Notre Damned,' I tried. I suddenly realized I was having to shout to make myself heard.

'Mister Adam!' screamed a queenly voice accusingly.

The door had flown open and there was Miss Hodge glaring sternly at Mr Adam and Miss Cocker, caught in verbal *flagrante*.

Quiet descended. Then scuttles, rustles, clangs as we stood up.

'Good-aft-ernoon-Miss-Hodge,' we wailed discordantly.

She reared up her shoulders, aimed a mighty sniff at the two miscreants, threw back her head and departed.

'Good-aft-ernoon-and-thank-you-Miss-Hodge!'

Miss Cocker dragged her eyes from the floor as we chorused again and gave Mr Adam a diffident look which simply said, 'Oh dear.' Then she walked quietly out.

'Good-aft-ernoon-and-thank-you-Miss-Cock-er.'

Mr Adam made to follow her. He got as far as the door, then seemed to notice that thirty eleven-year-old boys were in the room with him.

'Good-aft-ernoon-and—'

'Oh shut up you lot,' he snapped, and walked back to the desk.

* * *

Mr Mason-Jones was addressing the school assembly.

'And I'm sure, although of course Mr Adam assumes his new position in addition to his current responsibilities as Geography, History and Science Teacher, football-team coach and Cubs troop leader, we all wish him well in his capacity as Physical Education Instructor and Assistant Head.'

There was a ripple of applause to which Miss Hodge, notably, did not contribute.

'No rest for the wicked or the willing, eh Mr Adam?' the Head chortled.

Mr Adam's blue chops creased into a sizeable grin. He folded his arms in satisfaction, revealing the two leather patches on the elbows of his sports jacket like the patterns on a beetle's wings.

There were good-conduct badges in abundance, reflecting a recent dip in the crime rate.

' – and the second courtesy badge,' Mr Mason-Jones was suddenly jauntily announcing, 'goes to Timothy Armstrong, who, I'm sure most of you will be aware, is top scorer and recently appointed vice-captain of our soccer team.' He smiled broadly and added, 'Currently heading towards the Southpool Minor League Championship.'

Quite what that had to do with courtesy awards was left unclarified.

I followed Brenda Fairclough through the ranks of applauding schoolfellows. As always, the babies exalted in the rare ecstasy of being encouraged to make noise. Fifth Avenue ticker-tape parades are tepid by comparison.

We accepted our courtesy badges from Miss Hodge. Brenda Fairclough lavished her with gratitude. I forgot to say thanks.

It didn't trouble me. I was well aware that the finer niceties weren't prominent in my make-up. Courtesy? I thought spitting was manly. I laughed when people broke wind. I held belching competitions with Edmundo.

Prizes weren't given to the deserving, just the conspicuous. Honours and privilege feed off each other and multiply.

'Miss! Miss! Please Miss! Me Miss!'

The class was a phalanx of arms, erect and waving like spears. A horde of fanatical party faithful chanting 'Miss' instead of '*Sieg Heil*!' Linda Miller inched her way desperately down the aisle between the desks, throwing her hand violently towards the front as if she hoped it would come off and land in Miss Hodge's lap.

'Miss! Miss!'

Miss Hodge blinked and winced at the fine spray of spittle which must have been assailing her, but she seemed appreciative of the enthusiasm. Her grin was Caligulan. Her demeanour was Guinevere, selecting her champion.

The water in the fish-tank needed changing. When Miss Hodge appealed for a volunteer to clean out the fish-tank, the class reacted the way dire sinners in the Bible belt greet the prospect of salvation.

The point was that the job conveyed Miss Hodge's Stamp of Approval. It was her Supreme Accolade. An eleven-year-old could be exalted no higher in her favour.

Whilst everyone fought to be selected, only a few had any serious prospect of success. Nominees were frequently repeated. Her list of favourites seldom changed and going by the maxim 'by their deeds shall ye know them', there was rarely sufficient reason to admit a newcomer to the inner sanctum of fish-tank-cleaners.

But I couldn't help noticing, as she serenely surveyed the hissing, multi-tentacled mass before her, that her eyes would constantly return to mine. Yes, there it was again, there was no mistake. Could it be? Stranger things had been happening of late. Was the ghost of my incontinence to be laid at last? Was I about to run up yet another battle honour, collect a further gong? Her great head swung around towards me like a tank turret. My God, I was.

'Timothy!' she pronounced, proffering the fish-net like a sceptre. 'My little Stanley Matthews!'

If, at this stage in my life, I had an image of Divine Dispensation, something which symbolized the supreme authority in my existence, represented the lawgivers who demanded obedience, respect, fealty, it would have been a sort of Mount Rushmore with the gargantuan, granite faces of God, my dad, Miss Hodge and Stanley Matthews gazing down at me.

To be commended by one and compared to another was halfway to apotheosis.

I took the net between trembling fingers.

12

'Get on o'er to t' Tiller Girls,' Mr Adam said to me with a darkly adult laugh. It was Wednesday football practice. The end of the season was two matches away, the championship won and already there was even talk of a dinner in our honour with parents in attendance.

The 'Tiller Girls' referred to a necessary variant on training techniques Mr Adam had introduced, largely as a result of a lack of footballs. A pretty vital prerequisite to the game you might have imagined, and you'd be right, but we had two – one match ball and one practice ball. Consequently, if you weren't lucky enough to be actually kicking one, you usually had to pretend to be. At any one time half the team would be involved in propelling themselves on mighty run-ups of twenty or thirty determined strides, and then launching toe-ended assaults at the stationary practice ball. It was deflated and spongy and would wheeze in protest before loping lazily forward and then ambling to a halt. Frequently, the procedure involved the kicker travelling twice as far as the ball did.

The other half of the team would be banished to a

corner of the playground where they practised their kicking technique on anything to hand, or more precisely to foot – toffee papers, pebbles, even bits of the playground. We used to convince ourselves that we were being kept ball-hungry for match days, like Jimmy Greaves. I popped a Nuttall's Mintoe into my mouth, rolled up the paper, dropped it and then booted it in the direction of 2A. There was a vicious ripping scrape and my shoe sprouted a fresh white scar.

'Damn!' I hissed.

'Tut.'

I looked up and there was Miss Cocker, smiling fondly. Her hair was swept behind her ears and pinned with hairgrips, and she had on a light blue cardigan which hugged the swells and bumps of her ample torso so tightly that it looped into a series of convex bits between the buttons. She had her arms folded, and her matronly breasts swelled over them like a couple of fattened lemmings contemplating the drop.

'Don't swear, Tim love,' she admonished. But the fond smile was not for me. Mr Adam noticed her.

'Tiller Girls, you lot,' he bawled to the half of the team with a ball, and, oblivious to the groans, joined Miss Cocker. For a time they both fawned and smiled, chatting shyly. The air was filled with the sound of steadily degenerating footwear.

Edmundo took three spitcful swipes at a Reilley's Chocolate Toffee Roll paper, then paused with his hands on his hips. He eyed Mr Adam with ill-concealed resentment.

'Sir. Can we get skittles and play five-a-side?'

Mr Adam dragged his gaze reluctantly from Miss Cocker's rosy roly-polyness. 'Aye. 'Course, lads.' Evidently the playground was a lush meadow in balmy summer, and he a pastoral guardian fondly tending his young charges.

'You fetch—' he said softly, then paused and considered. 'No. Wait. Alice and I'll get skittles.'

He guided Miss Cocker towards the small storeroom where we kept odds and ends of sporting apparatus, including the wooden skittles which we occasionally used as goalposts. He unlocked the door and ushered Miss Cocker inside with elaborate consideration, then followed, glancing furtively to his left and right before closing the door behind him.

Seconds passed. Then minutes. Our assaults on the playground debris became half-hearted, then, as boredom set in, sporadic. Patsie Hunieghan landed his foot on Michael Atherton's expansive buttocks with a dull, solid 'whup'. There was a giggle, then a shout, and suddenly we were in the middle of an arse-booting competition. The noise swelled quickly, like a flock of startled tropical birds in a rain forest. Despite Edmundo's sober captain-like attempts to maintain gymnastic discipline, disorder soon prevailed. Billy Bibby shrieked as he shot past me with a protective hand cupping each of his skinny buttocks, closely followed by Frank Macnally skipping every few yards as he adjusted his stride and attempted to land a right-footer. They narrowly avoided colliding with Miss Hodge.

'*What* is going on here?' she demanded with Cleopatran resonance. We froze. Maintaining discipline and authority may be an issue in today's schools. Back then, we almost put our hands up and whimpered, 'Don't shoot!'

She waited with a thunderous glare. The silence fixed us in a tableau. Billy seemed to think she was addressing herself to him.

'Surely that's a rhetorical question, Miss,' he commented. This was possibly the first indication I had that he was destined to study Mathematics and Philosophy at Cambridge. Miss Hodge looked astounded, then irritated, then moved to clout him. He scuttled into retreat with a muffled squeak.

'*Where* is Mr Adam?' she boomed.

No-one answered, but, involuntarily, eleven pairs of

eyes swivelled towards the storeroom.

Without a further word, Miss Hodge marched towards it, heels tapping out her annoyance, grey mane billowing in her slipstream, jaw set grimly in determination to get to the bottom of this. She yanked open the door. There was a pause, then her right hand flattened over her chest and she let out a gasp which hissed like quenching steel. We could hear it clearly at fifteen yards.

Mr Adam and Miss Cocker emerged, looking shamefaced. For a moment, they blinked awkwardly as if they'd come into the light. Then, with an essay at defiance, Miss Cocker tossed her head and set off at a smart pace for the staff-room. Mr Adam shuffled uncomfortably. Miss Hodge's perfectly 'o'-shaped lips betrayed the fact that she was having difficulty assimilating what she'd just seen.

'Where the hell are the sodding skittles,' Edmundo ground out between clenched teeth.

'Where did you pick up language like that?'

John stopped what he was doing and questioned me earnestly. Up until then, my conversation had hardly interrupted his intent oiling, screwing, lifting, tightening, loosening, hammering and occasional puzzled frowning. We were in the back shed, which he used as a sort of a workshop, there being no garage. Morris Cowley innards lined the shelves and benches, and the floor looked as though a robot had just thrown up.

'School,' I answered shortly, starting to regret the enquiry.

He fixed me with a disapproving glare.

'Turn that manual back to page forty,' he ordered, nodding at the bench in front of him. His overalls were folded back at the cuffs and his hands and forearms were black with oil. I did as I was told, catching a glimpse of 'Methodology for Systematic Axial Regulation and Re-alignment of Gear Trains'. Lovely. I had a brief yearning to be oiled up to the armpits and using words like that.

'Well don't say it again. You're too young.'
He dismissed me with a determined jerk on a thirteen-sixteenths spanner.

'You little horror!' shrieked Nonnie. 'Get your filthy little tongue out of my room!'
She was sprawled on her bed in pyjamas with her knees drawn up in an easy, vaguely unfeminine way and *Marilyn* propped against her legs. Her hair was intertwined in brushes and her face a half-inch deep in Pond's Cold Cream. Drying nails dangled from drooping hands like ripe exotic fruit.
'Out!' She almost screamed. She went to throw the magazine at me but remembered her drying nail varnish. Instead, she sharply jerked one foot and despatched a pink, pompom-adorned slipper in my direction. Something she could do with uncanny accuracy.

Jim snorted. 'What do you want to know for?'
I was reluctant to be drawn. I just wanted an answer to a question.
'Someone at school did it.'
'Like hell they did,' he said with assurance. He squirted even more Fairy Liquid into the bowl and agitated the water until the sink was a cauldron of suds. Then he scooped up a handful and deposited some in the middle of my face, and, as I blinked, blew the rest into my ear.
'Well, what is it?' I asked again, dabbing away bubbles with the drying-up cloth. Younger brothers accept torment as a way of life. At least this beat being pinned to the ground with an ankle in each ear, patiently breathing in semi-asphyxiated agony whilst he banged out a winning fall with the flat of his hand on the floor next to my head. 'Awon . . . Atooo . . . Athree!'
He gave a bit of dried egg on John's dinner plate a cursory rub then released it with a clatter onto the draining-board. I picked it up and proceeded to dry it.

'Go on. Tell us where you heard it.'

'Oh – in t' playground. Someone said it in t' playground.'

He sounded very sententious. 'Aye, well,' he announced. 'Psychiatrists worry 'emselves daft about t' younger generation learning facts of life in t' playground.'

I waited expectantly. He felt around beneath the foaming mass and in rapid succession produced two cups, four saucers and a small armoury of knives, forks and spoons. For some reason he hated my drying to keep pace with his washing.

'So if I tell you, they'll have nowt to worry about, will they,' he said with finality. Soapy cutlery banged and rattled onto the draining-board.

'Go on, Jim. Tell us. What's it mean?'

It was no good. The conversation was over. He admired his reflection in the kitchen window and it must have reminded him how much he looked like Elvis Presley. He threw back his head and howled at the world that he couldn't help it he was in lo-o-o-o-ve, with the gurl of his best frurnd.

A tremendous explosion incapacitated the left side of my brain and the features of my face were suddenly numb to any sensation. The feeling was exactly what you might expect if you jammed a penny banger in your ear on Bonfire Night and lit the blue touch-paper. The blood sang through my head with a sonic whistle which blanked out any other sound. Desperately grasping for some explanation, I stared around the dinner table from right to left. My mother looked white with shock. Nonnie was smiling smugly as if at just deserts being meted out. John was slowly shaking his head in the sad way of one who has seen disaster looming. Jim was peering intently into the middle of his dinner, keeping his head down, an accessory after the fact trying to appear uninvolved. My father was mouthing judgement-day wrath and vengeance, silently lunging at me with a forkful of beefburger. Gradually, sound began to return. I raised a hand to my face and it met with ballooning cheek about three inches earlier than I had expected.

'How dare you say such a thing to your mother!' he thundered. 'By the left, if that's what you're learning at St John's we'll have you out an' double quick. Never! I have never heard such disgusting, foul-mouthed, vulgar . . .'

Shagging.

Patsie Huniegham had said that what they'd been doing in the storeroom was shagging. All the team had nodded sagely. I had asked my mum what it meant because no-one else seemed to want to tell me.

Quite quickly, it started hurting. Soon, bewildered tears were flowing over hot swollen cheeks.

13

I thought of the brick croft as an everyday aspect of the local topography, just like Whalley Square, the Co-op and the corner pub. I assumed every neighbourhood had one. It never occurred to me that it was something slightly out of the ordinary.

It had been around as long as anyone could remember. Presumably, at some time or another, the local ground had revealed itself to contain deposits of accessible clay, rich in the correct minerals. Whatever the reason might be, just a few streets behind us began an area of several square miles of rough, unbuilt land. Except for a small, makeshift processing plant in one corner from which curious roars, mechanical rattles and pulsing chugs emanated sporadically, the area was a wild irregular range of low hillocks, mainly grassed-over ancient workings. Between these, shallow valleys were threaded by beaten paths and a network of narrow tracking, along which unmanned skips trundled occasionally towards the chugging sound in the ramshackle factory, drawn on by some antiquated cable-traction system and loaded high with glistening loam.

Of course, signs everywhere informed you threateningly that trespassers would be prosecuted. But, as long as you kept away from the factory or the actual diggings, no-one bothered you. To a group of street-bound eleven-year-olds, it represented an opportunity too good to be missed. The shaggy hills and stagnant rain pools provided a perfect rendering of a stretch of Montana in the days of the Western frontier, or occupied Borneo under the Japanese, or even the alien ranges surrounding the landing site of the first British expedition to Mars.

I seldom went there except in a group. But this evening I had changed my route home from school, even taking myself out of my way. I had a headache. I wanted to be alone. Somehow, I needed air and time to think.

It had been an unusual day. When the bell had sounded at nine, instead of being herded into our classroom, we in the top classes had been told to report to the assembly hall. After our teachers had formed us into lines and taken register, we were allowed to file in. There, in regimental rows and at precision intervals, like tanks before an assault, were scores of desks each bearing two pencils, a rubber and a wooden rule. We were seated not in classes, but in alphabetical order. Mr Mason-Jones and Miss Hodge distributed thin booklets, placing them face down on the desk in front of us, then the teachers took up position at regular intervals along the walls, watchful keepers, and Mr Mason-Jones walked to the front.

'Is this the eleven plus, sir?' Billy Bibby asked.

'You think this is the eleven plus?' Mr Mason-Jones scoffed. His voice implied that comparing this to the eleven plus was like contrasting conditions in the Cubs with the Waffen SS.

'Yes I do,' Billy answered pluckily.

Mr Mason-Jones smiled indulgently and looked away. He raised his voice to fill the room. 'Read the instructions care–'

'Well is it?' Billy asked with gritty insistence.

Mr Mason-Jones' hand went up to smooth his balding crown and then moved to tickle the fringe of hair behind his ear in that intricate gesture of annoyance which pointed his elbow at you.

'Be quiet, Billy,' he said, his voice strained.

'It is the eleven plus, then,' Billy said, throwing back his head and informing the world. He sounded as though he had announced a confirmed case of smallpox. There was a communal whimper.

'This is not—' the headmaster began, gruff and irritated. No, he realized, he couldn't say that. That would be direct lying. His other hand came up into that self-imposed half nelson with which he prefaced true rage.

I didn't feel nervous. I felt petrified.

Mr Mason-Jones managed to contain his annoyance. He took a couple of deep breaths and continued in a calmer voice.

'Read the instructions carefully. Read the questions carefully. Write all the answers, er carefully. Do your best. No-one can ask more.'

'Are you going—' Billy began again.

'You have two hours,' Mr Mason-Jones broke in, eyeing Billy fiercely.

Susan Hopcroft began to cry. Linda Miller asked if she could go to the toilet. Several hands went up at once.

I turned the page, skipped the general guff and read at the head of twenty or so similar questions:

BLACK is to NIGHT as FRIENDLY is to . . . . . .

Golliwog? Pal? Wouldn't it make more sense if 'night' said 'white', then the answer must be 'hostile'. Was it a misprint? Should I ask?

I turned the page.

PICK the ODD MAN OUT from the following:
fish. toad. fox. fur. frog.

Toad didn't begin with 'f'. Foxes had fur. Toads had frogs. Or did they? Fish was a general word.

The next page was full of sums about decimals. I'd been off that week with my tonsils.

I wanted a wee.

They had let us out of school with sympathetic waves in mid-afternoon.

I walked the silent hills and valleys of the brick croft and let the wind play in my hair. To take my mind off things, I slipped into my part-time job as scout to a wagon train. I was astride my favourite mount, Brandy, a roan with a huge straw fringe of a mane. We were keeping a wary eye out for a Comanche war party. My left hand moved forward to take his rein, my tongue clicked out the sound of his hooves, I tossed spittle around my mouth to simulate the rustle of his harness. I urged him to the top of a rise, mouthing encouragement, and surveyed the next valley. There was a wagon.

No, I mean there *was* a wagon. Or rather, a van. It was stationary at the end of the long winding track that led from the main road into the brick croft. It was seldom used because it went nowhere.

I realized the van looked familiar. Number-plates meant nothing to me, but I recognized an Austin. Also it was green and black, the colour of Miss Cocker's van. I moved down the hill in the fading light. Even from a distance I could see that both driver's and passenger's seat were empty, but I pressed on anyway. It *was* her van. I recognized characteristic features, not least the rust.

I pressed my nose to the window of the passenger's side. Coats were on the seat. Keys. A wallet, a bag. I crinkled my eyes and nose in momentary puzzlement. I tried the door but it was locked.

Then I heard the noise. I knew straight away what it was. In the back of the van, someone was being given some very bad news. 'No,' they kept saying in long-drawn-out disbelief. 'No, oh no.' It was a groan of fathomless misery.

I moved around to the back doors, where I knew there were two windows. Standing on tiptoe I could just see in. There was a bicycle in there, propped awkwardly against one side of the van with its front wheel folded at right angles. Lying on some loose blankets next to it were Miss Cocker and Mr Adam. I could only make out their heads and shoulders. Mr Adam had his mouth right up to Miss Cocker's ear, and it was she who was so upset by what he was telling her in a low murmur. She gasped in horror even as I looked. He held her by the shoulders, tightly, afraid she might bolt. She was writhing to free herself. They weren't actually fighting, but it was certainly a desperate struggle. He was holding her so tight they were almost rubbing themselves into each other. She seemed about to cry.

I dropped back down to the soles of my feet. I felt disturbed, without knowing why. No, worse. What I had just seen frightened me. It frightened me in the same way I got scared when adults cried, or my parents fell out with each other, or said they were worried about something. It concerned matters, not just beyond control, but beyond comprehension. Things monstrously adult, like Uncle Frank dying of a cough, or Dad not having any money, or the Prime Minister saying we had to have a nuclear war.

I suddenly wanted very much to be home. It was late. The gloom was gathering and there was a chill in the air. I resolved not to let a living soul know I had been here.

I set off running, determined not to stop until I had the front-door knocker in my hand.

I rounded a low hill and came to a stop after a hundred yards. Two young lads were crouched together, busily preoccupied over something. With only minor surprise, I noted that one of them was Patsie Hunieghan. I didn't know the other but he looked something of a ruffian. I didn't want to stop, but I was somehow drawn on by the sound of their conspiratorial grunts and mean laughter, half growls, half chuckles. Patsie didn't wave encouragement, but the whites of his eyes shone with fascination at whatever was on the ground between them. I walked slowly forward. The other lad's arms were jerking purposefully and he was letting out animal snorts of excitement in rhythm to the movement.

Staked across a brick in front of them was a large frog. Its limbs were weighted with elastic bands and stones. With the ingenuity of human badness down the ages, they had contrived to introduce a bicycle-pump into the frog's backside, using a straw. The lad was slowly inflating the frog. It made not a movement nor sound. Its wide eyes rolled accusingly in passive, fishy condemnation. Its body puffed alarmingly at each stroke. Snooker ball, tennis ball, cannon-ball, football. Its skin was stretched so thin you could almost see through it. A veiny membrane, a living lampshade.

With a callous sweep of his arm, Patsie brought down a large brick he was holding and crushed the creature to death. At the resulting explosion of intestine and tissue, they each let out an earthy bellow of triumph, part snarl, part scream, such as you might have had to give out in the battles of the Dark Ages, as you plunged your blade into someone's guts.

14

An unexpected bitingly cold snap turned late April into midwinter. During morning playtime we huddled in coats and scarves, little clusters of stamping, jerking figures, too cold to discard outer clothing for a game of footer. A few feet away Miss Hodge, whose turn it was for yard duty, eyed us warily as if we were a chain gang on rock-breaking.

Linda Miller and Maureen Keene ran towards me trailing clouds of frosty breath behind them in discreet little puffs. Their freckled faces giggled cheekily from beneath jauntily cocked berets. I felt briefly elated.

'Favourite colour?' Maureen demanded without any preliminaries.

'Blue,' I said uncertainly, brow furrowing.

She aimed bunched fingers at me which were gloved into a paper contraption, intricately folded like the petals of a flower, over which figures and letters were mysteriously scrawled. She lifted the petal annotated 'blue' and then did some complicated shuffling.

'Lucky number?'

'Er, eleven.' This, because I was outside left.

'Between one and ten, dumbo.'

'Oh. Two.' For no reason. Not wishing to appear slow.

'Pick a letter.'

'What for?' I whined, getting fed up.

'Pick a letter.' Insistently.

'Oh, hell . . .'

'Ell. Right,' Linda said.

'For Little Lamb,' Maureen added with an enigmatic smile.

They turned towards each other and conferred, giggling. Maureen worked the paper petals of her contraption back and forth rapidly. It looked briefly like a Venus flytrap chomping on a largish bumble-bee. Then she lifted up one flap, stood shoulder to shoulder with Linda, and together they chanted at me like the angels' chorus in the school nativity play.

> 'A pig farmer is what you'll be
> A fishmonger your wife
> Together you'll have children three
> And lead a smelly life.'

Then they cackled shrilly like a pair of old crones.

I had expected better. From both Maureen's approach and my future. Also my ears were cold. I wanted to appear above all this.

'Oh clear off to the Fucking Palace Brothel,' I snapped.

The effect was explosive. They reared up, wide-eyed and incredulous, exhaling lengthy plumes of white breath hoarsely in disbelief. I felt immediate regret turn to panic as they moved off, throwing cautious glances over their shoulders as if fleeing from something predatory, in the direction of Miss Hodge.

She was talking to my mum. General Custer probably experienced a similar feeling of surprise alloyed with dismay on seeing several hundred thousand Lacota Sioux, armed to the teeth, painted up like Christmas and descending purposefully towards the Little Big Horn, to the one I felt at the sight of my mum talking to Miss Hodge in the playground. Their faces were grim and their arms folded in that way women have, though awkwardly because of several layers of winter woollies, and they were nodding towards me disapprovingly. Maureen and Linda skipped up to them chattering with excitement. Miss Hodge bent kindly forward, just as the word 'brothel' floated back to me on the wind.

My mother's head shook in disbelief. Her shoulders shrugged me off with a shuffling gesture of final dispossession, and she turned away. I watched her zip-up, ankle-length suedette bootees trudge slowly through the school gap in the wall.

Miss Hodge took Linda and Maureen by the hand and bore down on me, a destroyer flanked by two frigates. I fancied I could even hear a siren sounding battle stations. 'Woop-woop-woop!' Her red face loomed larger and larger until it was inches from my own, filling my entire view of the world. I flinched.

'I'll make you smart, young man,' she trilled. No idle threat. Deftly hoisting my coat she brought her hand down neatly with a sharp crack midway between where my short trousers finished and my long socks began. The effect on a bare expanse of chilled thigh was devastating. I leapt several inches off the ground and began dancing wildly around her, cantering in a circle like a circus horse as she held me roughly by the arm.

'Some people abuse popularity,' she barked. 'Some people can't handle privilege. Now who has been teaching you language?'

I screamed with my eyes closed, and pranced around, hopping obediently at each crack.

With each circuit of the little ring she was walloping me round, I recognized a new face. Some were glum, some sympathetic, some gloating. The pain was paltry compared to the humiliation.

And I knew it wouldn't end there. Might it go as far as the headmaster? Certainly parental retribution would be putting in an appearance just as surely as spinach in a Popeye cartoon.

15

'Nay, Hull City never got five.'

My father's voice held a note of desolation far too real to be attributable to something as trivial as a football result.

He was sitting forward in his armchair with his ear pressed against the wireless, a massive effigy in polished mahogany and textile, fronted with Bakelite knobs the size of train buffers and a huge white tuning dial which carried the name of every major city in the world. Normally the setting alternated between the Light, Home, and, as long as my father was out, Luxembourg. Occasionally, mysteriously, it would stray to Vladivostok, Sebastopol or Gdansk. This meant Jim and I had been playing 'Journey into space', a game he had invented which involved us tying bath towels around our necks and holding poker-swordfights against a background noise of Slavic monologue, overlaid with static. It usually ended with me tearfully nursing a soot-covered weal across the back of my hand.

'Hull, five. Did I get that right?' he asked, a bit desperately.

Nonnie was at the Odeon. John was outside under his car with a torch. Jim was at the table with his head immersed in his books, furiously proving that the opposite angles of a parallelogram are equal. I eyed my mother nervously. She continued knitting without returning my look. She hadn't spoken to me since the episode in the playground two days before. I was being kept in agonies of suspense over whether she was going to tell Him or not. If she did, it would probably mean the cruellest castigation in the Armstrong household since Jim was discovered over the grid in the front street, meticulously feeding down slice after slice of detested corned beef which he had filched from his plate into his pocket at teatime under cover of profuse and unconvincing 'yum-yums'.

'Five–nil to Hull. He never said that did he?'

Pitifully he waved the printed coupon in his hands.

It was the church sweep. His three numbers had given him Saturday's top scoring teams. That meant, provided neither Hull City nor Crewe Alexander scored more than three in their mid-week fixture, he had won a tenner. No small sum when you could buy a house for a couple of dozen of them.

Since Saturday he had been so nice and friendly to everybody, just like the time he brought home the oil-lamp which reminded him of back home in Ireland, and it had belched soot all over the living-room while everyone was out. When he had sent me for a packet of pipe cleaners the night before, he had told me to keep the change from a threepenny bit. Now he'd probably want to know what extravagances I'd lavished the three ha'pence on.

'Five?' he said incredulously. His voice was almost beseeching.

'Five!' my mother snapped, throwing down her knitting as though it had attacked her. 'Hull City five Crewe

Alexander nil. Brown-hat trick, Ellwood-penalty, Stone-own goal. Now will you shut up about it!'

For a second he looked a broken man. Then he breathed in deeply, clicked off the radio as though he hated it and became my dad again.

I sank down into my armchair.

So now they were both charged, primed and simply looking for somewhere to go off. Life would be a hazardous business over the next few days. It would take me a long time to forgive Brown his hat trick, Ellwood his penalty and Stone his own goal. My father never would.

16

The second-last match of the season saw us away to the tail-enders on a fine bright morning, though with a nip of frost in the air. The result was by now irrelevant to the outcome of the league championships, in that we couldn't be caught and there was nowhere to relegate them to. The clash was expected to be fairly innocuous: a mere skirmish rather than battle royal. And so it was for most of the proceedings.

But a series of incidents had revealed their right full back to be deliberately and outrageously provocative. He had been correct and polite before the match. He had hoped I had a good game. He kept making chummy conversation when we were both off the ball. At one point he even said 'well played' to me in the well-rounded vowels of a doctor's or solicitor's son. Added to that he was little and weedy, with long simian eyebrows, sticky-out ears and arms too long for his body. When contesting the ball with an opponent, he stood back and did a little loping jig from side to side which was supposed to impress you as a demonstration of skill. I simply stared at him as if a dog had just done him.

Halfway through the second half, I watched him advance slowly down the wing with the ball at his feet to about the halfway line. Directly behind him on the touch-line was an enormous pair of wellingtons inhabited by Miss Cocker, just visible in headscarf and mackintosh. Flanking her were Mr Mason-Jones, distinguished in deerstalker, and Mr Adam, reduced to the role of vociferous spectator since this was an away game.

The little full back paused in front of them and started showing his Hopi Indian rain dance to Michael Atherton. Thought he was Tom Finney, the little crumb. I bet myself that a goody like him had never had to prance about in chastised humiliation before his classmates, quake for days under the unrelenting threat of parental vengeance, suffer wrongfully and vicariously the reputation of having the mouth of a Calcutta sewer. He had probably coasted through his eleven plus.

Behind him was the first woman to trouble my sleep. Here was I, my manhood all untried and the molten lava of unrighted wrongs churning in my belly.

I started forward growling and snorting like a tournament knight, lumbered between Patsie and Edmundo who each glanced at me with a surprised, interrogative grunt, launched myself into full gallop and, as I bore down on him, leapt two-footed into the air, tore a five-yard furrow through the turf, threw out a wake of early-morning dew like a motor launch, and took him on the ankle.

A very young doe might make the noise he did if its foot were to stray into one of those spring-loaded steel-jaw traps. He went down like a bowling skittle and was wailing before he hit the ground.

'Tim!' I heard Miss Cocker scream.

'Armstrong!' Mr Adam thundered.

'Send that man off!'

That was Mr Mason-Jones. If our side felt like that about it, what did the opposition think?

As I lay on the ground, not over-anxious to get up, a large boot suddenly planted itself on either side of my head and I was looking up into the inverted features of a kindly schoolmaster. A long way up – he was inordinately tall. I listened to his voice as if from the bottom of a well.

'I have never witnessed anything like that in all my years of primary-school football,' his voice said, evenly and impassively. 'I have no idea where you picked up that sort of antic, young man, but you won't be using it here. Not while I'm refereeing, you won't.'

It was all very considered, matter-of-fact, no hint of enmity.

'Now I suggest you spend the rest of the game in the cloakroom and wait for your more civilized team-mates to join you there.'

It was the first sending-off in the entire history of the Southpool and District Minor League.

I sat in the cloakroom on one of the long benches under the numbered coat hooks with my head resting against the wall and my chest heaving. I didn't know why I'd done it. It was a gesture, an expression of something, like slamming a door or banging the table. OK, worse than that. I would have apologized, but I didn't know how. I wouldn't have known what to be sorry about. I wasn't sure what I was feeling. All I knew was that I was on the outside looking in. An outcast. A wrong 'un. And it was cold.

I changed into my shoes, put on my jacket and waited.

Soon I heard the clatter of studs on stone floor. I had held out vague hopes that within the team it might have been considered a ballsy sort of thing to do, that I'd be admired for showing that I didn't shy at a touch of rough-and-tumble when the occasion demanded. Any hope of that was shattered by Athers' first remark.

'You calmed down?' he asked laconically.

I just nodded. I quickly sensed that there was a general uneasiness about direct communication with me.

'He's walking again OK. At least, you know like, with help,' Edmundo told me in a misguided attempt at lightening matters.

Patsie sat next to me, leaned across into the clouds of my misery and whispered, 'Didn't know you had it in you. Do you take on contracts? May be able to put a couple of jobs your way if you know what I mean.'

Mr Adam marched through the busily chattering team, striding over outstretched undressing and dressing limbs and placed his mouth next to my ear.

'What on earth got into you, Armstrong,' he hissed urgently. 'Hasn't your mother fed you any red meat this week?'

He thrust his rancorous mug into my face, then took in my expression and saw he didn't really need to say anything.

'There'll be t' devil to pay next week,' he mumbled. 'Your headmaster is coming unglued.'

He blew in exasperation. I tried to dispel a brief vision of next week from my mind.

'Come on lads,' he said, straightening up and raising his voice.

Dejected, I trailed a group of others through the door and along a corridor, emerging onto the small forecourt, clear except for one or two cars and Miss Cocker's van. Cradled in her arms, Miss Cocker carried the huge brown paper bag which had held the half-time oranges and now held their peelings. Edmundo carried the bucket and sponge which, when filled with icy water, was Mr Adam's sole gesture towards first aid; Michael Atherton cradled the jug and empty lemon barley water bottle; Frank Macnally hugged the practice ball. One or two others followed. I brought up the rear. No-one spoke.

As we reached the van, a woman stepped out from behind it. She was small and plain, dressed almost shabbily in a light blue raincoat and black beret from which wayward locks of nicotine-blonde hair had escaped here and there in tufts. Her face was very pale except for vivid pink splashes at the cheeks and on the nose, and it was set hard.

'Going for our little Saturday ride out, are we?' she demanded.

There was a jeering note in her voice and somewhere a threat and it frightened me.

We all halted.

'Mary!' Mr Adam said.

'Because if you are,' the woman ran on, taking no notice, 'I thought it was about time you were aware a few other people have got to know about it too.'

Miss Cocker stepped quickly forward and confronted her.

'No, please. Mrs Adam let's just—'

The woman unleashed a vicious upper-cut which took the brown paper bag Miss Cocker was carrying full force, lifted it arcing high into the air and rained down bits of orange peel over all of us. They pattered like spent shrapnel.

'You!' she shouted bitterly. 'How dare you? Don't you dare address yourself to me you smutty little HAW!'

Miss Cocker stood back and went to cover her face with her hands, but didn't. She bowed her head in a sort of capitulation, folded one hand into the other madonna-like and then simply seemed to withdraw into herself. There was a quiet stoicism about her, as if she'd known she would someday have to face this and now it only had to be endured.

'And as for you!' The woman turned her wrath towards Mr Adam. 'You conniving, low deceitful ANIMAL.' Again her voice hissed dangerously along the sentence like a fuse before exploding on the last word.

The rest of us gazed in silent astonishment. Of course adults sometimes behaved strangely. One's parents argued. But this – in public, in daylight and in front of children. And from teachers, those everyday gods, whom you never suspected of having lives which revolved around liver and onions, *Rawhide* and football coupons. The very pillars of authority rocked before our eyes. Our shock would have been no more intense if Father Ryan had paused in the middle of mass to introduce a naked virgin and a blood-soaked cockerel at the offertory, or Miss Hodge had held up the Monday-morning assembly to do an Alma Cogan impression.

'Mary,' Mr Adam protested feebly, 'not here.'

'Not here!' she shouted scornfully. 'Why? Are you afraid it might do some damage to your –' she almost hawked and then spat the word, 'career! My dear God, that people trust innocent children to the likes of you two leaves me speechless.'

'Mary,' he said again. He moved forward just as she lunged out once more. His hat did a small bounce and then slid sideways from his head in a slow-motion tragicomic landslide, whilst his glasses flew from his face and skidded to a halt several yards away. He made a simultaneous grab for both and his bicycle crashed amongst the orange peel.

No-one moved to interfere, but no-one moved to leave either. Had we been adults we might have felt a shabby thrill at the intimacy of it. A touch of the morbid fascination that makes people linger at car accidents. Mean titillation at the public sight of soiled linen. Even ordinary human embarrassment. But, as children, witnessing this butchered dignity and hollow authority was awesome. We gawped.

'Woman, will you listen to me!' Mr Adam's voice took on force for the first time and he placed a restraining hand on each of her forearms. 'I know what you're thinking. But this is neither the time nor the place.'

'You know what I think! That's a good one! You know what I think do you John Adam?' Her voice wasn't calmer, it was spiralling towards hysteria.

I picked up Mr Adam's glasses almost as a reflex and went to return them, at the back of my mind some hazy notion that a civil act from a child might restore their adult sense of responsibility and put an end to it. I had no inkling of the enormity of what was being played out before us. Patsie placed a hand on my chest and shook his head silently.

'You know what I think? You know how I feel? Seventeen years of it. Seventeen years of working and scraping and saving. The bloody hours I've spent slaving. Building a home for you. You don't have the vaguest notion John Adam. You don't begin to understand what I'm thinking.'

She made a violent shrugging movement and took a step backward, freeing herself from his grip. Her raincoat was wrenched half from her shoulders and her face became flushed and crimson. She was panting like something being hunted.

'How could you?' Her voice almost squeaked in disbelief. 'The two of you? I mean it's not as if . . . I thought you . . .' Her body was shuddering with emotion as she strove to get the words out. 'I thought . . .'

There was something in her eyes which held you in horrible fascination. It went deeper than the hitting-out and swearing and insults. They were for the selfishness, the wasted years, the humiliation. The look in her eyes was for something worse than that.

'I thought you thought the world of me,' she breathed, in a voice so wounded, so accusing, so utterly assured that there could be no greater treachery than that.

For a moment it seemed the tears must come. She stared straight into his eyes, catching her breath, seemingly poised either to pounce or collapse. Then her face contorted in bitterness. She whispered slowly and evenly the simple word, 'Bastard'. A new word. A word with no meaning. For the rest of my life, long after it had lost any mystery, a word which would conjure up the scent of oranges.

Then she turned and was gone.

There was a long instant of silence before Miss Cocker took a step towards Mr Adam.

'John. I . . .' She didn't say anything else, but cast a look longingly towards the van.

'Yes,' was all he said.

She climbed in and drove away.

I handed Mr Adam his spectacles. He put them on with trembling hands and replaced his cap which had been clenched in one hand, taking a very long time to straighten it and set it comfortably.

'Thank you,' he said with almost comic formality.

Edmundo and Patsic raised his bike from the orange-peel debris. He sniffed a time or two as he took out the round metal clips from his pocket and placed them around his trousers. Gripping the handlebars and placing one foot on the pedal, he said courteously, 'Thank you lads. Would you please clean that up for me.' He nodded towards the bits of peel.

He surveyed us before leaving. A little knot of children ranged in rows, as hushed and attentive as a theatre audience. We gawped in silence. We had no response to a situation like this other than to gawp in silence. Life hadn't yet equipped us with one. Children have to be taught the art of pretence. We were what we appeared. Spellbound.

It wouldn't have seemed out of place if Mr Adam had finished with a rhyming couplet. But he mounted his bike wordlessly and rode off.

Almost immediately, a car coughed into life behind us and drove away, running quickly up the gears. I just had time to see Mr Mason-Jones behind the wheel of his big Rover. For him, it must have been like sitting in a private box.

17

Mr Mason-Jones wasn't a very good referee. He looked dapper enough in the new black and white outfit, but the authoritarianism which was his hallmark in everyday life seemed to desert him on the pitch. His refereeing was characterized by a sort of democratic legislative process and appeal to the finer virtues, expressed via a running commentary. 'Now, what was wrong there lads? Offside at the point of playing the ball forward yes? Try to keep in front of the last defender, young man. Don't look so upset now. Free kick. Direct or indirect? Yes, that's right. OK. Everyone happy? Off we go then.' Peep.

The pauses between play were longer than the match. The whistle almost seemed to beat the players to the infringement. It was manoeuvres, not active service.

For once, the pitch was lined with spectators. This, despite the fact that the day was grey and blustery with the certainty of rain. But it was the last match of the season. Presentation of the championship would take place after the whistle. There was a lady representative from the parish Board of Governors, a smattering of clergy, most of the teachers even including Miss Hodge, friends, brothers, sisters, parents. Not mine.

I looked down the line of figures to my left and right and said to Miss Cocker, 'Do you think there are any judges or lawyers in t' crowd Miss?' She frowned at me.

'Why?'

'Oh, just in case someone has to make a decision on a penalty. I think Mr Mason-Jones would appoint a jury,' I said dryly.

'Now, Tim luv, don't be sour. Mr Mason-Jones is just anxious that everyone knows t' rules and follows them.'

This of course set me thinking about fouls.

I suppose in a way I could count myself lucky that the school had been occupied the previous week with enterprises of greater pitch and moment than my cursing like a deckhand and upending an undersized full back. But the powers that be, in the form of Mr Mason-Jones and my dad, had still found time to deal with me.

It was interesting to note the natural deference to a supposed higher authority. 'Your father will know how to deal with you . . .' 'The headmaster will know how to deal with you . . .' In the end, neither of them seemed to.

But I was told by both of them, independently, that I wouldn't be playing for the school team again that year, which meant any year since this was my last at St John's. So even before the professional game had got round to dreaming up suspension for misconduct, I had been suspended. I could possibly claim it as my single distinction and sole contribution to the great British National Game.

It also meant that I spent the grand finale on the touchline next to Miss Cocker. Something which hurt more than I cared to admit. And certainly more than any hiding they could have given me. That came over as I watched the team from the wings. I had learned what vitally gregarious creatures we are by nature, and long before my first French lesson had experienced the strong pull, when not vicelike grip, exerted by what people call *esprit de corps*. Thankfully, it appeared that I might be rehabilitated for the gala dinner.

Unfortunately, not so Mr Adam.

'Good shot Edmundo,' someone called just to our left. There was a communal 'Ooh!' and concerted handclapping of a sort of which a St John's match had certainly never heard the like before.

As I say, not so Mr Adam. It often amazed me how little adults chose to tell children. Events fundamental to our existence might unravel around us, and our questions would be answered with 'We s'll see or 'Never you mind' or 'Get your tea'. On a recent Saturday morning I had been dragged early from a sleepy bed and mysteriously placed atop the lavatory to be soaped and scrubbed from head to toe; then adorned in my Sunday best and despatched onto the street with the instruction to keep out of the way of the feverish activity which filled the house whilst everyone, young and old, went through the same process, either self-administered or enforced. Whilst I hung about, Tesser Hallam had seduced me into a spot of birds'-egging. Uncertain of what this unusual day had in store, I had been careful not to scale anything too risky, and so returned an hour later with three thrushes' eggs, only a minor tear to my pullover, and the lightest dusting of tree bark to my clothes, hands, face, and the inside of my legs. Just in time to meet the cars departing for my sister's wedding.

So, of course, nothing was overtly stated. Mr Adam had appeared at Monday-morning assembly, been called to the headmaster's office afterwards, and then disappeared. Our class was broken up like a routed and leaderless battalion, and, for a couple of days, allocated temporarily to other teachers. Then we were told Mr Adam had left to take up a position at a school in Manchester. We wouldn't be seeing him again. On the Friday, Mr Mason-Jones introduced us to a pretty little birdlike thing in a print dress who blushed and giggled nervously. Patsie Hunieghan had whispered, 'Another ruddy Forces kid. They come and go like gypsies.' Mr Mason-Jones had said, 'Children, this is your new teacher, Miss Hargreaves.' Giggle, giggle. 'Er, at least for the time being, anyway.'

'Goal!' twenty voices roared.

The St John's team congregated around Kevin Lowe who had just tapped in a pass from Billy Bibby to make it six–one. I joined in the general applause, if a little listlessly. Miss Cocker noticed.

'Poor Tim.'

She put a hand around the shoulder furthest away from her, my left, and pulled me to her.

'Look at it this way,' she said. 'It only amounts to one game.'

I smiled bravely.

'Why *did* you do it?' she asked.

Of course, I knew straight away what she meant.

'Oh, I dunno,' I sighed. 'I was fed up wi' it all. Bein' t' best and everyone wanting to be my friend like, all of a sudden. And all t' prizes and teacher's favourite. Then just a couple of little things and I was a real wrong 'un, a villain. It was just like on t' fair, Miss. On top of a rise one minute and whooshing down the next. It weren't right. I think I went a bit addled.' I didn't mention anything about dreams.

She nodded. 'Those whom the gods would destroy . . .' she quoted.

I gave her a puzzled look.

'Anyway,' I went on. 'I didn't mean that little feller any harm. He just happened to be the one who was there when I got so fed up. If he were here now, I'd shake hands and say "sorry" to him. Really I would.'

She smiled and stroked my hair in that way she had. I chose not to mention the part she had played in my Berserker behaviour! How could I tell her that when I went to dream 'Flash Gordon' at nights, it wasn't Queen Azzora of Mars that the knights of Ming threw back their splendid cloaks and knelt before, it was Queen Alice of Southpool. And that my Flash Gordon episodes frequently deviated to explore little avenues of emergent sexuality which Buster Crabbe didn't seem quite up to yet.

'After, I felt bad about it, Miss. I was a bit surprised at myself to be truthful.'

'Yes,' she agreed. She lifted her head up and the wind whipped her hair around her smooth, full cheeks and sprinkled the first few drops of rain into her face, setting her blinking. 'Yes, I know what you mean. We live our lives from day to day. Doing our best and always believing that we have a very fixed idea of right from wrong. A line which we won't cross. We may even find ourselves in the self-righteous position of judging others who've crossed that line, because to do so is to cause hurt and suffering. And that can never be right.'

She was looking much further away than Terry Welsh, who was fixing to take a free kick over on the far wing. And I wasn't sure that she was talking to me any more.

'And then, one day something happens. And you let it. Even though you know it's on the other side of that line. Because you're tired of listening night after night to the same piece of Chopin which is your life tinkling away.'

There was something almost noble about her staring

into the wind and talking like Greta Garbo. Though if I were her, I thought, I really would get that tooth seen to. I waited a few minutes, to leave her alone with her thoughts, then said, 'Yes, Miss. That's just what I were thinking.'

She looked down and treated me to a smile that spread as far as her eyes. Just then, the heavens opened and umbrellas sprang up like desert flowers, though black ones because, like cars, there was no other colour.

Miss Cocker raised hers, unbuttoned her coat, pulled me inside with her and wrapped it around us, saying 'Brrr' as if taking me into her bed. It was warm and giving and smelt of something damply human that I couldn't get enough of.

But my thoughts remained only vaguely carnal. I turned my head up to speak to her and a ponderous but yielding weight almost fell into my eye like cup and ball. For a time I was happy with my left-eyed vision of the world. There was a damp cheer which greeted our seventh goal, but I didn't stir.

'Mmph hmph mmp bmbl mpp pmpf?' I said into her pullover, just left of her midriff.

'What, love?'

'I said, "But you're all right now aren't you Miss?"'

I had meant the enquiry to be considered specifically in terms of the orange-peel assault, but she took it much more generally.

'Oh aye,' she said, patting my shoulder gratefully. 'I'll be all right. Don't you worry about me, young Tim. I'm tough.'

I doubted it, but she did seem steelier than of old.

'Tougher than you, I think,' she said, giving my hair another sympathetic stroke.

That faraway look came into her eye. She stared across at the line of teachers which centred on Miss Hodge.

'And them.' She jerked her head in their direction.

Then, after a time, 'And him. Poor love.'

I was pretty sure I knew who she meant.

PART 2

Kicking Forward, Passing Backward

18

My father was waiting on the front step to meet me. He couldn't have been home from work very long, because he hadn't even taken off his collar and jacket. He had the envelope in his hand.

Parents up and down the entire country had received such envelopes that day from the local education authority. They contained an important communication concerning their children. The communications were printed either on blue paper, which was good, or yellow paper, which was bad.

'Have I passed, Dad?' I asked anxiously as I walked down the familiar path to fourteen George.

Tibby took advantage of the open door to nip in ahead of me.

'Aye lad, you have,' he said. He put his hand on the back of my head and guided me gently in. 'Your mother would have been proud of you.'

So, contrary to Jim's foretelling, it was to be grammar school. But 'would have been proud', you notice.

You seldom know what happiness is in life, but you sometimes know what it was. A mellow voice with a Celtic lilt, preaching wisdom that righted all wrongs. Enfolding arms as soft and heavy as pillows that loved and protected. An eternal, inviolable queen in a realm that was always redolent of warm baking, fresh ironing and the BBC Light Programme. Words that prick your eyes. Peace, safety, home.

My mother had died after a short and shockingly

unexpected illness. As the youngest, it was assumed I must suffer the most. That the long hours I spent alone, kicking small stones up and down the pavement, wondering, were evidence of a withdrawn and melancholy personality in the making.

I felt an overwhelming sense of loss, but I was too young to grasp the enormity or finality of it. The hurt would come later. Rather than devastated by grief, what I mainly felt was bewildered.

The others were not cosseted by such innocence. Their memories were longer, their impressions and shared experiences more vivid. It took them much harder, and my sister hardest of all. She did her crying alone, but it was a long time before her eyes lost that swollen red stare which evinces recent tears. My brothers, trying, not always successfully, to be the men which they weren't quite yet, were stoically silent and uniformly miserable. My father managed, and despatched events with a quiet dignity hitherto not suspected in him.

For a brief period a host of aunts and female cousins descended on us, and the house swarmed with fresh-faced women and young girls from the west coast of Ireland. They were refreshingly uncomplicated, invigoratingly direct, infectiously brusque and practical. Life to them was *doing*, everything else was to be idle or to mope. They were also profuse and demonstrative with their sympathy, and my unappreciative little head spent more time being prodigiously stroked, kissed and enveloped lovingly between female breasts than it was destined to do for, well, than it was destined to do at all now I come to think of it.

Then, as suddenly, they were gone and Nonnie returned to her new husband. Fourteen George Avenue became the residence of Robert Armstrong and his three sons.

'Like *Bonanza*,' Jim said one night at tea, and we all laughed together, it seemed for the first time in months.

We would get by. But, for all of us, things were never going to be the same, ever again. 'A life changed, not ended', as my mother's requiem mass had it.

How much life had changed was probably best illustrated by the evenings at home after tea. The family collage was gone for ever, departed with the women. John still meddled with his engines, but now could afford one which actually ran, and was proving popular with a series of young ladies who enjoyed being chauffeured between cinema and coffee bar. My father increasingly found the lounge of the Saddle and Anchor more companionable than his own, and who could blame him? Frequently, the house would be empty in the evening except for Jim and me, the crowns of our heads pointed towards each other as we pored over our grammar-school homework at the front-room table.

Jim, in his final year, would be racing through his work to get to the TV before eight. I, in my first, slightly confused, floored by the newness of it all, would be taking it slowly and deliberately in a determined effort to get things right. For Jim, intelligent but not academic, education was something to be got out of the way so that life could begin.

Our industrious scratching would occasionally be disturbed by a conversation along the lines of:

'Jim, what's "contours"?'

Without pausing or raising his head, 'Lines on a map joining points of equal altitude.'

'What's "hinterland"?'

'Country inland of a port.'

'What's "relief"?'

'What I'll be feeling when you belt up.'

Following Jim through grammar school wasn't going to be all that easy.

19

Like most grammar schools with pretensions, St Michael's had a small chip on its shoulder about not being a public school. So we had our 'prep' school, and, though in a very small minority, 'boarders'. And also a range of school traditions in the Tom Brown vein. Some unique – the single sanctioned deviation from a strictly-enforced school uniform was the green cravat worn by the head boy. Some pious – fasting in Lent and a week-long religious retreat prior to Easter. Some mundane – sports days, speech days, masters' gowns, a choir, an orchestra and a school song with a chorus in Latin. And some frankly eccentric – an unswervable insistence that Friday lunch consist of fish cake, chips and beans, considered nourishing, rather than peas, considered common.

Sometime in the 1920s, the running of the school had been taken over by an Irish religious order, the Christian Fellowship. Not priests, not monks, as they used to tell us, but a teaching order dedicated to equipping young men with a balanced temporal and spiritual make-up with which to face the world.

All of this might not have impressed an Old Etonian, but it certainly impressed me. And my father. People still talked of a 'grammar-school education' and, for the likes of Jim and me, the least we could expect from St Michael's was that it would introduce the letter 'h' into our diction and soften our northern accents. My father would never hear of us going to school. It was always 'to college'.

But, ranging high on the list of traditions, certainly above anything merely academic but perhaps lacking the singular cumulative aftermath of seven hundred plates of beans on a Friday afternoon, was the game of football. Meaning rugby. The football you played with your feet was referred to scornfully as soccer and mocked and derided as the *other* game, no doubt as a result of some complex esoteric strain of English school snobbism. It made some of us feel rather bitter.

And the pre-eminence of 'rugger' at St Michael's was in no small part due to the efforts and influence of one man. O.X. O'Connell, otherwise known to his confederates as

Oxo. Oliver Xavier O'Connell, rugby fanatic, former Irish county prop forward, school rugby trainer, physics and chemistry master to the sixth form, and Irish Christian Fellowship Father. The pegging order is the one he probably would have chosen himself.

In youth probably built like a mountain, by middle years Oxo's figure had suffered major landslides, resulting in a shape not unlike a gargantuan pear-drop. Like Mr Adam, he had a booming voice which was the product of touch-line bawling, but accentuated in his case by the daily need to communicate with his fellows across the broad landscape of his own belly. His nickname was based on his initials, but the bovine connotations were not inappropriate. On a rugby pitch, civilization ceased at his hairline, above which nestled a full head of neatly coiffeured fleece greying to the perfect shade of leaden silver which can complement real looks and mature sophistication. Below Oxo's scalp squatted two hundred and fifty pounds of raging moo-cow. He was a large flabby animal with a film-star hairdo.

Possessed of that ruddy complexion which people used to call a healthy glow and associate with fresh air and active living, but nowadays in perhaps less innocent times put down to booziness, it may in his case have been attributable to either, neither or each in equal part. As pupil to teacher, of course, I never saw him drink, but, as I got to know him, couldn't help finding some of his behaviour and *sotto voce* asides left him, as they say, dancing slightly out of formation.

He was most often to be seen on the school playing-fields outside classroom hours. Sporting a pair of shorts which contained enough material to rig a schooner, and his county jersey, an unfortunate arrangement of hoops and bizarre colours which on him created the overall impression of a dangerously pregnant rare species of tropical bee, he would hover around the scrum, gallop through the ruck and bounce after the backs, shorts flapping and midriff undulating rhythmically, like something in one of those slow-motion television advertisements for stuff that softens your woollies. Occasionally his cheeks would balloon at the whistle dangling from a ribbon round his neck and the field would echo resoundingly to parade-ground Irish encouragement, or enlightenment, or admonishment, usually punctuated by evidence of severe cardiovascular punishment.

I came across Oxo soon after arriving at St Michael's. Lunch break had just finished. As we new boys stood in line, shop-fresh blazers, pink bewildered faces, like virgin soldiers to be marched off to our classroom by the prefect sergeant-majors, Oxo appeared. His vast bulk bulged the lines like netting as he moved between them. Looking around appraisingly, he proceeded to prod childish unfleshed ribs and pinch puny biceps between thumb and forefinger, like a cannibal king sizing up a batch of missionaries for the pot. In answer to our puzzled frowns he would only wink knowingly. He was much given to knowing winks, but the knowns were all on his side. Most disconcerting.

'Sheep trials,' was Jim's laconic response when I asked him what it could mean, and would reveal no more.

Shortly afterwards, Oxo spent a lesson with us as a fill-in for our sick science teacher. He couldn't take twelve-year-olds seriously when it came to physics, so spent most of the lesson expounding to us on the vagaries of socialist economics and the threat posed by comprehensive education. Just once, in a little sub-discourse on the school's heating bill, he touched on the convection of heat, using as an example the flow created by the radiator. Suddenly, in a display which held the class silently transfixed, he launched off into an animated impression of a heated-up molecule. Pumping his arms in and out, pirouetting slowly, he moved diagonally across the front of the class, at the same time maintaining a fluid discourse on triaxial motion, colliding gently with the furniture or gliding gracefully around it, for all the world like a syrup-filled barrage balloon.

Later, to revive a drowsy pupil, he despatched Newell's *First Principles in Scholarship Physics* on a lethal torpedo pass across six rows of desks with a speed and accuracy which would have awed Gareth Edwards. And probably Albert Einstein as well when I think of it, though conceivably for different reasons.

As he left the class, on the way to the door he resumed his little pantomime of a pulsating sub-atomic particle, winked again knowingly and said, 'See you at the trials, boys.' Then, peeping back through the closing door, bleated, high-pitched and plaintively, 'Baaa!'

Conversation, which had been suspended for an hour, gushed like a flash flood.

'So what *are* the sheep trials?' I asked Jim again a day or so later.

This was at what I had to keep reminding myself to call milk break rather than playtime, and in the yard not playground, both descriptions reflecting our maturer status in life. Jim was the centre of a small group of first-years, each cradling a small bottle of milk which Her Majesty's government had just bought for us. The group consisted mainly of the remnants of my primary-school friends. Edmundo hadn't survived the cut, so to speak, having received the wrong colour of envelope on the fateful day when life's lottery tickets were dished out, and Patsie had discovered he had a vocation, and was away training to be a priest. But Michael Atherton was there, and Frank Macnally, still begloved and tucking a football under his arm like a symbol of office, and Charles Vart, less freckled as puberty threatened, and skinny, very brainy, now heavily bespectacled Billy Bibby, far too tall for his age, and Kevin Lowe still snorting back nasal pea-soupers between gulps at his milk, which you tried to avoid watching because you suspected that there might be momentary intermingling and the fluid going down Kevin's throat was actually a delicate shade of chartreuse.

We were very privileged to be addressed by a fifth-former, even though he was my brother. Older pupils totally ignored our existence except to cuff us or try to terrify us into incontinence with tales of what the school had in store for us.

'Sheep trials?' Jim repeated, with the smugness of one who has endured something testing which you have yet to get through. 'That's when Oxo takes a look at the flock and picks out his sacrificial lambs.'

Things were becoming clearer, but not much. Jim seemed inclined to lead us on a bit further, then, apparently tiring of the joke, came clean in a tone of bored irritation.

'First-year rugby trials, you dopes.'

There was a chorus of 'oh's' as enlightenment dawned.

Charlie Vart said, 'When?'

'Soon.'

'Why sheep?'

'Mindless,' Jim snapped without hesitation. 'Like anyone who allows themselves to get picked. Bloody silly game. Don't know why we can't play football like the Secondary Moderns.'

As if in emphasis, he leaned forward, eyes raised heavenward, following the flight of something. A football from a nearby game sailed into our midst, and, effortlessly, without pausing almost, Jim returned it neatly with a perfectly-timed sweep of his forehead through a fifteen-degree arc. Then he flicked a nylon comb from his pocket and repaired the nominal damage to his quiff.

'Is it so bad?' Charles persisted feebly.

'Bad? It's bloody calamitous. The game consists entirely of either lying face down in puddles while people walk all over your back, or attempting to belt along on a north-north-westerly course at a great rate of knots, while some snorting lout attempts to take your legs south-south-east. The rules are so obscure that no-one has a clue what's going on except Oxo. There are more infringements of the rules in five minutes of schoolboy rugby than there are breeches of decorum at a Mothers' Union tea party when the toilet won't flush, the vicar's flies are open and the cat's got flatulence.'

There were murmurs of assent.

'Added to that,' he went on, 'it means practice after school on Mondays, Wednesdays and Thursdays, and matches every Saturday, sometimes in places like . . . like,' he sought for somewhere universally detested and came up with, 'Liverpool!' He spat out the name of the as yet pre-Beatle, therefore still not respectable metropolis. It was still a year or so before we all acquired lazy vowels and said things were 'gear' and called girls 'Judies'. 'Meaning,' back to Jim, 'that you just get Sundays off from Oxo and this place.' His voice had risen in indignation.

There were grunts of discontent.

'And of course,' he added, now matter-of-fact, 'if you want to play a decent game . . .' again, apparently fortuitously, his eyes rose skyward as if tracking a trajectory. This time he appeared to break off prematurely to look straight into Billy Bibby's eyes, a warm smile spreading gradually across his features. Seconds later, the ball took Billy an almighty, brain-jarring thud on the back of the head, catapulting his spectacles into the centre of a group of nearby preps who were playing tig. Feet danced daintily around them for a second or so, until, with a sound like a boiled sweet being crunched between molars, they were pulverized. Billy scuttled forward with something between a stifled scream and a whimper.

'. . . for the youth team or the YMCA,' Jim continued, his head turning nonchalantly towards us again, 'or even go and watch 'Pool or North End or Burnley, then naturally – you're stuck.'

This time there were growls of disapproval.

'So what do we do?' Charles asked anxiously.

'Well,' Jim said, as one pointing out the obvious, 'you make sure you don't get picked.'

There was silence as we all waited for him to go on. Everyone watched intently and one or two even squatted on their haunches before him, like insurgents before a guerrilla leader at a tactical brief. Veteran rebel, Jim coached us patiently in the art of failure.

'I mean, it's simple enough. Even you lot ought to be able to manage it.'

He breathed out slowly.

'As I've said, the rules aren't exactly simple. Go out of your way to show absolutely no comprehension whatsoever. Total inactivity is a bit too obvious. Jump up and down and squeal a lot. Just think of a bunch of girls playing netball and you can't go far right.'

There were one or two eager nods.

'You have to remember that what they're looking for is a general ballsyness, a sort of see-if-I-care-if-you-break-my-body attitude. So bite your nails. Wring your hands. Keep your lower lip wobbly. If you do happen to find yourself in possession of the ball, shriek and throw it vertically upwards.'

Behind a veil of freckles I noticed Charlie's lips were moving as if he were committing this stuff to memory.

'Then there's the coughing, whimpering complaints about asthma, the urgent appeals to be allowed to go and pee, the stumbling, hands outstretched "I can't see a thing without my specs" pose.'

'I can't see a thing without my specs,' Billy said, rejoining us. He was squinting behind the shattered remnants of his bifocals, a wreck of tortured metal and cracked glass, which dangled from his face. He looked like he'd not quite come through a motorway head-on.

'There you are then,' said Jim, clapping him on the shoulder then shaking hands. 'Welcome out of the team. Good to have you overboard.'

Billy smiled vaguely.

The bell sounded for the end of break. Cauldwell, one of the prefects, came skirting the yard ready to round up shirkers and tail-end charlies. Fresh, blond and manicured, he approached us with a condescending grin, neat and adult in his prefect's black to our silly schoolboy maroon.

'Corrupting the young, Armstrong?' he said to Jim, like

tolerant prison officer to time-served rogue, and then, glancing at me, 'I presume the consanguineous to be beyond redemption.'

Jim ignored him magnificently.

Conspicuously addressing himself to us, he said in a grand and paternal voice, 'So remember, children, mortal sin demands far more courage than banality,' and shepherded us possessively towards the classrooms.

Charlie sniggered.

There were times when I really looked up to Jim.

20

As Jim had predicted, the rugby trials took place soon after.

It was an October evening but winter was coming early that year. A light but steady rain which had been falling all day was reinforced by traces of sleet as the evening chill descended. The topsoil turned slimy and you could take your choice of puddles to lie face down in.

We first-years, about sixty strong, shivered in ranks at the edge of the pitch. Silent, cowed by the cold, striped, convict-like in maroon and yellow, we could have been the inmates of a Siberian labour camp on roll-call.

Reinforcing the impression, Oxo stood at the front, an overfed overlord, and surveyed us dispassionately. He was even flanked by henchmen. They were actually the captain and vice of the first XV, here for Lord knew what reason, but given the overall scenario you could be forgiven for thinking it was to administer the lashes. Arms folded, gaze unswerving, biceps bulging like Bantu battle chieftains, I couldn't help reflecting that if they failed their 'A' levels they had jobs for life doing exactly what they were doing now. See any low-budget movie featuring powerful but wicked foreigners from 1920 to 1962.

Not without relish, I thought, Oxo announced, 'A certain amount of violent contact will be inevitable.' Then he proceeded to march briskly down the lines, and run a rapid but practised eye over each youngster. Once in a while he would stop, scrutinize more closely, then jerk his thumb towards the front. Evidently we were being subjected to some process of selection, a sort of 'go', 'no-go' gauge like the Egg Marketing Board used before stamping the little lion.

As an ill assortment of overdimensional specimens slowly broke rank and collected at the front, his criteria soon became obvious. Since rugby is a physical game, it follows that physical characteristics play a significant role. Where Oxo, man of science, differed from established sporting opinion was in the strict application of the arithmetic to the axiomatic. Plus, of course, a total indifference to any consideration of aptitude. Putting it bluntly, anyone over a certain weight or height was in.

This somewhat cut across Jim's advice, so Michael Atherton and Billy Bibby both looked stunned as they were herded, hippo and giraffe, to the front. Oxo netted quite half a team like this. I glanced nervously at Charles Vart. It was like watching your comrades in arms go down in battle.

'Sir. I CAN'T RUN,' Michael said with the air of one repeating a Great Universal Truth.

'No matter mi boy,' Oxo answered cheerfully. 'The first requirement of the circus bearded lady is that she is not clean-shaven.'

As if in illustration, he prodded a very confused Michael chummily in the midriff. Subject closed.

Billy cast darting glances around him like a very small bird feeding, wrung his hands and set his bottom lip trembling so convincingly you were tempted to applaud, until you realized he was genuinely terrified. Built to prop up a clothes-line rather than a scrum, he would no more make a rugby player than a sumo wrestler. He was computing the contribution to his physical well-being implied by his current predicament and coming up with lots of minus signs. As a result, he had difficulty getting his line out between chattering teeth.

'S-sir I c-can't sss . . .'

'. . . see a thing without your specs?' Oxo ran on obligingly, voice rising in question. 'I know, I know, neither can I. Fortunately the game of rugby needs no directional sense whatsoever. There is only one way to go. Forward.'

Billy contemplated his future like a condemned soul.

The next ten minutes saw us arranged in circles of a dozen or so a few yards apart, languidly tossing a rugby ball to each other across the diameter. Whilst the sleet swirled around us, Oxo moved among us making searching enquiries about our sporting prowess.

'Ever played rugby before?'

'No.'

'Ever played rugby before?'

'No.'

'You?'

'No.'

'You?'

'No.'

The muscle-bound equerries from the first XV watched with mouths disparagingly downturned, but offered no advice or instruction.

Next, we were lined up like cavalry at one end of the pitch and instructed to charge *en masse* to the opposite try-line and then back again, as fast as we could.

As we set off, the sleet came down again in earnest, this time turning to real snow. It froze on your cheeks and tickled your eyes, and, with each stride, your boots acquired a ponderous layer of sucking silt that had to be jerked from the ground with a smacking sound which, multiplied by sixty pairs of feet, sounded like applause at a children's Christmas party after toffee-apples have been handed out.

One or two of the lads bunched their hands inside their sleeves from the cold and attempted to pull their jerseys up over their ears. Finding myself accompanied by one of these headless, limbless apparitions fleeing blindly through a snowstorm, lent the proceedings an unexpectedly spooky air which gave me a bit of a start.

The snow shower ended as abruptly as it had begun. We arrived back, sweating steaming and snorting like horses, to be appropriately corralled into seemingly a winners' enclosure, a losers' enclosure and a bunch which could only be destined for the knackers' yard and the glue factory. I had come joint twenty-third. That's the sort of thing you notice as a twelve-year-old.

Oxo placed his hands on his hips, a gesture which gave him a total width of about seven feet, and addressing this latter group shouted, 'OK you lot. Better luck with the school choir. Go.'

Release registered briefly on their faces before they turned and fled, a cheering charging wave, hitting the changing-room as if it were Omaha beach.

The two remaining groups were about team-size and were now referred to as Probables and Possibles. Charlie, Michael and Billy had been assigned to the former for no apparent reason; Frank Macnally and I, with equally compelling justification, to the latter.

Oxo, with ball in one hand and whistle in the other, marched us onto the field and posted himself at the centre spot. He looked like a marquee with the stripes going the wrong way. The Possibles he directed to one side and the Probables to the other and instructed us vaguely to spread out. Realizing that, for most of us, this would be the first rugby match of our lives, he summarized the thirty-six laws, forty-eight clauses and ninety-one sub-paragraphs which comprise the rules of the game of Rugby Union Football.

'Pass backwards. Kick forwards.'

Before he could start us with a blow on his whistle, a voice came from the midst of the Probables.

'Can we head it sir?'

Oxo smiled leisurely across at Charlie as one who appreciates a good wag as much as anybody.

'I would advise you to avoid risking anything vital,' he said. Then, seemingly as an afterthought, 'Before we begin, we have to exclude the danger of what I believe the military call blue-on-blue kills.' His voice lingered lovingly on that last word. Eyes widening, he glared intently at a particularly frail-looking youngster. 'Fratricide,' he said in emphasis, the way some people say 'Cheers' when licking at the froth on a fresh pint.

So the Possibles had to turn their jerseys inside out, which got rid of the yellow stripes. Humming in the cold like insects, we metamorphosed. Then Oxo hoofed the ball in a mighty up-and-under and we were away.

If you've ever witnessed one of these Spanish festivals where they let a bull charge around the village streets, and the unmarried male population try to take ribbons from its horns, in turn chasing it, fleeing from it, sitting on it, falling off it, tweaking its tail, squeezing its nuts, trampling or being trampled on, or simply hiding in abject terror, substitute for the bull a glistening black oval leather slug with a highly unpredictable bounce, and you have a fair impression of what followed. Or have in mind one of those enormous battle paintings that were popular pre-Renaissance, where each square foot tells a separate story. Acts of extreme heroism, base cowardliness, wanton cruelty, and downright perversion in a single collage.

In the first five minutes I was butted, kneed, rabbit-punched, bear-hugged, kicked, bitten and bollocked. Much worse was happening to anyone who actually hung around in the vicinity of the ball.

After ten minutes or so, I had the immensely satisfying sensation of thwarting the intention of a Probable of considerable mass and velocity who was on a vector closing rapidly on the chemistry lab, by deflecting him briefly onto a bearing for the bike sheds, before bringing him to a complete stop, accompanied by a gratifying thud and splat which couldn't have been louder if he'd been pushed off the Empire State.

Seconds later, I emerged from a game of pass the parcel

which was being played between four Palaeocene clay monsters, to find myself actually carrying the ball. I managed to slop along for a full ten yards, blocking a flailing arm from the left and smothering an enquiring face from the right, before turning and almost reluctantly popping the ball into the arms of the first lumbering giant I saw wearing a similar-coloured jersey.

It suddenly occurred to me, with a registration of mild surprise, that I was having the time of my life.

Not so everybody, it seemed.

Charlie was proving the most assiduous of Jim's disciples. Having seized a couple of chances to show real incompetence on the ball, he was determined to follow them up with a comprehensive demonstration of general tactical ineptitude.

At the mere suggestion of a rush from the opposing forwards, he took to shouting 'Give ground' loudly and authoritatively, which, in the predominant atmosphere of inexperience, caused at least half his side to fall back in disarray.

'Let 'em run lads,' he advised at the next attack, and, later, making capitulation sound technical, 'concede possession to the right flank.'

Perhaps exhilarated by success, perhaps heady with power, perhaps merely showing a fatal bent for dramatic emphasis, he began to wax theatrical. In the middle of one gruelling onslaught, he plucked the ball from the centre of an aimlessly churning loose maul and suddenly bolted for his own line, calling, 'Scatter! All is lost. Flee!'

There was a shrill blast on Oxo's whistle.

'Vart!' he barked.

After the usual chorus of Yes-sirs and Certainly-sirs followed by raspberries blown on the back of hands, the intended implication being that in obedient, youthful eagerness to please, this had been innocently interpreted as an instruction, Charlie came slowly to the fore, smiling sheepishly.

'Tell me Vart,' began Oxo, sorely provoked but in a tone

of reasonable enquiry, 'why do you wish to persistently encourage your team-mates to move in the wrong direction.'

'Tactics, sir,' responded Charlie brightly. 'Like in battle.'

Oxo was not ignorant of the workings of a twelve-year-old mind, or entirely unaware of its purpose. He adjusted his gaze.

'You consider cowardice a central element in strategy, do you?'

As far as one can in footwear which has taken on the weight and proportions of deep-sea diver's boots, and whilst standing knee-keep in sludge, Charlie shuffled uncomfortably.

'Rugby,' Oxo called loudly and grandly, 'is the opposite of *sauve qui peut*!'

I couldn't do it. I could not do it. It wasn't a question of honour. It was more important than that. It was a question of sport. If my school played rugby, then rugby player I would be.

The last little exercise in Oxo's ordeal appeared to be specific to the borderliners. The ones who, if they weren't careful, would end up in the permanently depressing role of permanent reserve.

The first XV captain stood in his keeper-of-the-keys-to-the-dungeon pose, and you were invited to knock him over.

'What's your name fella?' Oxo asked me when my turn came.

'Tim Armstrong, sir.'

'And what did you have for breakfast?'

You got used to this sort of thing with Oxo.

'Porridge, sir.'

He gestured towards his captain.

'Well, good Timothy, whose limbs were made in England, show us the mettle of your porridge.'

I had watched people go in too low and brain themselves on his kneecap. I had watched people go in too high and end up embarrassed and giggling in an ineffectual embrace. Those who had gone in at the right height had slithered down his thigh with dislocated shoulders.

I put down my head, ran at him from twelve yards, and butted him in the genitalia. He didn't so much fall as disintegrate, like a building which has had its foundations dynamited away.

Standing up and rubbing my head, I was aware of Oxo, smiling as he wrote something into his notebook.

21

So, from adolescence to manhood, rugby became my game.

Monday, Wednesday and Thursday evenings in any of the non-summer months between my twelfth and eighteenth years would find me sprinting furiously between two wooden-framework 'H' posts with my face contorted in exertion, or frozen in foetal self-preservation whilst booted limbs hacked and writhed around me, or closing like a bounding predator on a pair of flying heels whilst a Judgement Day voice with a Donegal lilt boomed out, 'Get in low! Take his legs! TAKE HIS RUDDY LEGS TIM ARMSTRONG!'

It was Oxo's permanent refrain. For six years I used to hear it in my sleep.

Crammed into hired coaches, we toured the wet and windy alluvial plain between the Lancashire coast and the Pennines, visiting like-minded grammar schools, a few not very distinguished publics, even the odd seminary. Each Saturday morning, our ritual of civilized violence began with thirty robust, garishly attired adolescents engaging each other across a minty-white expanse, their boots tearing green scars through the frost and their nostrils flaring condensation as they closed, and ended with tea and Bakewell tarts.

A time of change. Your friends' voices grew deeper,

their shoulders squarer, their chins fluffy and then stubbled. And that was the girls. No, just kidding – girls were a species you were interested in, but you had never met any personally. You knew someone who knew one.

I pretended not to worry about the changes that were happening to my body – mainly pimples – and the ones that weren't: mainly shouldn't I be hung like a rhino by now? And, whilst my hormones fought it out amongst themselves, I played rugby.

The norms of years were blown away. Kevin Lowe's catarrh disappeared overnight and he sported a head of spun-gold flax which was to make him the dream of every pubescent female in Southpool. Michael Atherton's puppy fat turned to solidity and he changed from a figure of fun to a revered mountain of muscle. Frank Macnally ceased wearing gloves and carrying a football under his arm and became lead guitarist in a pop group. Billy Bibby was shaping up as the fastest winger the school had ever produced, and, for him as for me, a trial with West Lancs Schoolboys was in the offing.

So it was as no less a dignitary than captain of the first XV that I duly collected a crop of 'O' levels and moved on to the sixth form, where I could dress in a fetching shade of Gestapo black and be cruel to first-years.

Of course, all this was happening against the historical backdrop of the Swinging Sixties. That meant colours got louder, trousers got wider and music got better. Singing 'You've got to hide your love away' sure beat the hell out of singing 'How much is that doggie in the window?' And sexual intercourse was invented.

However, not much of this cut any ice at St Michael's. Two boys were expelled for writing to Radio Caroline and allowing Mick Jagger to suggest to two girls at the local grammar that they spend the night together. And the rugby team were given detention for singing 'Norwegian Wood' with its line about her saying it was time for bed. Oxo had lumbered down the aisle of the coach in a sort of hasty samba muttering 'Godless, shameless' and

'Detention, suspension' like a menacing Gregorian canticle.

Possibly over-hormoned and under-exercised, the boarders invented a game called 'rasping' which involved taking people unaware by thumping them hard in the privates. For a time they all limped around like oversexed wildebeest towards the end of a highly active mating season. Perverse little bastards. Problem was, no-one was safe. If we were to hold a class reunion today, it wouldn't surprise me in the least to find that half of my year are childless.

Liberated Sixties be damned. The only male I knew who was getting any was Tibby, and we had him neutered. That must have been the week England won the World Cup. Funny, the things you remember.

22

'I wouldn't advise evenings,' Oxo said, lighting up a cigarette and settling back into an armchair in the corner of the staff-room, 'but then, I wouldn't advise anything.'

Even as one of the half-dozen or so sixth-formers occasionally allowed into the teaching staff's inner sanctum, it still shocked me to see one of them smoking. It was after all, an expulsion offence for ninety-five per cent of the school's population. It seemed to expose the moral code as a bit of a sham. Follow my instruction, not my example. Also, it set me busting for one.

Something of this must have been showing in my face. Oxo caught my expression, checked my fingers automatically and spotted the rusty smears which a matchbox edge didn't quite remove. He cocked a thoughtful eyebrow.

'So, I've got your permission?' I said, hurriedly clasping my hands between my knees.

'If you must take a part-time job,' he said, dismissively flicking ash, 'but at least try and make it something useful. Don't for heaven's sake go delivering newspapers.'

I didn't need to point out that three nights' rugby training a week precluded any such possibility. People wouldn't wait for their *Southpool Sentinel* while Oxo worked out his latest tactical variation on scrum-half to stand-off exchanges. Besides, I had been scared off the idea for life by witnessing three years of Jim's choking protests as the old man force-fed him a disgusting concoction of raw egg, milk, pepper and HP Sauce which he was obliged to imbibe before being discharged into the winter mornings.

'Oh no,' I said acquiescently, 'I'm hoping to find something ehm, community-minded. Public-spirited. The money is really a . . . well er, secondary.'

'Quite.'

The money was in fact bloody vital. Seventeen-year-olds live adult lives on childhood incomes. My old man's notion of pocket money didn't allow for such teenage essentials as checked button-down shirts and knitted ties, let alone five fags a day and a half-bottle of QC sherry before youth club.

The door slammed and Syme, the young geography teacher, marched in, his feet clattering on the parquet and echoing loudly in the sparsely furnished room. He grimaced disapprovingly at the back of Oxo's head for taking up the easy chairs and coffee-table – and with a pupil for heaven's sake – and, seating himself noisily at one of the desks, thumped down a set of exercise books and proceeded to daub irritatedly at them with a red felt-tip.

'Evening Mr Syme,' Oxo called over his shoulder without turning. I could almost swear I detected a wink in my direction.

'Father O'Connell.' And then, in a much lower voice, 'Armstrong.'

It was generally known that certain of the teaching faculty considered Oxo's infatuation with the game of rugby conferred a privilege or two too many on certain selected pupils. I was unfortunately aware it was a charge felt with some conviction.

'By the way,' Oxo said, sitting forward and reaching over his sprawling waist, with difficulty, to stub out the cigarette, 'I've made a couple of changes to "Radioactive Disintegration".' He pulled paper and pen from the inside pocket of his black cassock, and laid them on the table, suddenly becoming very animated.

I sighed inwardly. This might take hours.

He drew an oblong on the paper in front of us, put a small 'H' shape at each end, then proceeded to decorate it with circles and crosses, explaining excitedly, with grand sweeping arrow signs and sudden agitated hand movements, how the circles could be brought to converge on the 'H' at the top end.

If rugby was Oxo's love, then tactics were sex.

He had an infatuation with strategy that was almost obsessive. He would spend hours dreaming up schemes on drives, thrusts and penetration and commit them to diagrammatical illustration like a sort of substitute *Kama Sutra*. I had watched him work out scores of these things lovingly like this on scraps of paper, talk through their feasibility, introduce them at practice sessions and clap his hands with joy as the ball was thumped down behind the posts.

And here he allowed the only encroachment, or perhaps fatal conflict would be a better description, from the other big love of his life. Each set piece, once drilled to perfection on the practice ground, was fondly christened with a code-name culled from the realms of science. A strategy not without its practical side, actually, since it was important that the enemy had no notice of what to expect, and confusion would be maximized by an apparently totally disassociated code-word. But no 'plan A' or 'number ten' for us. It had to be 'gravitation' or 'magnetism'. And, as the ploys became more elaborate and cherished by their inventor, he seemed to feel that their description merited appropriate sophistication. Moves with labels like 'Osmotic Infusion' and 'Electromagnetic Induction' crept into our repertoire. And I was the chump who had to announce these things at the top of my voice in the middle of a rugby match.

'Well, what do you think?' he concluded eagerly.

'Radioactive Disintegration,' I said, trying to keep any downbeat modulation out of my voice. 'Right. Three in the line, hand off to Barker, forwards bind and drive, peel off to the threes. Got it.'

He nodded with a that's-my-boy smile.

'We'll give it a whirl on Saturday.'

My face clouded.

'Saturday's all fixed up then?'

'Of course,' he said, looking pleased with himself.

As a grammar school which put on airs, it was always a feather in Oxo's cap to set up a fixture with a public school. It lent a bit of class. Flemmings in Cheshire could even be considered a minor coup. It was one of the north-west's top public schools. Oxo beamed at the prospect of a paragraph or two in the *Sentinel*.

But, I couldn't deny, I faced these occasions with more than a touch of trepidation. It wasn't the intimidating historic gothic façades or the overtones of privilege, like the full-vowelled young gentlemen who went around calling enigmatic phrases like 'Olly Olly Big School!' and 'Shunters you chaps, this minute!' It wasn't the undeniable difficulty of finding common ground. After the first match I had played against a public school I sat down with my thirteen-year-old opposite number across the Bakewell tarts ready to discuss 'Fireball XLV' or Southpool Rovers' chances of promotion, to be asked conspiratorially, 'Don't you consider that our American cousins have rather bitten off more than they can chew in French Indo-China? Do you think they've ever heard of Dien Bien Phu?' I had never heard of Vietnam, but then I wasn't being brought up to be Foreign Secretary.

Of course, you got used to that sort of thing after a time and realized it wasn't their fault. It was simply that they were being matured at three times the normal rate. See any teenager who's behaving as if he's suffering from an advanced case of middle age, and you can guarantee he's being extremely expensively educated.

No, it was just that these visits inevitably involved me as captain in bits of weird ceremony with which I was as yet ill-equipped to cope – votes of thanks, speeches of welcome, three bows and a do-se-do with the opposition's rugby master – anything could happen. Second nature to the sons of the landed gentry, but a source of protocol nightmare to someone from George Avenue.

'So best behaviour Saturday,' Oxo said. 'You know what I mean?'

He meant creep. I felt like telling him to keep his nose out of our class system.

'Oh by the way,' he added, as if he'd been listening to my thoughts, 'you are invited to take tea with their captain in his den after the match.'

'In his what?'

'Den. Study, I suppose. Room. You'll find out.'

I blew softly. Study. I had only got my own bed as a result of John's nuptial capitulation.

'Right sir.'

He made a couple of vain efforts to rise, setting his vast bulk oscillating, and by about the third rock had given himself enough momentum to keel forward out of the easy chair.

'I'll get you a print of this,' he said, waving the rough draft of 'Radioactive Disintegration', 'so you can chew it over before Saturday.'

He left to go to the print room. I stood up and idly wandered about for a while, hands in pockets. Syme noiselessly continued to work through his pile of geography homework.

I toyed with a couple of rock specimens on a side table. Mused over a miniature rowing cup inscribed only 'School House 1953'. Blew the dust off a pile of files. Realized I was standing in front of a copy of the Pure

Mathematics mock 'A' level examination paper.

Suddenly very still, I began furiously attempting to commit questions to memory.

'Wouldn't like a drink while you're waiting would you Armstrong? There's a bottle of Scotch in the cupboard above your head.'

I turned to see Syme's clean-cut visage scrutinizing me behind a sarcastic smile. Very groomed and spruce as always he was, with his feet folded neatly and placed straight out in front of him under the table. It was impossible to look at him without imagining pips on his shoulder. They nicknamed him 'Tash'.

I made a show of stooping to look out of the window towards town.

'Not for me thank you sir. Not till the sun's gone down behind the British Home Stores. You go ahead if you can't wait.'

The bugger didn't have any idea what being rugby captain entailed. Not all gravy. Anyway, I'd dropped geography.

23

Armed with a finger-length column of penny pieces and the sits-vac page of the *Sentinel* suitably annotated in red, I camped down in the phone box at the corner of George Avenue and Phillip Street. In the fleeting seconds between the burglar-alarm buzzes, coin-inserting crunches and piggy-bank tinkling with which the good old GPO chose to blight coin-operated telephone calls – presumably the aim was to frustrate or embarrass you into installing your own phone – I conducted the first job interviews of my life.

'You experienced then, rock rolling?'

Being near the Blackpool part of the coast, a fair selection were based on a tourism of sorts. Not quite your Malibu Beach lifeguard or St Anton ski-instructor brand, but still an industry innocently dedicated to assisting people in realizing holiday dreams. Like breaking their teeth on Blackpool rock.

'No.'

'It's an experienced job, rock rolling is.'

'Surely not for all rock rollers?'

'What jer mean?'

'Well, they must all start somewhere.'

Silence. Then, 'Aye, but that were somewhere else. It's an experienced job, rock rolling is.'

Since people apparently waited years for their big break in roll and rock, I tried the next one. Babysitting.

'You're a boy,' a young woman's voice said accusingly.

'Yes.'

'Oh, no boys.' You could almost sense a shudder of distaste.

'But, I—'

'Boys is unreliable, boys is.'

In those days people didn't have to say things like, 'We are an equal opportunities employer.' They could say, 'The following half of the human race need not apply.'

The third voice sounded harassed and appeared to be coming from the middle of a violent altercation involving a shoot-out with automatic weapons.

'You ever operated a football-pools-coupon-folding machine before?'

Rat-tat-tat . . .

'No, but it's the sort of thing I've always wanted to do.'

Tat-tat-rat-tat . . .

'Nah, nah. Anyone could say that.'

Sometimes, you feel wit is wasted.

'I could take you on as a coupon checker.'

Rat-tat-tat . . .

'Same money?'

Tat-tat-tat . . .

'You must be joking. Half a crown an hour.'

'I'll think about it.'

The final number was an advertisement for two

waiters, Sundays only, to serve at 'a select, seaside family restaurant' in Tedderton, an up-market coastal resort. It was a lengthy bus ride away but I was getting desperate.

'Tollivers?'

'Aye.' The voice sounded dispassionate. Disinterested to the point of hostility.

'I'm calling about the job.'

'Aye.'

'The Sunday job. Waiters.'

'I need two.'

'Pardon?'

'I said, I need two.'

'Er, I know.'

'Can you bring a friend?'

'Eh?'

'Can you bring a pal. Next Sunday.'

'Well, er . . .'

'Come at ten. Job goes to t' first pair I like t' look of.'

The line went dead.

Odd.

24

As anticipated, Flemmings was an imposing country house centred on a crenellated tower, clothed in rustic creeper. Or rather in summer it would have been. In colourless, leafless February it looked as if the walls of the building had been skinned to reveal veins beneath.

The young boy posted to greet us at the gate called up, 'Just follow the drive, sir. Then right at Old Hall. Jobbings are straight in front of you.'

I heard Oxo mutter as he retook his seat, 'Why can't these people call anything by its proper name.'

As we took the field, rather than the usual two first-formers sullenly clutching handkerchiefs and press-ganged into service as touch judges, there were quite fifty or so spectators lining the pitch, mainly uniformed youngsters from the lower school. Their enthusiastic, high-pitched reception was however drowned by Oxo, executing a couple of vaguely social hooting exercises towards the opposition rugby master by way of limbering up his vocal cords.

At the centre spot, their captain Guy Lavelle introduced himself with a firm handshake. He was lithe and tallish with a thick head of dark red hair, straight and long, and very bright blue eyes, the sort that you could tell had a lot going on behind them. He also had thick sideburns covering his cheeks and almost meeting at his chin, very fashionable just then. At St Michael's they would have got him expelled.

'You must be Tim Armstrong. Guy Lavelle. Glad to meet you, Tim. We're having a chin-wag afterwards aren't we? Looking forward to it. Can I introduce Bob Lockett. Bob's very kindly dragged his head out of the *Economist* long enough to ref for us this afternoon. Bob. Tim.'

Bob looked a bit too old to be a pupil but the introduction had given nothing away.

'Pleased to meet you, er sir, Bob.'

'Oh not quite yet,' he said smiling pleasantly enough, 'but who knows. Perhaps the Birthday List, eh Lavelle? Heads or tails?'

It was the way they seemed to get everything right that floored you. Their social ease. Even down to the disarming touches like finding out your name in advance. You felt beholden to them from the first, charmed and yet awkward and graceless in return.

The thought of this damned tea was weighing heavy on me. I had a mental image of sherry with cucumber sandwiches before a coal fire in the fading light. Politically orthodox noises. Cultured conversation. I'd probably commit some horrendous gaffe treating his 'fag' like a human being or something.

Perhaps it was the preoccupation. From my kick-off which didn't go ten yards, 'Scrum back, sir,' Guy Lavelle called perkily, to my fumbling knock-on three strides from the try line, 'Oh, tough luck, Tim,' to being exquisitely sidestepped for their winning try, 'DON'T GO GETT'N' YER TOGS DIRTY NOW, ARMSTRONG,' I played a nightmare. To make matters worse, all attempts at 'Radioactive Disintegration' resulted in critical mass and random collision.

As I strode despondently towards Guy at the final whistle, Oxo fell in briefly beside me to hiss bitterly, 'I told you to be polite, not defect. Enjoy your tea, Judas. Ah young sir, a fine game. Well played.'

'Thank you Father O'Connell,' Guy said, shaking hands with the familiarity of years. And then, to me, 'Get yourself showered Tim, and I'll pick you up outside the changing-rooms in ten minutes, OK?'

He did. We marched side by side across courtyards, along oak-panelled corridors, through vaulted halls, up squeaking wooden staircases, Guy keeping up a steady monologue evidently considered obligatory, and delivered like a recitation without feeling. Confiscation of the lands and house from the Duke of Monmouth's brother after the rebellion in 1685, building of the old hall by a grateful queen for one of Marlborough's returning captain generals, 'or perhaps that should be captains general, anyway—,' addition of the last wing by his son, conversion to a military hospital, 'the graves are under the tennis courts'. Eventually we arrived at a school. The elm tree opposite the entrance was nearly three hundred years old. 'Now this bloody Dutch stuff has got at it,' he added, the first touch of emotion getting into his voice. As if in answer to an unspoken question, he waved a hand vaguely at the stately paintings and ageing photographs which lined the walls. 'A liberal mixture of historical nonentities and various pre-war first fifteens.'

At last, he stopped outside a door which was identical to several dozens of others we'd passed, and turned, with his hand on the door knob.

'Can I ask you something?' he said, possibly provoked by my silence.

'Sure.'

'Why did you keep shouting out chapter titles from an 'A' level Physics book all through the game?'

I looked carefully back at him. The bright mischief in his eye warmly invited you to give at least as good as anything you might get.

'A tactical device designed to confuse,' I told him. 'As public-school lads, steeped in the classical tradition, we were convinced you'd be rendered clueless by the mention of anything that happened within the last century and a half. We expected you to hit back with epigrams in Periclean Greek.'

He threw open the door with a snort.

'Hey, you two, meet Tim.'

The room was not, as I had anticipated, panelled oak, walnut writing-bureaux, leaded windows and a huge grandfather clock ticking away reverentially in one corner. It was in fact rather meanly furnished with a ten years out of date vinyl three-piece, Formica-topped coffee-table, and little else. Wide shelf-like work-benches ran the length of two walls in lieu of desks, and were covered untidily with books, papers, clothes, jars, tins, two guitars and more books.

At one of these, a corpulent young man with dark tightly-curled locks and thick spectacles was writing listlessly, and a second was perched in the centre of the room in some kind of cross-legged pose of meditation, head erect, eyes closed and hands extended in a permanent 'gimme' gesture. His lotus position was not strictly orthodox, largely because his legs were restricted by an enormous pair of zip-up Chelsea boots which extended three-quarters way up his calves. But he wore, over bell-bottomed trousers, a silk shirt in appropriate midnight blue, and had very straight shoulder-length blond hair, almost bleached and obviously blow-dried, which was curled inwards at the ends in a kind of medieval pageboy style. In front of him, joss-sticks smoked in a milk bottle, and sitar music whined tunelessly from a cheap portable gramophone on one of the benches.

'Gavin and Alastair,' Guy said, gesturing first at the one then at the other. Striding nonchalantly over the milk bottle and around the meditating figure, he spoke over his shoulder, 'One thing I cannot understand about our generation is this current obsessive veneration for the culture and philosophy of a country which can't even manage to feed most of its own population.' He flicked at the arm of the record player and the sitar music was terminated with an abrupt 'zurrup'. 'Everyone for toast?'

Neither of them showed the least sign of irritation. Opening his eyes, the Brian Jones impersonation climbed into one of the easy chairs with slow, feminine movements, folded his arms and said in a lazy Oxford drawl, 'Home the warrior hero. Did you ahm, put down the scum?'

'Yes,' Guy answered. 'Tim here captained the scum. He's here for tea. Where's the bloody toaster?' He became very active, opening drawers, lifting objects, moving piles of books.

The portly one abandoned his writing and produced a rusty toaster from amongst a disordered array of mugs and jars. It was one of those old-fashioned prism-shaped types with spring-loaded sides that you levered outwards and then used to clamp the toast against glowing filaments. It looked as if it had seen much service. A couple of decades' worth of crumbs clogged its workings.

'Then we must do our guest honour,' this one, Gavin, said and rummaging around in a set of drawers below what was evidently his corner of one of the workbenches, produced a clinking of heavy glass and then triumphantly thumped three bottles of Newcastle Brown on to the coffee-table. He returned to forage for another.

The effeminate one seemed suddenly to come to life. Looking at me eagerly he announced, 'Shit?'

I had seldom been less certain how to go about answering a question.

Without waiting for a response he leapt to his feet, dropped his trousers to his knees, thrust a hand inside the pair of white girl's knickers he was wearing for underpants and produced a small plastic bag secured with elastic bands and about the size of a golf ball. Almost like a third testicle. Rearranging his clothes, he too rummaged in a set of drawers, this time in the opposite corner of the room, and returned with cigarette papers and a tin of tobacco. Seating himself again, he quickly and expertly began to roll cigarettes, lacing the tobacco with the crumbly dark green powder from the plastic bag before licking the papers closed.

'We have a party,' Guy announced happily.

He began lavishly buttering toast and handing it across to Alastair, who stacked it, plateless and without ceremony, onto the coffee-table in front of him. Gavin located an opener and attacked the bottles of Newcastle Brown which each came to life with a click and a gasp. By the time Alastair had rolled four smokes, there were twenty or so slices of toast forming a buttery stockade in front of us. Guy selected some records from a stack of LPs laid inconveniently in a flat pile, slipped one from its sleeve and dropped it onto the turntable before joining us. We clinked bottles and drank.

There were several minutes in which we chomped and gulped with the single-minded dedication of hungry adolescents. After a period of undiverted bodily gratification, the bottles were empty and a half-dozen or so unwanted pieces of toast littered the table amongst patterns of granular black dust. We lay back sighing happily, as at the end of a brief orgy.

Gavin produced four more bottles of brown ale saying, 'Careful with the empties, there's threepence each on them.'

Alastair belched roundly and handed out the doctored cigarettes which he lit from a petrol lighter produced from his pocket. They each made an absurd little ceremony of drawing in the smoke with a startled gasp, holding it, and then relaxing in a staged serenity intense enough to be post-coital. I copied all this to make it look like I'd done it before.

No-one spoke for a while. The music seemed to get louder.

'You like West Coast bands, Tim?' Guy asked as the sound of a tortured lead guitar gave way to grumpy bass.

I was about to mention one or two pop groups from Blackpool and Fylde, when it suddenly occurred to me he might not be talking about the west coast of Lancashire.

'Yes, right enough. Beats Harray Krishnaw anyway,' I said with an impish glance at Alastair.

Alastair paused in his ecstasy to open his eyes and stare at me wonderingly. He had a habit whilst talking of running locks of his long blond hair between finger and thumb.

'What an intriguing mode of diction you have,' he said aristocratically. 'Do all your family talk like that?'

'Yes,' I answered and added, speaking very slowly, 'it is called English. Many people use this language in the country called England. England begins beyond the big elm tree outside Old Hall.'

The others laughed softly.

'Inglund,' Alastair repeated slowly, as if turning over a new idea. 'My education has been so limited. My existence so . . .'

'Cloistered?' I suggested.

'Yes.'

'Cloistered and privileged?' I asked.

'Thenkfully.'

'Let's drink to that,' I said, raising my bottle. 'From the sons of those who drive lorries for a living to the sons of those who drive aeroplanes. Cheers.'

'How did you know Alastair's father is an airline pilot?' Gavin asked.

'An inspired guess.'

Guy appeared to be enjoying himself hugely. Smiling,

he raised his bottle to his lips and sucked thirstily at the neck.

'Cloistered and privileged and homosexual,' Alastair announced, with the air of one making an important amendment.

'Oh hell, here we go,' Gavin said, 'arses to the wall chaps.'

The two of them began a long and involved altercation which was evidently the latest skirmish in a protracted war. It was fought elegantly with the subtle little jabs of an épée, and brutally with the swinging clubbing insults of a barbed mace. The phrase 'consenting adults in private' was lobbed back and forth like a dead sheep from a ballista.

I noticed that Guy now seemed to be chuckling at things which I was pretty sure weren't intended to be funny. Or alternatively at things which were going on nowhere except inside his own head.

Momentarily excluded from the flashing exchanges, I felt a need to assert myself. I sought to cut in wittily. Casting around the room for inspiration, my eyes happened upon a cheap printed poster, crudely fixed to the wall with masking tape, in which a pyjamaed Vietnamese peasant in a sampan was advertising a 'US Out' rally in Trafalgar Square. He held a Kalashnikov loosely under one arm and brandished a closed fist at the end of the other.

'Don't you agree,' I began grandly, 'that our American cousins have bitten off more than they can chew in French Indo-China? Do you think they've ever heard of Dien Bien Phu?'

'I can't sleep safe in my bed at night,' Gavin answered.

'You can't sleep, fatowl, for the sound of the bed rattling whilst you play with yourself under the blankets. Podgily squinting through your jamjars at *Penthouse* by torchlight. Matron says you go through more handkerchiefs than the rest of the sixth form put together,' Alastair answered.

'I should imagine so, Tim,' Guy answered smiling. 'When my father was posted to the consulate there they were running coach parties to it. It's quite a popular picnic spot now.'

I noticed the Vietnamese peasant broaden his grin, move his clenched fist to stifle a chuckle and then point his rifle at me mockingly. Something was becoming decidedly odd. He fired a burst which sprayed a rainbow.

The air was sweet with blue smoke. The music became louder still, each guttural twang seeming significant, though signifying something just outside my grasp. How could the Mamas and Papas have suddenly become so esoteric?

'Charlie Cong shoots rainbows,' I announced.

Alastair and Gavin stopped arguing to agree with me solemnly. Guy paused in his quiet laughter to ponder it, and then drew on his joint, making the end glow fiercely. He picked up one of the discarded pieces of toast and chewed on it without enthusiasm. Staring intently at the poster, he quoted:

'What passing-bells for these who die as cattle?
Only the monstrous anger of the guns.
Only the stuttering rifles' rapid rattle
Can patter out their hasty denizens.'

There was a somewhat bleary pause whilst we contemplated.

'No. Orisons,' I commented.

'No *horizons,*' Alastair said, aspirating like a gas leak and looking at me condescendingly.

'Exactly. No future. No chance. What a bloody war,' Gavin commented.

'Just the point, Tim,' Guy agreed, smiling at me appreciatively.

The point I had been trying to make slipped tantalizingly in and out of swathes of sweet blue smoke.

'Denizens,' I said, articulating very precisely.

'Usurpers. Non-natives.' Then, speaking in a way which expanded and contracted the entire lower half of my face like latex, 'Implantees.'

'God, you're deep,' Alastair commented respectfully. Then spoiled it somewhat by adding, 'If you dig deep enough.'

There was a knock at the door.

'Abandon all hope, ye who enter here,' Alastair called.

The door opened and a small boy entered, wearing a school uniform of surprisingly intense and interesting blue.

'Lavelle,' he squeaked, 'the scum captain's missing. Their boss is in a frightful wax. Someone said – oh . . .'

I spread my arms and rose without the use of my hands. It seemed appropriate.

It was decided they would all escort me. There was a great deal of discussion and preparation, as if for a long journey. I should finish my smoke. I should take some toast. I would need something to read. Alastair offered me *The Road to Wigan Pier* in Penguin paperback, then withdrew it mumbling that it might give me ideas. 'Something to move on from,' he affirmed, and replaced it with *Brideshead Revisited*. I should wrap up warm.

The preparations for my departure became intense. Cloaks were mentioned, provender, warnings about dark ladies and magic potions against sorcery. All possible eventualities were examined. Halfway down the stairs, Gavin was sent back to retrieve my jacket.

The gardener was weeding. At one side of the driveway was a wheelbarrow full of discarded common weed. Bird's-eye, buttercup, lion's tooth: constellations of crimson and gold in an emerald heaven. The sky at night seen from the depths of one of Pluto's ammonia seas. A riot of psychedelia. I persuaded the others that, if I took a good run at it, I would be able to fly over the top and land at the coach.

'Shove off, you bloody little shirtlifter,' the gardener growled.

Loath to provoke, we proceeded on our way.

The coach, which previously had been red and cream, and slightly tarnished versions of both, was now miraculously scarlet and ivory. Its wheels shone like mirrors and its windows sparkled like lead crystal. Oxo protruded from one side, floating several feet off the ground, his head bobbing like a balloon against the top of the door. His powers of levitation seemed natural, but as we approached I could make out that he was standing on the topmost of four steps, impatiently awaiting my return.

'Father O'Connell,' Guy called, as if saddened that they had been forced to spend two hours apart.

'Mm-hum . . . it only remains for me to thank you gentlemen for your generous hospitality.'

He began shaking hands all round. I slipped past to the sound of inane pleasantries and mounted the steps to the coach.

And there I was confronted with a real surprise.

The inside of the bus was gaudy yellow and white baroque church with touches of neo-Santa's grotto. I could hear no sound as I was in a hermetically sealed but totally transparent bubble being wafted along from row to row, but I could tell the air was filled with excited chatter.

As I floated gently down about half the length of the coach, I looked towards the back for familiar faces. Between me and the first fifteen – I noticed the firsts as always had commandeered the back four rows – were the fifth-formers, next to us in age, jealous of our authority, emergent untried rivals and would-be challengers. They were dressed as a set of chess figures in deep purple velvet with silver trim. Their faces were painted smooth as marble, dissected perfectly by a vertical line, the one half crimson, the other silver.

Damion Moone, smooth-skinned and flaxen-haired, as beautiful as any girl, was their queen. He smiled at me in a cool superior way as one seeing through sham. I hung in helpless suspension.

The queen's knight, Michael Blake, leaned over and begged leave to challenge.

He fixed me with cold eyes set in that sinister segmented face, then slowly brought down his lance in a wide arc which bore on me fiercely. His painted lips smiled cruel vengeance. The tip of his lance pierced my bubble with the vicious sigh of phosphorus thrown on water, and the bus exploded into sound.

I staggered forward and flopped down next to Michael Atherton. I must have looked as shaken as I felt.

'Christ,' he commented.

I grasped his wrist urgently.

'Beware the purple knight,' I urged.

He looked as if he wished I'd sat somewhere else.

I seized his other wrist, and whispered harshly.

'I think I have suppressed homosexual desires for Damion Moone.'

The uneasy tension in his face relaxed somewhat. Disengaging his hand to pat mine reassuringly, he said, 'Join the club, ducky,' with only a slight hint of camp.

Oxo remounted the coach. There was a pneumatic hiss as the door closed behind him and the engine rumbled immediately into life. He raised himself onto tiptoe and peered towards me, wearing an expression of enquiry perhaps tinged with concern. Or perhaps menace.

In one of the wisest moves of my life, I promptly fell into a deep sleep.

25

The following Sunday morning, after a lengthyish bus ride, I emerged from Tedderton bus station and headed for the sea front.

It was a grey day with a stiff wind and a heavy hint of rain. The place seemed to be populated exclusively by pensioners in plastic pac-a-macs, berets, and freshly whitened pumps.

On the one side, a dishwatery sea languidly tossed grey-foaming breakers across sand the colour and texture of wet cement. It looked as inviting to bathers as only the Irish Sea can, but one or two plastic caps bobbed and jerked among the waves, their owners quite understandably releasing the occasional scream.

Facing the incoming waves was a gaudy array of amusement arcades, bingo stalls, cafés and fair rides. Quiet at this hour and without the flashing bulbs and neon lettering, it was eye-catchingly colourful all the same. 'I SEE YOUR STARS' howled one sign in luminescent orange. 'YOUR EVERY DREAM FORETOLD' shouted another. And a third, as if in answer, 'JUGS OF TEA FOR THE SANDS'.

I stopped an ancient couple who looked as though they were wearing binliners with buttons and matching headgear and asked if they knew Tollivers Café. There ensued a protracted and heated debate. 'That were t'place our Agnes went wi' Doris.' 'Worrit?' 'Aye!' 'Nay, that were t'Blue Dolphin.' 'Nay, tha's addled. Blue Dolphin's pub where our George allus goes fer Thwaites's.' 'Tha's as reet as cheese at fourpence. George allus swears by t'Blue Lantern Licensed.'

I left them in contented contradiction, and asked someone else. Left at the rock stall, right at the pub, dead ahead for fifty yards.

'Don't go down the pit Granny
There's plenty of slack in your pants'

A ditty of my father's kept going through my mind. Not that I was going down a mine exactly, but I had never done a day's work in my life – real work, you know, the sort somebody pays you for – and I found this shanty constantly jingling in my head. First I would chant it, then invent a tune for it. Nerves, I suppose. Finally, I was walking in step to it.

Tollivers was in the street which ran parallel to the

promenade. Here, the sea breeze had lost its freshness and picked up the scent of donkey dung. Also you had to watch your step for fear of picking up last night's hot-dog and chip wrappers. Or even, in some cases, their remains, purchased apparently more in the euphoria of the moment than from hunger. As I approached Tollivers, I had to step gingerly between a half-eaten meat and potato pie and a splash of vomit. The former presumably from one who'd drunk too much to get it down and the latter, too much to keep it down.

'Come on Tim, you're late,' said a sort of familiar voice.

I looked up to see a face which was also sort of familiar, though not immediately placeable. Shining eyes and boyish smile, framed completely by long auburn hair and sideburns à la West Coast. Guy Lavelle.

Public schoolboys appeared at places like Tollivers about as often as Lobster Thermidor appeared on the menu.

'What on earth are you doing here?' I asked in genuine astonishment.

The question was greeted with a silent stare. Then a faintly embarrassed smile.

'You don't remember?'

'Eh?'

The smile flickered, vanished, reappeared.

'You invited me.'

'Eh?' I repeated, a semitone higher.

'After the match the other day.'

There was a pause whilst I wound back a few reels in my mind then replayed them, waiting for a familiar bit.

Nothing.

'You said Alastair, Gavin and I didn't so much live in an ivory tower as an ivory Manhattan,' Guy said helpfully. 'You said we should come down occasionally and sample life as it's lived by the human race.'

I looked at him blankly.

'You said privilege not only nurtures aloofness and

complacency, but breeds contempt and poisons minds. You said no character could be fulfilled without struggle.'

I thought I'd let that go without comment.

'You said that, like most people from ordinary backgrounds, you were obliged to find work to support your studies. You needed someone to go with you because the job was offered on condition you brought a friend. You dared us to take it on. You said the experience would revolutionize our outlook.'

I cleared my throat quietly. Guy's voice lightened a bit.

'You said my forebears had forced your grandfather out to work at the age of nine. As a chimney-sweep's apprentice. You said he'd had to start as the brush.'

It appeared that a combination of wacky baccy and Nuking Brown had left a great big hole in my head where some brain cells used to be. I made a mental note to be a bit more cautious with my poisons in future, and decided bravado was probably the best course of action.

'Well, where the hell are the other two?' I asked Guy testily.

Unruffled, he answered, 'Only two jobs.'

'Quite.' Then, 'Well let's get on with it.'

We turned and bounced roundly off the centre of an unyielding bulk which barred the doorway.

'Can I help?' a voice asked with more sarcasm than polite enquiry.

The voice's owner was dressed in a shabby white smock and apron of extravagant proportions. They needed to be. He had the figure of something a lorry had dumped at the side of the road. His face fell in layers from a balding crown and finished in a sort of solid ruff of blue-shaven flesh. Across a great barrel of a chest, he folded forearms which might have been more gainfully employed propping up a grand piano. The rest of him spread like pudding towards the ground. The eyes that fixed us were the sort you see on bloodhounds, but whereas there they inspire sympathy, here they conveyed a feeling of faintly malevolent indifference.

I squared up for my job interview, trying to forget that it was taking place on a doorstep.

'We've come about the job. I called you. Tim Armstrong. You said bring someone. Guy Lavelle.'

He surveyed us, pawing thoughtfully at rasping chins; after a few moments of this he seemed singularly unimpressed.

'Got yer aprons?' he asked at length.

I was just about to explain why a couple of experienced, go get 'em, sure-fire helluva pair of waiters like us should be temporarily minus the tools of our trade, so to speak, when Guy said, 'No. We don't have any. We've never done this sort of thing before.'

The big man sniffed. Put him in a trilby, tasteless check, give him a dicky bow and stick a big fat Havana between his teeth and you had a youth-club boxing promoter. Telling enthusiastic young bods like me which round to take a dive in.

'Aye, OK,' he said abruptly. 'I'm Joe. Joe Tolliver.' Nothing was offered to shake. 'I'm gaffer. See Doris inside. Tell her to fix you up.'

Guy took my arm and hustled me through.

It was immediately apparent that to describe Tollivers as a 'select, seaside restaurant' was conferring on the establishment a status to which it had only a very tenuous claim. I mean the seaside, and even that was a couple of blocks away.

The place was narrow and arranged on two floors not much wider than a double-decker bus, with stairs just as difficult to negotiate. The tables were simple, Formica-topped and regimentally arranged as permanent fixtures to the wall. Each bore a small tray on which were the condiments and bottles of sauce, HP and ketchup, which even at first glance, judging by the collar of congealed dross they sported, were of substantial antiquity. On the floor was plain linoleum, on the walls cheap paint and the décor was completed by a series of yellowing prints, depicting a range of glum but defiantly inedible-looking sea creatures. At the near end was a huge edifice in chrome and stainless steel in which the fish were fried, the chips cooked, and the pies kept warm. At this hour it was beginning to steam and hiss softly like a stationary locomotive.

Doris emerged from behind it, evidently disturbed from firing it up, whatever that entailed. She too was dressed in white, but her outfit included a plastic overall, cap and rubber gloves, which put you disconcertingly in mind of a ship's surgeon.

It transpired she was Joe's wife. She proceeded to give us a brief run-down on the necessaries. Middle-aged and motherly, she spoke mechanically, preceding everything she said with 'mm, mm' as though unsure whether it was about to bring down the wrath of the behemoth on her. She had an air of having been worn down, defeated. You couldn't look at couples like Joe and Doris without imagining them on their wedding day. Or, heaven preserve us, their wedding night.

'Mm. Mm. Float's a quid. No gyps, now. Fish is "in". Wi' peas it's "away". Mm, or if it's beans it's "brown away". There's prices.'

Guy and I struggled hard to keep any lack of comprehension from our expressions. We even attempted an encouraging nod or two, which neither of us seemed quite able to make emphatic.

She gestured towards a huge wooden board fixed to the wall at the far end of the room. Meals and prices were garishly painted in bright red on a cream background. If it hadn't been facing inland, it could have been read from the Heysham ferry at twenty nautical miles. Everything with chips, and everything three and sixpence, or three and nine with peas or beans.

At the top, a banner headline proclaimed that tea, bread and butter were inclusive, and, at the bottom, 'Children's and OAPs' portions given', was treated slightly less sensationally than some newspapers would handle the news that a Martian battle fleet was hovering over Trafalgar Square.

'You'll soon get used to t'prices,' she assured us. 'Here's your aprons. Mm. T'others are buttering up. I'll take you down.'

We followed. I'd been warned work would be different from school, but how could a simple job like waiting-on be so complex? I had joined the ranks of the workers, and already I was a duffer. What good was education for heaven's sake, if it didn't teach you what mattered in life? I felt mild panic as I considered: how did you float a pound? What was a gyp? A fish was 'in' what? The peas were 'away' where? I looked at Guy and he mouthed, 'Bootering oop?' in frank incredulity. At least I could understand the words.

We followed Doris's hermetically enveloped ample hips through a door marked 'Staff Only' and down a narrow wooden staircase, all the time hearing her murmur, and straining to catch the next bit of advice in some vain hope of amplification. But it soon became obvious that her truncated humming was used not just as the precursor of speech, but also to punctuate silences. Our training was at an end.

Below decks, the restaurant's cellar reminded me of the ratings' quarters on an eighteenth-century man-o'-war. The place was low-ceilinged, dimly lit, and you could see at a glance that space was sacred. In one corner, a white-tiled square bath several feet deep was filled with peeled potatoes over which a rubber hose was gently playing water. A large vat of batter stood on a mechanical mixer, and a nearby freezer was overflowing with pieces of frozen fish which looked like heaped lemon ice lollies. Racks and racks of dishes towered precariously over a sink the size of a paddling-pool. All this in a space not much larger than the average one-car garage.

''Scuse me you lot,' Doris mumbled. 'New lads.'

She hadn't asked our names, so pointed to each of us in turn.

'Tim.'

'Guy.'

In the centre of the room, a man and three youngsters were seated at a table directly below a single naked bulb. They were almost obscured by pillars of sliced bread onto which they were diligently slapping margarine from a plastic tub in the centre of the table. The man was in his thirties, two of the youngsters were about our age, and the other was just a boy of twelve or thirteen. This one said ''Lo' to the room at large.

Doris told us to muck in, then left. As we sat, one of the lads said 'Watcher cock,' to each of us in turn. He fetched us knives and pushed a pile of sliced bread nearer to us. The other two said nothing. I didn't like the look of either of them. It was more than their lack of welcome, their general demeanour was about as reassuring as a slumbering crocodile. Reluctantly I took a place opposite the younger, with the older bloke on my right.

He slowly lifted his head and stared at us intently. He was thin and wiry, but very solid-looking. He was dressed in a lumberjack shirt and jeans and around his waist was an enormous leather belt adorned with various metal studs, knobs and incidental ornaments. It looked like the sort of thing Henry Cooper might have hanging in his lounge. His face looked as if it had been chipped from wood, and indeed, there were some men, older and much larger than us, who did call him Pinocchio. When he spoke, it was with the jarring nasal vowels of an Ulsterman.

'Aim Jack. Aim gaffer,' he said to us slowly.

I nodded and smiled what I hoped was my complete accord. He nodded in return. He repeated the process with Guy, whose nodding was vigorously enthusiastic. Among male chimpanzees, in order to establish rank and hierarchy, submissiveness or unwillingness to fight are indicated by the weaker monkey showing its arse to the stronger one. Guy and I had our backsides pointed at the Pole Star.

Incongruously in one of his age, Jack's grizzled hair was styled in a 1950s teddy boy – swept back at the sides with a cluster of curls teased forward over the forehead. One particular Brylcreemed strand swept down in a great arc to the tip of his nose. He looked like he had a ski-jump down the middle of his face. When he nodded, it coiled and rolled like an iguana's tongue despatching a fly, but curiously enough, I found it very easy not to find this amusing.

'Spread, lads,' he invited, banging the table sharply with the butt of his knife-handle. 'Spread!'

We scooped and splattered.

For a time we worked in silence. I was aware of a vaguely disturbing tendency on Jack's part to glare at me, as if daring me to stare him out, so I surveyed the others. The one opposite me was unusually short, you could tell that, even though he was seated. He had a pasty, unhealthy complexion and sported untidy facial fuzz with dingy blond locks which fell in greasy coils almost to his shoulders. Sleep filled his eyes. His eyelashes were caked in the stuff. He chewed gum noisily, occasionally baring grey teeth. I bet myself he didn't have a girlfriend.

The elder of the others seemed amiable enough, and winked as he caught me observing him. He was rather ugly but not in a self-inflicted way, with bulging eyes, enormous sticking-out ears, and an oval mouth. God had given him the sort of face you usually see carved on a totem-pole but he didn't seem to hold any grudges. The young boy looked as if he might be related, though fortunately for him the features were less pronounced.

Still no-one spoke.

The atmosphere was indefinably charged. It was like a poker game at the Crazy Horse Saloon just before the gunfight breaks out. Except of course that, instead of aces and queens, people were slapping down slices of bread and marge onto the table.

I noticed Guy was producing about one slice to everyone else's five or six, mainly because he was conscientiously ensuring every square inch was covered, then slicing each piece diagonally like your mum does for

Sunday tea. He seemed deeply contemplative. I gradually realized why. I dreaded some quintessentially public-school conversational entrée, and began to try and think of a way of heading him off. Too late. He cleared his throat. I winced.

'Well,' he began, 'we seem to have closed a chapter in the cold war with the Czechoslovakian débâcle. I can't help feeling the West should have adopted a firmer stance from the outset.'

It was like dropping an antelope into a bear pit. The air was ripped apart by an explosion of growls, roars and muffled screams. The boy tittered, the totem pole said, 'Good one, cock,' and the silently hostile ruffian ceased chewing to call, 'Awf awf. Heyah, heyah.' Loudest of all, Jack's brassy voice fanfared over and over again, 'Little Lord bloody Fontelroy! Lord flaming Haw-haw!'

Very gradually, they desisted, and the room was filled once more with sticky thuds and tacky scraping.

We got down to the last loaf without further incident. Perhaps there would be no shoot-out after all. The young boy began not quite whistling, more faintly blowing, 'Let It Be.'

'Nige. Shut yer trap,' Jack barked.

Guy cleared his throat again. I groaned inwardly. He wasn't being provocative, he just hadn't understood. He was genuinely interested in drawing a conversation out of these people.

'Paul McCartney eh, er Nigel. Do you know he wrote that song about his mother? The "Mother Mary" bit has no religious connotation, it's intended to be taken literally. Most of the lyrics are a repetition of childhood homilies. "Let it be" is of course a representation of the sort of thing all mothers advise – leave well enough alone, don't aggravate a problem, don't get in over your head, don't get excited over what you can't control . . .'

'What the fuck do you know about it?'

This came – unmistakenly confrontationally – from the

silent ruffian with the dirty blond hair. There was what's called a pregnant silence.

Well, I decided, if I had to go for my gun I'd rather draw on this one than Jack.

'If you'd listen he's trying to tell you,' I said evenly.

Without a word of warning, his eyes swivelled towards me, his cheeks puffed out then contracted, and with a menacing 'phut' he spat his chewing-gum across the table at me. It hit my chest, bounced off, and plopped onto the surface.

We all stared at the lump of distastefully gnawed grey goo, slowly shedding a small puddle of spittle. I was aware of people putting down their knives and bread and marge very slowly. Adrenalin began pumping and there was a high-pitched whistle in my ears. This was it. Draw!

'You disgusting little tyke,' I growled.

The chairs shot back with a violent guttural scrape and, there being no Colt .45s, we lurched forward, fists up and the wild light of battle (in his case behind the manky stuff) in our eyes.

I was momentarily gratified to note that he came no further than my midriff, before his chest met with the flat of Jack's hand and he bounced back into his chair.

'Cool it! Mickie! Cool it! Not yet!' Jack demanded.

Mickie ricocheted off his seat, shot back in my direction, and this time was restrained by Jack's hands on each of his shoulders.

'That'll do Mickie lad! Leave it! Later!'

I was on my feet with my fists bunched and knuckles white. Guy was beside me, wearing an expression of someone intrigued, concerned and vaguely disgusted. Rather as if for the first time in his life he'd happened on two dogs copulating. Mickie panted and snarled like a baited bear at its neck chain. The other two began to finish buttering the last loaf of Sunblest.

'You'll get yer chance later, lad,' Jack said soothingly. He patted Mickie's shoulders and chuckled without humour, like one using forced jollity to front darker emotions.

I was grateful for his intervention, but couldn't escape the suspicion that it was less a policing action than a delaying tactic. Bearing in mind the 'laters' and 'not yets', I could be forgiven for thinking he had something in store for me. Something perhaps more dastardly than a punch-up.

'Waiters up top! We're open!'

It was Doris, who had descended a few steps and bobbed her head briefly below the line of the ceiling.

Guy, myself, and the lad with the bulging eyes moved towards the stairs and slowly ascended.

'Lads! Hey, lads!' Jack called as we were leaving.

We turned to see him pluck the chewing-gum from the table and lob it with a plop into the vat of fresh batter on the mixer.

Then he laughed, a little madly.

26

The third waiter, who was called Gordon, turned out to be friendly but not very communicative.

Guy and I, visibly shaken by our first hour in salaried employ, sought desperately to put things in rational perspective by investigating some of the background. Gordon wasn't really the person to ask. He would have had difficulty giving you the background to his own birth. He rarely produced a sentence of more than four words, and, invariably, one of those was 'cock'. He lived in this environment day in, day out, but it interested him about as much as your average bird is interested in ornithology.

The three of us stood together in the centre of the restaurant, trays under our arms, awaiting the arrival of what Gordon called 'the punters'.

'Jack and Mick,' I said tentatively. 'Are they – er – all right?'

'What do you mean cock?'
'Well, they seem a bit touchy.'
'Aye.'
'Are they always like that?'
'More or less, cock.'
There was a pause. Guy asked, 'What does Nigel do?'
'Gets thumped mostly, cock.'
'By Jack and Mick?'
'Not by me.'
I nodded towards Joe who had now managed to inject his vast bulk between cooker and counter and was manoeuvring trays of pies.
'Why doesn't Joe do something about them?' I asked.
'Upstairs-downstairs, cock.'
Again there was a pause.
'But they don't just seem aggressive,' Guy commented, 'I would almost say they were violent.'
'Oh aye cock. Bad buggers, pair of 'em. Villains.'
He appeared to tire of the subject. 'Now Tim, you take those tables over by the door. Guy, you take those over there by the toilets. I'll handle the rest.'
This was probably just as well. A more loquacious character than Gordon might have been able to help us decipher the less obscure aspects of Doris's initiation, but we quickly learned that most of them were a simple short-code.
A few orders, and things began to settle into routine. Then tedium. Within an hour, I had cracked the last great mystery of the job when I heard Gordon charge a shilling for a bottle of pop for which he had only paid ninepence. The gyp was the bottle deposit – already discounted by Joe. But the punters didn't know that.
Over lunch it was damned hard work. Joe and Doris occasionally disappeared completely in swathes of steam, to emerge blinking and sweating like people waking from a nightmare, then howl, 'Who's on?' We ran, shouted, struggled to remember orders of a dozen meals at a time, swerved round prams and over children,

sweated profusely, and, in between, tried to be polite. The customers were mainly either pensioners, who praised the fish as the flakiest they had ever eaten, insisted their special thanks be conveyed to the chef for the crispiest, most golden chips they had ever tasted, said the tea was even better than our Joan's and stood for the Hallelujah Chorus when it came to the mushy peas; or teenagers, who, if male, wanted to take up a table for an hour while they sipped a Coke each, if female, wanted to take up a table for an hour while they sipped a Coke each, giggled, screamed, cheeked the waiters and backchatted the lads at the next table; or middle-aged men with families, who said the service was disgusting, the food was revolting, the prices were insulting, suggested you should be publicly flogged and burned for the heinous crime of spilling tea into their saucer, then left you a tanner tip.

As lunch-time drew towards an end, I'd collected a warm inner glow from the first group, the possibility of a couple of interesting nights out from the second and just under five bob from the third. Not bad when you were only getting thirty shillings for the day.

At two o'clock Joe called, 'Tim, Guy, break-time. Do you want your dinner downstairs with Jack and Mickie or to take out?'

'Oh, I think we'll take a breath of fresh air if it's all the same to you, Joe,' Guy answered without asking me.

The day had brightened, and a watery sun now shed pale lemon light onto the street. There was a pub called the Moon over Water on the corner, but we were at that age when drinking is still more a matter of swagger than a true pleasure. We walked the length of the street gorging contentedly, then retraced our steps.

Next to the restaurant was an amusement arcade. We drifted in and soon were anchored to a pinball machine and squealing like sea birds as the great big silver bolly chugged and pinged, setting lights twinkling like a night incendiary attack and the score-counter clattering away like an AK-47 on automatic.

I was suddenly aware of a figure appearing at my right, leaning casually onto the machine and then bringing his knee up against its side. The lights went out, the noises ceased, and the ball bounced dully off the bumpers, tumbling sadly and silently to oblivion, like an erection that's been told, 'But I don't want to ruin our friendship.'

'Oops. Clumsy me,' said Jack jovially.

Little Mickie appeared and parked himself on the opposite side of the machine. He glared at me with the eyes of one of those snakes that can spit venom with pinpoint accuracy over ten feet. Or perhaps I just had a slow-motion *idée fixe* of a chewed-up ball of gum spiralling through the air towards me. I gave him a look which I had never used before, but had practised a lot in front of mirrors.

'We missed yous for yus dinners, lads,' Jack said, still maintaining a tone of mock-*bonhomie*. 'We was looking forward, wasn't we Mick lad, eh?'

'We were that, Jack.'

They had a sort of Jolly Roger laughing session together.

'We decided to dine out,' Guy said.

Coming from me it could only have been sarcasm, but they weren't sure how to take Guy.

'Shame, shame,' Jack said, 'because we was needing to have a little chat with you.'

Jack seemed now to address himself mainly to me each time he spoke.

'It's about a little house custom we have fellas. We forgot to mention it this morning with all the excitement.' More pirate laughter. 'It's to do with you lads having all the fun upstairs while poor Mickie and me slogs away in all the muck and steam and dark. Galley-slaves in the dungeons.'

I wasn't about to pick him up on his mixed metaphors. For one terrifying moment, I thought Guy was.

'Oh yes. What is it then?' I cut in hurriedly.

'Well it's always been a pals' agreement with the waiters, seeing as how they has the cushy end of the job, seeing as how they earn all them tips, and chat up all them girls and such, and seeing as how if there was no-one down below to peel tatties and batter fish and keep pots and dishes coming and all, there's always been a chummy agreement that half their tips comes down to us. Is that not right Michael?'

'Right enough, Jack.'

'Fair and square don't you think gents? Team spirit and all.'

I pursed my lips and looked at Guy. He shrugged.

'And Mickie and me having the experience like, and knowing what's what. We reckon on a day like today you're probably doing ten bob each, right?'

I breathed deeply and said nothing. Guy said, 'Tan bawb?' which is exactly how Jack had pronounced it. Jack nodded.

'Five bob each all round, son. Fair and square. Even shares eh?' Jack laughed a hard laugh like a very old goat and gripped my upper arm fiercely. 'Eh Tam? Fair shares eh?'

Again I pursed my lips and breathed in through my nose. I looked at the silent pinball machine and then sideways at Guy who was scratching his hairy cheek thoughtfully. A few yards behind him there was a comfortingly enormous attendant who was eyeing us inquisitively. He wore a brown coat and carried a huge bunch of keys, but, more important, he had arms and a forehead like a creature from the Cro-Magnon era.

'And just suppose, purely hypothetically,' I said, buoyed by what I'd seen, 'and I don't want you to run away with the idea that this is our final answer, but just supposing we were to say "Mickie and Jack suck on this."'

I raised my middle finger vertically upward, but at the same time smiled disarmingly and cocked my head to one side in the classic gesture of reasonable enquiry.

Jack laughed even louder, his quiff coiling and uncoiling like a leaf spring as his head shook.

'Then you'd be a plucky little bastard with a broken finger, Tam.'

Mickie reached into the side pocket of his imitation leather jacket and withdrew a rather grim, if faintly fantastic weapon. It was a toilet chain, complete with a heavy wooden handle. Fixing me with his eyes, he wrapped a length of chain around his knuckles, leaving about twelve or fifteen inches dangling free with the weight of the handle. Then, suddenly and without warning, he swung the chain and lashed the handle viciously down on the base of the machine, putting an enormous dent in the small metal plate which tells you how many points you have to get to earn a replay.

I was determined not to enter into an exchange of gradually escalating bravado. It would be nerve-racking in the extreme, particularly for me as the unarmed party. On the other hand, total capitulation was probably a very bad idea indeed. I was healthily wary of Jack, but suspected Mickie was largely bluff. The idea of a five-foot tough guy is after all slightly absurd. Besides, there was an attendant the size of a polar bear standing not three yards away.

'Well Guy,' I said cheerfully, 'what do you expect to find on the end of a toilet chain but a little shithouse.'

Even I realized I'd overdone it. There was a roar of outrage mingled with a disbelieving shriek. Mickie flew at me as if he wanted to bite a piece out of my face, but again Jack's restraining arms were around him like a mental patient's male nurse fumbling for the strait-jacket.

'No Mickie! We'll sort him later! Not now lad! Not yet!'

I turned calmly around, expecting our protector to pad over like Mummy bear about to cuff one of her cubs, to see him feverishly locking himself into the little cubicle which served as his office.

'Christ Guy, run!' I shouted.

27

The afternoon provided a welcome respite. The few customers were of the 'cup of tea and a Kit Kat' sort, except two young girls in black kiss-me-quick cowboy hats, one of whom called Guy over and in broad Liverpudlian asked for 'Fish and chips for her and a coffee and ten Players for me.' When Guy told her we served tea only, she shook her head silently and disparagingly.

I plodded my patch like a bobby.

During one of his chattier moments, Gordon told me that Jack had done time and Mickie had been to approved school. Guy commented that they certainly seemed determined to widen their institutional experience.

'Who would have thought,' he said with irritating detachment, 'that there would be a gangland Tedderton in among the pensioner's portions, donkey rides and jugs of tea for the sands.'

I had a suspicion that if I took the problem to Joe, he would be impatiently dismissive. Of course, it could be that Mickie and Jack would simply let the whole episode drop. To types like them, threats and bullying probably came as naturally as snarling and clawing the air came to a big cat, and could be just as meaningless. On the other hand, I bet they too got a wanton satisfaction from making things bleed. I found myself glancing nervously at my watch with unnecessary frequency.

As I passed close to the two girls for the third or fourth time, the one who was eating suddenly barked into her food. Then she threw her hands to her throat as if attempting self-strangulation and said, 'Ugh! Guroo!'

'Excuse me, waiter,' her friend called to me in a calm, polite voice.

I went over. The crisp professionalism was becoming a bit shop-soiled by now, and I was somewhat preoccupied. Still, I tried to look respectfully helpful. The girl with the food was now mainly choking sounds under cascades of dark blonde hair. The other looked up at me with very large, beautiful eyes. I admired the way she managed to look upwards deprecatingly.

'My friend Doreen,' she said, smiling sweetly, 'has just found some chewing-gum in her fish.'

I had to tear my gaze away from hypnotically intelligent eyes, which, even in a moment of panic, I couldn't help noticing were complemented by a perfectly-shaped mouth and skin as clear as meltwater, to verify that there was, indeed, a lump of chewing-gum in the middle of Doreen's cod. In the shock of recognition, I almost blurted something about returning it to our kitchen staff. Then, recovering some composure, and desperately seeking to master a situation with which I was ill-equipped to cope, I smiled inanely. Since the girls were about my age, my first reaction was to make light of it.

'And if you once mention,' she went on, gaze steady and unblinking, 'waiters, flies in soup, or any variations on the theme, I shall go immediately to the nearest telephone and phone the Health Department.'

You could tell the scouse accent was real because she was trying, very slightly, to tidy it up. At this time, everyone else our age was mildly affecting one. She pulled hard on her cigarette, so that when it left her lips it had a pink band around its base, and scrutinized me through smoke.

'Ah. Right. Yes.'

Second thoughts were to pass the buck. I turned to the other girl, bent forward, and, peering intently through the curtains of blonde hair, discovered a grimace.

'Might I ask who served you?'

She stopped attempting to throttle herself long enough to utter the words, 'The 'ttractive one.'

'Tractive means pulling something, Doreen,' the other said, a little tetchily. Then, with a glance across towards Guy, added to herself, 'Though you might have a point.'

I scanned the room, meeting only with Gordon's large round eyes bulging inquisitively, huge ears protruding and mouth pushed forward in concern like an exhaust-pipe.

'My friend is not referring to the colleague who looks like the last of the Mohicans chipped his face out with a tomahawk,' she told me.

I went and got Guy, then hid behind him.

'Hello, I'm Marjorie. This is Doreen. Doreen has discovered something inside her fish which we suspect it didn't pick up at full fathoms five in mid-Atlantic.'

Guy peered at the plate. I was annoyed to notice that Marjorie peered just as intently at Guy.

'Good Lord, how disgusting,' he said in perfect honesty. 'Would you like me to get the management?'

She widened her eyes.

'A place like this has management?'

'No, not really,' Guy said. 'But there's Joe. He owns it.'

'Forget it,' Marjorie said, taking a last drag on the ciggy and stubbing it out in the middle of Doreen's fish. 'Just don't present us with a bill.'

'Of course not Marjorie –' she cocked an eye at that – 'please do accept our profound apologies. Is there anything at all we can do for you and – er – Doreen?'

Marjorie picked up their cowboy hats which had been sitting one inside the other on the bench beside her, replaced hers and plonked the other unceremoniously onto Doreen's head.

'Two things,' she answered very definitely.

We waited. They rose to go.

'Firstly, replace the ketchup and HP. In 1760, when Voltaire said that the English were a nation possessed of forty-six religions and two sauces, he must have been talking about the contents of these bloody bottles.'

I didn't know about Guy, but I couldn't get enough of those huge eyes flashing in vexation.

'*D'accord, mademoiselle,*' Guy bowed with a flourish. '*Et l'autre chose?*'

'Meet us at the entrance to the pier at eight. C'mon Doreen.'

Guy and I had no time for discussion. A coach party flooded in and began to settle on my patch. Gordon called, 'Tim, Doris wants to see you in the cellar.' I was halfway down the steps before it occurred to me I might be the victim of a strategic ruse.

Sure enough, Doris was nowhere to be seen. But then, neither was Mickie. It was hot and steamy, and I could dimly make out Jack, stripped to the waist and sucking greedily at the neck of an upturned bottle of cream soda. His Adam's apple chugged like an engine until he finally pulled the bottle away from his lips with a satisfied 'Aaah!'

'Hello Tam lad,' he said. He wasn't smiling, for about the first time since I'd met him, which suited me. I was getting heartily sick of his idea of *bon* sodding *homie*.

He held out the bottle. 'Thirsty work Tam, in all this heat. Will you have a drink?'

I shook my head. To my left, I was aware of a noise which sounded like rain running down a gutter. I turned and there was Mickie, casually peeing into an empty cream-soda bottle. It looked like they got through a lot of the stuff.

'Not even time to go upstairs for a pee,' Jack called. 'No rest for the wicked.'

I didn't stray too far away from the bottom of the stairs. Jack moved around the table towards me. His physique, as I had expected, was wiry and firm. Muscles glistened in the naked light like wet marble in sunshine. He had a tattoo of a scorpion on one shoulder, and a fancy escutcheon with 'Doris' enscrolled on the other. I thought of asking him jokingly if Joe knew, but couldn't summon up the courage. The intricate contraption which held his pants up, his Lonsdale belt, gave him a gladiatorial air which scared the hell out of me.

'I just wanted to make sure,' he said, coming much closer than he needed to, 'that we had an understanding.

After our little conversation at dinner-time. You and Guy seemed to have to leave all of a sudden, so we never got finished.'

There was a hurried clatter and Guy appeared on the steps behind me, then a pause while they took him in.

'Guy,' Mickie said jovially, 'have a drink.'

'Well, thank you Michael,' Guy said in the manner of someone who's been offered the peace-pipe and is determined not to cause offence, 'I could do with a swig. My! Warm . . . you chaps do have a tough time down here.'

'Mickie's just peed in it Guy,' I said hurriedly without looking away from Jack.

There was a hasty 'Argh!' and a heavy clunk as Guy thumped the bottle down somewhere.

They chuckled.

'But there's another small matter I forgot to mention,' Jack said, with his voice slowly becoming serious. 'Another little house custom that'll affect you before you go home tonight, Tam.'

I swallowed, but said nothing. When he resumed, his voice had shed any humour. It was pure menace. You could almost believe he was acting, but of course the back-slapping heartiness was the act.

'We have a little initiation ceremony for the waiters. A sort of baptism. A sort of "welcome to Tollys".'

He looked over to the tiled bath which that morning had been full of peeled potatoes. I followed his gaze. Now it was full to overflowing with cold water.

'That's right Tam lad. Baptism. Just a bit of good-natured fun.'

When he spoke his bottom lip was curled so far forward that I could count his lower teeth jutting like fence-posts. His voice fell to a gravelly whisper.

'You're going in. In yer woy fronts, or in yer clobber. But you're going in, lad. Tonight. After work.'

So that was it.

I turned and mounted the stairs, knowing for sure this custom had been instigated exclusively for me.

28

The teatime rush was not on the same scale as lunch. All the same, my preoccupation with what Guy now called 'the two scorpions in a bottle' made itself sadly evident. The enthusiastic rushing to and fro slowed to a lethargic lope around the tables. My personal target of faultlessly recalling an order for over twenty meals became an effort hopelessly beyond my concentration. And the youthful effervescence with which I had greeted my first customer lapsed into snappy irritation.

Thus, exchanges along the lines of the following became not uncommon at the counter:

'Five in, three away, sausage egg in, 'am in, pie away, double egg away brown.'

'One in, one away, sausage in, sausage egg away brown, double bread, two Cokes.'

'Ehem, three er in, no – away . . . one, oh damn.'

To which Joe would gaze at me impassively through clouds of steam, like Buddha from amongst the incense.

Or, at the tables:

'We didn't order that.'

'Are you sure?'

'Yes. Andrew doesn't eat peas, do you love?'

'Oh. Well, couldn't he eat them this once?'

'Andrew's never eaten peas.'

'Just this once Andrew?'

'Andrew's never eaten peas.'

'Well isn't it about time he started?'

Sharp intake of breath.

Or again:

'Excuse me young man.'

'Yes?'

'Could you reckon that up again?'

'What?'

'What we had.'

'But you paid ten minutes ago. How do I know what you had?'

'I'll tell you.'

Long list of comestibles, calories in, cholesterol away, heart attacks by the plateload.

'Twelve and six.'

'You charged us twelve and eight.'

'Did you say a children's sausage and chips?'

'Yes.'

'Well, we won't ruin our day over tuppenceworth of offal and breadcrumbs will we? Here!'

'Really!'

My heart simply was not in it. My head pounded with the effort of finding a way out of the dilemma.

It wasn't that I was frightened of physical confrontation. Several years of playing rugby had inured me to sustaining the odd knock here and there. But I wasn't certain just how far Jack and Mickie might be prepared to take that sort of thing. Either way, I was pretty sure that their idea of a fair fight was unlikely to coincide with Guy's or mine.

I had also been imagining my old man's reaction when I splashed into the house, having dripped my way home for forty minutes on the number three bus, to sneeze and say, 'Bid of fud at work, Dad.' On the whole, I thought facing Jack was slightly preferable.

But, at bottom, it was a question of personal honour. I could hear Mickie's derisive laugh as I climbed out of the bath. I could see him grin as we handed over the money. There really is no short-term response to coercion. When someone pushes you around in life, you have to come to a decision that you can live with afterwards. I was painfully aware that neither Guy nor myself were built to inspire physical intimidation. Jack was.

I thought of the people I would normally go to for advice and tried to deduce what it might be. Nonnie would tell me immediately to find a policeman: the pragmatic woman's solution, totally ignorant of, and unconcerned about, male vanity. John would say meet them head-on, get stuck in; even if you took a hiding you'd be showing them they weren't going to get away scot-free. Leave 'em something to remember you by. Jim's would be the negotiated settlement: propose a reasonable percentage of the tips – making dead sure they had no idea what a hundred per cent was – and offer to stick your head in the bath as a token gesture of goodwill in deference to custom. Tell them you'd get them a pint later in the pub and part as pals. Or at least as near as you could ever come to it. I could hear my father saying, 'And why didn't you get this idiot Joe to do something about them? They work for him for God's sake. It's his responsibility.'

All too soon, we were handing over to the evening waiters. We paid Joe his float and obtained the locker key from Doris, who was getting our money ready. At the top of the stairs Guy said, 'What are you going to do?' I said, 'I don't know,' and started down.

I still had a vague hope that it was all a bit of a macho joke and that they would simply leave us in peace. Mickie and Jack were busy with some dishes, and said nothing as we entered. We walked to the lockers, opened the door and slipped on our jackets. I left the key in the lock and turned to go. There they both were.

They'd positioned themselves to block our way back to the stairs. Mickie, slightly to the right and behind Jack, was whirring six inches or so of his toilet chain idly, like an aeroplane with its propeller on taxi. Jack had taken off his enormous belt and was slowly and very deliberately wrapping it tightly around his right hand. He arranged it so that the buckle, which was a huge silver lion's head, was positioned squarely across his fist to serve as a knuckle duster. I found myself thinking up stories about having walked into a door-knocker.

'Bathtime,' was all he said.

We faced each other like one of those stand-offs that took place at Checkpoint Charlie at the height of the cold war. Tanks, barrel to barrel at point-blank range, each one waiting for the other to make a move. Even Jack seemed strangely reticent to act.

The seconds ticked by. My succession of advisers whispered in my ear.

'Get a policeman.'

'Stick one on him.'

'Tell him to break out the cream soda.'

'Call for the boss.'

The silence grew to be thunderous, the inactivity interminable. The voices began to chant, quicker and louder.

'Get a policeman!'

'Stick one on him!'

'Offer a compromise!'

'Get the boss!'

Jack continuously massaged the lion's nose on his belt-buckle with the palm of his free hand. It gleamed like a pencil torch. Next to me, Guy licked dry lips and it sounded like a handclap. The voices were shouting now.

'Policeman!'

'Punch-up!'

'Powwow!'

'Boss!'

All of a sudden a deep sepulchral voice boomed inside my head like an invocation. It drowned the babbling of advice like a sonar wash and overwrote it with one single unmistakable command. It had a rumbling Godlike authority which would have figured on the Richter scale. And an Irish lilt.

'TAKE HIS LEGS TIM ARMSTRONG! GET IN LOW! TAKE HIS RUDDY LEGS!'

I dropped my head and launched myself forward like a guard dog off the leash. Instinctively, I gave Jack my right shoulder and took him perfectly three inches above the kneecap. Before he even had time to register surprise, his legs buckled, his slight frame lifted off the floor, and his head flew backwards through the air and crashed into one of the storage cupboards. It hit with a muffled, spongy thud, rather like a report from a field cannon fitted with a silencer, and to my amazement went *straight through* the cupboard. They were evidently made of the cheapest laminated cardboard. The thing detached itself from its fixing and Jack slowly slid down the wall wearing it. He had a great big cube for a head like a cartoon robot.

I released his knees from my grip, and squirmed around on the floor to see Guy and Mickie involved in a two-man scrummage. Mickie had the fire and the rage, both very necessary qualities in the loose scrum, but Guy had the technique and the weight. He began a forward drive which took him past the batter, between the two chippers, around the edge of the table and pushed Mickie right up against the tiled bath. I could hear almost the Twickenham west stand groaning 'Heave!' Guy gripped Mickie around the waist and attempted to hoist him, backside first, up the side of the bath, presumably obsessed with the illusion that getting him in would be the equivalent of a pushover try.

Jack began to stir. He made the sort of noises that people make when they wake up with a cupboard on their head.

'Guy. Come on!' I called.

Guy made one last gut-wrenching effort to get Mickie over the side of the bath, failed, so planted an enormous up-and-under between his open legs.

Mickie's eyes momentarily widened to the size of saucers, and he let out a sound like a lawnmower misfiring. I ran over, grabbed him by the arms and nodded to Guy who seized his legs.

'ARCHIMEDEAN IMMERSION!' I shouted.

We pitched him over and in, with a splash like a depth-charge, then turned for the stairs. As we passed Jack, now tentatively exploring the unfamiliar, cuboid contours enveloping his own bonce, I thumped down as hard as I could with both hands on the top of the cupboard.

'KINETIC DISSIPATION!' Guy called.

As Guy scampered up the stairs, I stopped and turned. Mickie's sodden head was just emerging over the side of the bath. I adopted the classic posture of derision, left arm across the crook of the right, fist raised, and bellowed, 'ARTIFICIAL INSEMINATION!'

We ran.

Up the stairs, out into the street, around the corner, down two blocks onto the promenade, across the road and along the sea wall.

All the way people stared at us – there is a conspicuous difference between people who are running *to*, which is mundane, and people who are running *from*, which isn't. We jinked in and out of the crowds and didn't stop until we had put five minutes between ourselves and Tollivers. Past the fair, through the arcades, along a Victorian terrace of bed-and-breakfast boarding-houses.

Eventually we slumped with our backs against a bus shelter, and sucked air into our lungs through heaving chests. For a time we just let it hurt. I thought I could detect a smile in the darkness.

'And with one bound, they were free!' Guy panted.

We began laughing. It hurt, but we couldn't stop. We laughed even though we couldn't breathe. Guy kept saying 'Jack' and then, unable to draw breath or frame the words, began drawing square shapes around his own head. His face contorted in pain. I asked, between sawing at the air, if he thought Joe would send us our wages. He shouted 'No!' and detonated a crescendo of hysterical hooting and cackling which left us both with tears in our eyes.

We counted our tips. A little under twelve bob.

We waited at the entrance to the pier until eight thirty, but Doreen and Marjorie didn't show. They had evidently got a better offer.

We found a quiet pub with a good jukebox and drank halves of bitter until it was time for the last bus. Then we set off for the bus station, keeping a wary eye out for small men wielding toilet chains.

PART 3

The Siren of Extra Cover

29

I experienced my first orgasm – of the non-autogenous kind – as a result of a game of cricket. I'm aware not a lot of people can say that.

I could add that the game probably cost me early promotion to high office and was instrumental in my saving a life. But, as they used to say in novels, I anticipate.

'Parents,' Jim said one spring evening, sprawled across his bed, 'draw lines in the sand from which they are obliged to retreat, generation by generation.'

It was raining softly, but we had both window and door slightly ajar. The latter to provide early warning of my father on the stairs, the former to create a steady draught which cleansed the air of smoke from the illicit packet of Cadet tipped we had half consumed.

Through the window, warm rain glistened on the rooftops, and the elm tree in our back garden was a slimy coal-black, speckled with green shoots.

'Eh?' I said.

He tutted.

'This, for example,' he said, waving his cigarette vaguely at the room and sitting up on the bed. The bed and room were his, newly inherited from recently-married John, who in turn had inherited them from Nonnie when she had married.

I looked around questioningly, but didn't see the point and said so.

'Not the room, dumbo,' he whined, exasperated. 'The fag. Smoking.' And then at my uncomprehending shrug, more emphatically, 'Taboo. Not allowed. Against house rules.'

I shrugged again.

'So?'

'The point is, we still do it. Nonnie would sooner have married a darkie.'

I considered.

'But, we do it in secret. Without permission.'

'Well, yes,' he conceded, his voice mellowing, 'that's because we haven't fought that particular point yet. But over the course of the decades, ground is ceded. Parental jurisdiction is constrained. The rules are less stringent from generation to generation. Easier.'

He puffed grandly, as if in emphasis.

'I don't see it,' I said candidly. 'It's always seemed to me to be "You'll do as I tell you till you leave school." Then "Till you're working." Then 'Till you're twenty-one." Then "As long as you're living under my roof." By that time you're almost ready to impose curfew and martial law on your own kids.'

'Nah!' he insisted, flicking at an ashtray balanced on his lap, 'that's because you don't think globally. And I don't mean Roosevelt's Four Freedoms or anything like that. That's just the sort of global guff you would think. The freedoms that matter to you and me are the freedoms to do what you want, where you want, with whom you want, and when you want.' He paused. 'Meaning usually as late at night as you want,' he added as an afterthought.

'Mm.'

'Nonnie and John went through hell to win some of those freedoms. Think back. When Nonnie was your age, there was a list of fellas she would have been skinned alive for being seen in the same street with. Even those on the approved list had to have her back on the doorstep at ten on pain of emasculation. John was forbidden to go to coffee bars. Or youth clubs. I can remember one particularly violent skirmish over polo-necked sweaters, for Christ's sake. Our front room has been the scene of more spectacular battles than anything staged by Eisenstein.'

'Well, I suppose . . .'

'The point is, our nip, I am on the verge of extending those freedoms by a quantum. I am no child. I earn my money. I pay rent for my room. I should not even have to ask.'

'What, then?' I asked, a hiss of excitement in my voice.

'You'll see,' he promised. He stabbed out his cigarette with conviction.

This was typical Jim. Lead you on. Carry you to the climax. Then leave you in the air.

'Your pigeon,' I muttered, mildly annoyed.

'Wrong. Yours too. It is in the nature of things that the hard-won freedoms of one generation are automatically inherited by the next. Nonnie, John and I will have shed blood for you to reap the ultimate spoils of adolescence under a benevolent autocracy.'

'Oh rubbish—'

'Which I suppose,' he ran on, grinning mischievously, 'might be construed as you bringing your future girlfriend back at three in the morning and taking her roughly from behind on the hearthrug, whilst the old man seethes upstairs at the sound of her hooting hoarsely like an anguished moose.'

My face froze and I became very still. At this time in my life, I found it immensely important not to be intimidated by this sort of talk. It was essential to look and behave as if sex between man and woman was an ordinary, healthy, natural, everyday aspect of everyone's life. This was because my entire experience of the female species had amounted to sporadic exchanges of saliva with three not particularly attractive specimens.

'Oh,' I said, floundering a bit. 'I'm not so sure . . .'

'You, unsure!' he broke in mockingly. He lifted the ashtray, swung his legs off the bed and proceeded to seclude the cigarette packet in his underpant drawer. 'If I were you, I'd pray that my children are very bright or very stupid. You are cursed with just enough intelligence to be unsure about anything.'

I cleared my throat defensively.

'There are some circles in which I'm considered pretty bright,' I asserted.

'Aye. Academics,' he said dismissively. 'The silliest of all silly buggers.'

He slammed the window. Presumably my signal to depart.

But I couldn't deny he had struck a chord. I lived in an all-male household. I was being educated at an all-male school. When something female walked into the room, I found myself jumping and taking three steps backward. I began to feel that my development was being stunted in one vital direction. It was all too easy to convince myself that unbearable restrictions were being imposed by authority. My natural expression was being thwarted by overbearing parentage. A recent letter from Guy Lavelle had expounded at length on the importance of a rounded development, and the need to identify strengths and weaknesses at an early stage by exposing oneself to as wide a variety of experiences as possible. So here I was, determined to expose myself to the opposite sex.

At tea that evening, the three of us munched away in silence. Our meal was not a seething casserole comprising a herd of Aberdeen Angus and half a market garden of vegetables, because it had not been made by my father. It was not a mouthwateringly tender steak and kidney pie decorated with courgettes, baby carrots and *pommes de terre dauphinoise*, because it had not been cooked by Jim. It was two slices of luncheon meat and a quartered tomato each, because it was my turn. My father was finished, but, apparently just for the sport of it, continued to chase a bit of tomato around the rim of his plate, stabbing spitefully with his fork.

Jim put down his knife and fork and folded his hands delicately under his chin in the classic pose of after-dinner conversation. It looked a bit out of place among the sauce bottles and abandoned luncheon meat.

'I was thinking of buying a motor bike,' he offered in a voice of casual amusement.

The old man's reply detonated like a report.

'No you're not. Chrome-plated coffins. You can wait till you're twenty-one. Not while you're living under my roof.'

Jim's face collapsed. He looked like a defence lawyer who had just completed an hour-long impassioned summing-up, to find the jury blowing raspberries at him.

Apparently unconnected, I found myself saying, 'I was thinking of starting youth club, Dad.'

'Good for you lad,' he said, spearing the tomato with a decisive clack and popping it into his mouth. 'Get you out and about a bit. Might even meet a lass or two.'

30

I wonder if youth clubs have changed much. Perhaps they have. Perhaps, these days, rambling purpose-built complexes house sports and entertainment facilities to rival Club Med. Perhaps counsellors with Ph.D.s in Adolescent Trauma lead discussion groups on 'Coping with Spots', 'The Urge to Masturbate' and 'Where Will Hair Grow Next?' There must at least be programmes for Social Action? Environmental Encounter Groups? Surely Aerobics?

In the 1960s, most youth clubs consisted of Not Locking the Local School Hall One Night Each Week.

In my case, the school in question was Clarence Street, a small primary in neat Sixties red brick with a hall about twice the size of a single-car garage and a playground about half the size of a carport. The One Night Each Week was Friday.

I couldn't deny I was on the upper side of the age bracket for youth club, but licensed premises could still be a source of tortuous embarrassment if you were asked your age, or, worse still, the ultimate blow to your manly pride, refused service. Besides, having a year or two's edge wasn't going to hurt, was it? Sophistication, confidence, a head for drink, taste in clothes. I sniffed proudly at John's aftershave – strictly accurately, it was after bum-fluff trim with the scissors in my case but I still swelled confidently. Pure bloody Sixties girly fantasy, I told myself.

I had taken care with my appearance. To a pair of glossy bronze trousers in Terylene, I had added a high-collar nylon shirt surreptitiously filched from Jim's top drawer in the precarious expectation of being home before him. My jacket was of a shiny blue textile of indeterminate nature, lined with sponge to make it ultra-light. I rustled when I moved, exactly like the silk stockings on a plump lady's thighs. It was an interesting age for clothes. Briefly, people believed cotton and wool had had their day, and preferred material concocted in a plastics factory. Most of the stuff I had on hadn't so much been woven or knitted, as patented.

The raunchy beat of Ray Davies singing 'You really got me' thumped pleasurably into the gut as I crossed the playground. There were one or two youngsters standing around at the door, either looking sheepish with their hands behind their backs, or with their hands behind their backs, giggling vacantly. When they realized it was someone of their own age, the hands reappeared clasping bottles of cheap sherry, which they guzzled recklessly.

As I pushed open the door, I was confronted with a scene of tribal ritual from which only the missionary in the cooking-pot was missing. A line of silhouetted figures shuffled more or less haphazardly to loud drumbeats. Strobe light flashed and flickered like the flames of a camp-fire. Nearby faces were glazed and entranced, QC sherry having much the same effect on the mind of a young adolescent as chewing coca leaves has on an Amazonian Indian. Against a bare expanse of wall, a light show projected florid oily immiscibles which writhed together like dimly seen shapes orgying. The whole was suffused in an eerie violet glow.

Faces began to take form in the gloom. Lining the walls, three deep like farmers on market day and concentrating with a similarly discerning intensity, was the male population of the hall.

Surrounded and cut off in a small square under the lamps, was the female half. Scores of pubescent female beauties bobbed and jerked around their handbags in an absolutely divine orgy of pert breasts, ripely gyrating buttocks, and, after the fashion of the moment, acres of wantonly exposed thigh, stockinged in every conceivable colour.

I smiled inwardly, feeling like a lion on a hill surveying a Serengeti full of frolicking game. I had come to the right place.

For a time I simply enjoyed the view, twitched to the backbeat and savoured the expectation, trying to look merely interested rather than transfixed. Teenage girls possess a purity of beauty unique in nature, one even teenage boys can appreciate. Put them in their finest and set them lightly perspiring to rhythmical music under subdued lighting, and it's enough to make you sing. In fact, a few of the lads lustily joined voice with Ray Davies on the rallentando that accompanies the 'Oh Yeah!' bit. One ecstatic soul even broke into an air-guitar solo. I appreciated how he felt, and couldn't quite dispel the impression that I was in on something anthropological. Anticipation and excitement merged like tributaries to form a river of ruttishness.

As the next record started, I moved confidently forward, well-stocked with a repertoire of polite banter which Jim had assured me was indispensable on such occasions.

(a) I like your dress
(b) I like Roger Daltrey
(c) I like the way you dance
(d) (In emergencies) I hope this isn't your bloody handbag I've got my foot wrapped up in

and approached a particularly sweet and understanding-looking one who appeared to be a loose satellite to a stellar cluster of Dolcis' leather articles. I tapped her on the shoulder just as her elliptical trajectory hit apogee.

To my astonishment, she began shaking her little head vigorously before I could even get the question out.

Retiring somewhat sobered to the perimeter, I decided it was best not to hang about and brood over one minor setback, but return immediately to the fray with redoubled effort. A second refusal, this time from a dusky blonde in a little backless number, was delivered mainly by a sharp spin and a wriggle of the shoulder-blades, a surrogate bum if ever I'd been shown one.

Now definitely taken aback, I staggered to a small Coke bar I had noticed in one corner, where an enterprising owlish youngster in braces was camped behind upturned crates, shifting ninepenny bottles at a bob. I moistened my rapidly drying mouth. Thankfully in later years there would be Newcastle Brown to fortify one in such moments. Now, I could only gulp and let the bubbles cascade from my nostrils. I stared disbelievingly back towards the dance floor, as twin rivers the colour of milkless tea foamed onto Jim's shirt.

Two more equally sharp rebuffs had me murderously surveying the spectating males for any sign of spiteful laughter. Giggling in mild hysteria myself, I was prepared to tear off limbs at the least sign of mirth in any male around me. There was none.

What on earth was *wrong* with me? Feverishly, almost in panic, I compared my appearance to the rest of the lads. We all seemed to show the same predilection for clothes based on petro-carbons. We all shared hairstyles which traced their antecedents to post-republican Rome. Now I came to notice it, we were even virtually unanimous in making the same statement of nonconforming individuality via the knotted red neckerchiefs. I sweated coldly.

My fifth attempt met with the most favourable

response I had yet received, which was still 'No' but at least she had spoken to me. After two further rejections, one reinforced with acerbic verbal discouragement, I retired, white-faced and shaken, to a small room I had noticed at the far end of the hall. It was lit normally, a sort of cloakroom now pressed into service as a leisure centre, and a dozen or so lads were playing desultory games of darts and table-tennis.

I slumped despondently against a heap of coats and jackets, prepared to contemplate a life of prayer and meditation. It was with only mild surprise that I noticed Charlie Vart and Billy Bibby were languidly patting a ping-pong ball back and forth across the table in front of me. The ball clicked perkily in my direction. Charlie came to retrieve it and chummily clouted me on the crown with his bat. I looked up into the carroty curls and constellations of freckles.

'Get blown out then?' he asked with an annoying chuckle.

Bruised male vanity had me prepared to be testy. But there was something about Charlie Vart that tended to make antagonism pop like a bubble.

'Well,' I answered moodily, 'you'd have thought I'd just shuffled out from behind some bushes in the park for goodness' sake.'

'You mean sexual assault wasn't on the agenda? Not even low down, after the half-bottle of cheap sherry?'

There are some possibilities you don't like to admit, even to yourself. I only managed a half-puff of indignation.

'No, thank you. Although it does seem to be the accepted seduction technique around here. I was merely asking the young ladies for a dance.'

'Mm, so we observed,' he commented, like a suspicious copper. Then, after a pause, 'Anyway, they don't dance with grockles.'

'Pardon?' I said, not managing to keep the irritation out of my voice.

'Grockles,' he said again. 'Outsiders. Newcomers. Non-members.'

'My experience entirely. Why ever not?'

'Well, half of 'em just want to get done up in their shortest mini and have a good bop. Natter with their mates and scoff a bag of chips on the way home. The other half are probably being picked up by their dads at ten.' He considered. 'And of course, half of 'em have got steadies and get a kick out of saying no.'

'A cruelty entirely natural to their age and sex,' Billy Bibby broke in, loping over and placing a lank hand on Charles' shoulder. 'By the way, you've dropped maths, haven't you Charlie. I shouldn't like to see you let loose on statistics.'

'Put like that,' I grumbled, still a bit petulant, 'you make social ostracism on the dance floor sound positively reasonable. Not to mention unavoidable. So how do you get to know the little loves?'

'Club activities,' Billy announced with quick conviction.

'Like?'

'Well, we're desperately short of cricket players.'

I frowned.

'You have female cricket players?'

'No, stupid – we have active female support.' Billy smiled condescendingly.

'Very appreciative active female support,' Charlie added with a definite roguish leer.

Cricket. Not a sport that sparked my imagination. At school, the summer sports were divided between those who could run, jump or throw – who did athletics – and those who couldn't – who did cricket. The team was run by an ancient genteel cove called Mr Warner. A teacher of Latin. No Oxo he. All dusted in chalk and pickled in prehistory, in his heather-mixture dicky bow, patched tweed sports jacket, suede brogues and Oxford bags, smelling of pipe smoke.

'Oh well,' I sighed with the air of one lacking a better

idea, 'let's give it a whirl. When? Where?'

'Well, as it happens,' Billy said, reaching out a long arm and helping me to my feet, 'the gentlemen you should speak to are right at hand. However,' he added, indicating the way with open palm, 'don't let them overwhelm you with their torrent of conversation and the breadth of their anecdotal wit.'

He led me across to another table where two copiously blond-haired youngsters, evidently twin brothers, were playing table tennis. Properly, I noticed. At least, the ball corkscrewed devilishly when they hit it, in contrast to the docile parabolas prescribed by the plonkers Billy and Charlie had been patting to each other. Also, we had to pause while they completed a rally, seemingly a very rare occurrence in the game as played at Clarence Street Youth Club.

Hair flying and arms flailing like hard-rock lead singers during the guitar solo, they were engaged in a sizzling exchange which saw both of them fielding wildly arcing trajectories from yards beyond the table. Then one of them noticed us and caught the ball in mid-flight.

They came together a bit sheepishly, like children caught in the middle of something venial.

'Janosc and Stanislav Pederewski – Jan and Stan – this is Tim Armstrong,' Billy announced. 'Tim wants to join the cricket team,' he told them.

They were dressed identically and rather shabbily in crumpled flannels and grey school shirts, open at the neck and rolled untidily up the arms. As they stood, their blond hair settled into Old English sheepdog fringes which concealed half the face.

'He hasn't played much, but then we're desperate,' Charlie Vart offered helpfully.

They looked at each other, shuffled, nodded and smiled brief encouragement at me. The deference was almost oriental. I half expected them to smother the smiles with a hand, the way Japanese women do.

'Stan and Jan,' Billy said, to them as much as to me,

'captain the team alternately because we couldn't choose between them. They open the batting and open the bowling. They also do most of the fielding. It would be churlish to call them the backbone of the team. Even skeleton, flesh and blood would be selling them a bit short. In fact, continuing the analogy to its extreme, you could probably say that the rest of us equate to a light walking-stick.'

I wasn't sure whether I expected this eulogy to cause them to wink in agreement, howl in modest protest or collapse in fits of laughter. What it did do was produce further shuffles, surreptitious sideways glances and intense contemplations of the toecap.

'Most of us expect them to become the first blond, Polish émigré identical twins to open for England,' Charlie added.

One smiled, the other frowned. Then they both produced that sweeping flick of the hair and hesitantly shook hands. Jan said what sounded like 'Porridge.' I took it to mean something welcoming.

'So you'll be seeing Tim at practice,' Billy said, by way of taking leave.

They repeated their curt nod, hands clasped respectfully in front of them, before resuming their positions at either end of the table. Polite interlude over, back to what mattered. Stan restarted with a complicated pendulum motion of his bat, despatching the ball on a humming hyperbola which almost took the ball round, rather than over the net.

We turned and left them to it.

'Would that be the first blond, Polish émigré, non-English speaking identical twins to open for England?' I asked in a low voice.

'What women call the strong silent type,' Billy responded.

'What night is practice?' I asked, on a slightly different tack.

'Oh, any night. Every night. When you like. Thursday,'

Billy pronounced, hesitantly then with finality, like a gunner bracketing his target before homing in.

I tried not to look harried. 'Loose arrangement then?'

'Carson's Field. Know it?' Charlie asked, ignoring me.

'Yes.'

'Good,' they said together.

We had returned to the door of the main hall. The waves of sound and flashing lights hit us like stun grenades.

'Well, Tim,' Charlie nodded towards the dance floor, 'game for another attempt? Or shall I get Fatowl to stand us a coke?'

'Thanks, I could do with a drink,' I said, thinking: what is it about me? My intention had been to leave with a delectably rampant bit of totty on my arm, and I end up taking away an invitation to play cricket.

Tut. Sigh.

31

Carson's Field was a stretch of open council land near the edge of town, which throughout the year served a whole range of sporting and social uses – kickaround soccer, rounders, kit-flying, dog-walking, and that sort of thing – all of which were forbidden by municipal authority as represented by various warning notices placed around the perimeter. Also, it was a place where you had to be a bit careful when you chose to be athletic. It had been the scene of very mixed feelings in my early childhood, when I had dived into a pile of dog dirt and found one and ninepence.

Cricket, for some obscure reason known only to the inhabitants of Southpool town hall, was allowed. In one corner, between a leaden grey concrete machine-gun post of the sort which only finally disappeared from the English landscape forty years after the end of World War Two, and a wedge-shaped brick edifice of indeterminate function which hummed like a hive and had large access doors with a sign proclaiming it to be the property of the North Western Electricity Board, was a pavilion of sorts. It was in fact a small rotting green hut from which the windows had long since been knocked out. The roof leaked, and inside it was damp and smelly and mildewed. Decrepit benches and hooks on the flaking cream walls revealed that it had once been used as a changing-room, but its present condition rendered that unthinkable. Like the machine-gun post a relic of a bygone age, it served only to provide dismissed batsmen with somewhere to walk towards.

In order to eliminate the vagaries of pace and spin essential to the game, and the need for a groundsman, the council had constructed a wicket which consisted of a twenty-four-by-two-yard slab of concrete. As I arrived the Thursday following my youth-club début, this was evidently firmly in the control of the Pederewski twins. Jan was bent at the crease, resolute and intent, prepared to face a delivery from Billy Bibby. Stan leant nonchalantly on his bat at the other end.

My experience of cricket was limited to a domesticated version of the game designed for the limited confines of our own back garden. Using a roughly carpentered bit of next door's fence as a bat, the drainpipe as a wicket and an old tennis ball, Jim and I played out innings in which even the meekest of hits got you a run, a push to the garden fence a couple of yards away two, a knock past the bowler four, and anything into next door's was six and out. The standardized scoring system was a practical solution to the problem posed by a large rockery which traversed the wicket about halfway down and made running between the creases hazardous in the extreme.

The lack of any element of caution in Jim's make-up meant that he inevitably went for gold. His scores were wildly various, but always directly divisible by four or six. My style didn't quite encompass his *élan* or, depending upon how you viewed it, show the same reckless instinct to gamble. A defensive push was sufficient to bring the ball securely as far as the garden fence and chalk up a steady two. A block got one. In the classic tradition of the unsure, unaccomplished or just plain incompetent, I often found that I was mouthing elementary instructions to myself as Jim began his run-up.

'Weight on the front foot
Angle the bat
Smother the bounce
Two to the garden fence.'

I knew no strategy except stonewalling, and no stroke except the forward defensive. On a full-sized pitch, I could probably stay there all day, but wouldn't be able to score a run to save my life.

The only spectator was a girl of sixteen or so. She was a dozen yards away from me, lying on her side, head erect, in the long grass which skirted the boundary. She was couched in a little den of flattened grass, as regal and serene as a lioness, and appeared to have concentrated the outfield in a formation which couldn't possibly have any basis in strategy. A group of four or five fielders lingered vaguely in her vicinity, and seemed far more intent on swapping smutty innuendo with her than following any event around the wicket. As I listened, I heard her enquire of one of them after the power of his drive and the length of his googly, and follow it up with a hoarse barmaid's cackle which tommy-gunned across the field, causing another couple of curious fielders to edge towards her.

Even to my unpractised eye, the proceedings lacked the air of communal commitment which characterizes most sports training sessions. The batsmen and bowler seemed to be going about their tasks diligently enough, as evidenced by the sound of regular solid whacks and scuttling interchanges of position by the Pederewski twins, punctuated by the occasional groan from Billy Bibby. But, even allowing for the fact that the young lady in the long grass had lured half the team into covering the same ten feet of boundary, the arrangement of the rest of them seemed to leave the field dangerously exposed. Inner fielders may have started out with the best of intentions, but with the passage of time appeared to have drifted together for company and casual conversation. The slip fielders were reluctant to stray far from the transistor radio parked on the ground between second and third, hammering out Radio Caroline at full volume. Without relinquishing his position, the back stump had discarded one glove to enjoy a bag of chips which had just been delivered to him by a youngster on a bicycle – an event which hadn't even caused a pause in the bowling. There was a general air of laxity fringing on insubordination. Youth clubs existed to keep youth off the streets, so here we were. In a field.

Eventually, Billy 'took his sweater' as they say, and tossed the ball to someone called Dobbin. He walked towards me, sweating and red-faced, the former a bit more freely than you usually associate with cricket, the latter not exclusively from exertion, I suspected. I'd heard he rated himself somewhat as a bowler.

'None for ninety off five overs,' he told me, 'not bad I suppose, considering.'

I decided that didn't need a comment.

He panted and sniffed for a while, recovering himself.

'You made it then?' he asked at length.

I decided that didn't need a comment either.

He seemed to notice the little congregation around the young female spectator for the first time.

'Oh Christ, look at Sharon,' he said to me. 'She draws them like moths to the candle. The bloody siren of extra cover.' He raised his voice. 'Oy! You lot!' Then, clapping his hands, 'Come on now! Is it any wonder they've made a partnership of two hundred and eleven in less than an hour?'

They looked towards him exactly the way a trespassing Alsatian does when you clap your hands at it. What's it got to do with you. Sod off. Wuf.

'Come on lads,' his voice took on a blend of encouragement and appeasement. 'We're a team, not a duo. Let's not have them offering to give us three bat handles again.'

It was management by consensus rather than authority. But it worked. Slowly, reluctantly, they began to fan out.

'C'mon,' he said to me, 'you can take this stretch of the boundary.' Then, intriguingly, 'She doesn't know you.'

He trudged off after the dispersing group, herding them towards a more effective distribution. I nodded briefly at the girl, then turned my back on her – registering casually that she had large bright blue eyes, shoulder-length hair as black and shiny as a raven's wing, lips that rose like a pink ripple in a sea of milk, a beauty spot on her neck just below her right ear, wore a dark pink cheesecloth blouse that hugged her promisingly ample bosom and in so doing defined new parameters for Young's Modulus of Elasticity, a blue miniskirt which made her seem sexy and accessible yet cherishably feminine, black shoes with a square heel and gold buckle over schoolgirly white ankle socks, and that her general pose and demeanour reminded me of a mermaid – then I took up a position a few yards inside the boundary: a semi-crouch, hands outstretched as if I were warming them at a camp-fire; muscles taut, eyes ranged like precision radar on the batsman forty yards away; a trained athlete, a warrior on the eve of battle, a primed weapon, a coiled snake ready to strike.

I remained perfectly stationary without incident for twenty-five minutes.

There was a cough behind me.

'You're new aren't you?' she said.

'Yes,' I said over my left shoulder, without taking my eyes off Jan Pederewski.

'You don't *have* to stand like that y'know. Not out 'ere.'

Her accent was heavily central Lancashire.

I relaxed a bit, concerned only that she might think I was one of the sort that have to try harder than everybody else.

Just at that moment, Jan hopped down the wicket to meet a shortish ball, dropped to one knee, and with a grand sweeping motion of his bat hooked it high over backward square leg. It soared thirty yards before punching a hole through the feeble roof of the decaying pavilion with a sound something like 'crump'.

'Bee-ay-yoo-tiful,' Sharon screamed delightedly, breaking into spontaneous applause. 'See that! Oh, baby-baby! He could have waited and clipped it off his toes – square leg drive fer four – but it were that bad it deserved a six. What a sweep! Down on one knee like a bloody knight. Luvly. Brian Close did same thing to Wes Hall in t'second test. To WESLEY HALL mind you!'

She threw a lot of emphasis onto the name as though it should mean something to me.

I turned. She winked one of those huge blue eyes. It suddenly occurred to me that she was everything I'd taken up cricket for.

'Are you ah keen on cricket then?' I asked.

'Bloody fanatic, baby-baby. Eh – has anyone ever told you you look like Ivor Churchward?'

'Ivor . . . ?'

'Churchward. Dead ringer.'

'Who's . . . ?'

She tutted and rolled her eyes. Her hair fell forward rather fetchingly.

'Captained Lancashire, 1921 to 1928.'

A loud chorus of warning voices erupted like a cheer from the direction of play behind me. Just as I turned, the ball sped past, a foot or so to my left, and tripped merrily over the boundary.

Sharon smiled, immediately smothered the smile with her hand, then dropped her jaw in mock tragedy. It was only another four, after all.

I retrieved the ball, the first red 'corkie' I had ever held. Feeling all eyes upon me, I thought I had better attempt to make something out of what was, after all, my premier action in Clarence Street cricket. I studied the ball leisurely and knowledgeably and gave it a vigorous rub against my groin as I'd seen the professionals do on TV. Then I returned it to the stumps with a creditable throw which fell a few yards short but certainly had the correct line.

Looking down, I was mortified to note that my best ice-blue jeans now carried a stain which suggested that previous evidence of my right testicle having been blown off had failed to come out in the wash.

'Not a bad throw,' she said. 'By the way, I'm Sharon.'

I made a small ceremony of turning my back on her, placing my hands on my knees.

'Hello Sharon. I'm Tim.'

Ten long minutes passed. No action. No sound from behind me except sparing applause as Stan and Jan clocked up the three hundred.

Was I here to play cricket or what?

'What brings you to watch Clarence Street at practice, Sharon?' I said over my shoulder.

'Oh, I come to all t' matches as well,' she answered.

She had to be what Billy Bibby had called our 'active female support'.

'Why?' I asked, genuinely intrigued, but my eyes remaining determinedly fixed on Jan.

'I luv cricket,' she said brightly, 'you're t' nearest team,' in a tone which suggested it was something of a penance. 'I'm staying in that house over there.'

Of course I had to turn round to see where she was pointing.

Sharon Battersby, as her name turned out to be, was from Padiham near Burnley. As part of a standing family arrangement, she spent her six-week summer holiday with an auntie near the seaside. In every other conceivable way, Sharon was an evidently – nay laudably – normal, blossoming young woman. Her only eccentricity – and so I have to consider it in a woman, she being the only female I have met before or since who even saw the point, let alone understood the rules – was her boundless passion for the game of cricket.

The reason was not difficult to piece together as we talked. She was the only daughter of Sid Battersby – perhaps I had heard of him, well no actually – who had played for Padiham CC, Burnley CC, Manchester CC, finally Lancashire and oh so very nearly, England. And of course Sid, who had no doubt yearned for a son to lob leg breaks at in the back garden, and oil the bats, had failed to notice that God had blessed him with a daughter instead.

It's a forgivable trait of parenthood that we hand on a lot of what we know a lot about. Even the most imaginative minds move within the limits of experience. When H.G. Wells sought to describe a time machine, what he did describe was a very elaborate bicycle. H.G. knew about bicycles. Sid knew about cricket.

'A good fielder combines the pick-up and retrieval and returns to the back stump at chest height,' Sharon told me critically as I completed my second piece of the action. I had thought I was just giving them their ball back.

Consequently Sharon, though visibly no tomboy, at sixteen had no better measure of a man than how he handled the fast ball. She let slip she had a photo of Colin Cowdrey in her bedroom. That was like the *Catholic Herald* doing a centrefold Play-nun of the Month. Arriving in Southpool, she had quickly sought the nearest source of virile young men in whites. Finding Stan and Jan Pederewski, she thought, 'OK. Forget the whites.'

'WOOHOO! Baby-baby!'

A frustrated bowler had bounced a loose one at Jan's head. With an intricately spiralling flourish I'd seen previously performed only by a drum majorette, Jan clicked him over the machine-gun post.

'The lad's a god!' Sharon squealed.

She was on her feet, cheering, clapping, and jumping in excitement.

The light was fading. There seemed to be a general feeling that Jan's six was an appropriate moment to call it a day.

This was it. Perhaps already, the culmination and termination of my cricketing career. Thrusting my hands into my pockets, I said, 'What are you doing afterwards, Sharon?'

'Fish and chips wi' Jan Pederewski,' she said in the way a girl might say, 'Being picked up in a helicopter by Steve McQueen.'

She skipped over toward the approaching crowd and fell happily in beside him. He nodded and smiled. What else? Arm in arm they sauntered off in the direction of the Jolly Bloater, via the pavilion.

I began to muse on possible uses a teenage couple might have for a disused, isolated pavilion at dusk.

'Not bad for a first time out,' Billy was saying to me as he walked up. 'Two misfields and an overthrow. You'll be pleased to know you've made the grade. Talent, skill and experience do not necessarily guarantee your place in the team at Clarence Street.'

I was still staring after Sharon and Jan. Billy mumbled to himself, 'Turning up guarantees your place in the team at Clarence Street.'

He followed my gaze.

'Yes. I noticed you seemed to be getting on famously with our little cricketing lexicon. A honey isn't she? Taken. For this evening anyway.'

I didn't miss the significance of the last bit.

'What does she see in him? What do they talk about? How can he possibly keep her interested?'

Charlie Vart had come over from the other side of the boundary, where he'd been posted all evening, just in time to hear that. I caught the look he threw Billy and coloured a bit. The last thing you want to be considered at seventeen is naïve.

'Sort of personalized Man of the Match award,' was what he said, with a matter-of-factness which lit up my imagination like a torchlight vigil at a gasworks.

So there it was. The way to this seductive creature's heart, and God knew what other more immediately accessible bits of her, was to be found on the cricket field.

With the consecrated dedication of sexually-possessed youth, I determined that, should it require me to become as debonair as Ted Dexter, as fiery as Fred Truman, or indeed as hairy as W. G. Grace, I would achieve that goal.

32

Obviously, there was much to be done.

I dragged Jim into the back garden at every opportunity, doggedly defending the drainpipe against his relentless, medium-paced attack.

Weight on the front foot
Angle the bat
Smother the bounce
Two to the garden fence.

But it was useless. As a batsman, I was supernumerary, the Pederewskis saw to that. Uncharted reaches of hyper-space separated them from every other player in the league. A Clarence Street innings usually involved the rest of us settling back to watch as they whacked and scuttled through the gathering dusk, mute but intent, blond hair whirling like the rollers in a car-wash, until victory or bad light stopped play.

Having developed a yorker which fairly consistently defeated Jim's golf-drive of a batting style, I determined to try my hand in the team. I insisted on being given an over one practice night. Everything I threw down, Stanislas Pederewski cracked to the four points of the compass. I was forced to bowl a wide deliberately to avoid setting a negative one-over record. Out on the long grass beyond the boundary, Sharon's enormous lemon blancmange of a hat turned slowly and sadly left and right.

That left fielding. If I were to impress her, it would have to be via my prowess in the field. But VCs are not awarded in the Pay Corps. That meant moving closer to the front lines.

Most of the key fielding positions were reserved for established team members.

But there is a position in cricket which is in the direct line of fire of the natural batting movement – right to left across the body. At a safe distance from the wicket, because it is in the middle of the batsman's 'on' side it is called mid-on. Nearer to the wicket, because cricket balls are very hard, it is called silly mid-on. I had noticed it was not particularly popular.

This, then, would become my specialization.

I dispensed with Jim's reluctant participation and developed a solitary form of training which suited my specific needs. It involved throwing a ball at a walled corner of the garden and catching the return. I started at a dozen yards distance, pitching gently; moved in to eight yards, putting a bit more pace into it; then, at three yards, lunging as hard as I could. From the left. From the right. With the process of time, movement became trance-like, anticipation inspired. From the left, from the right. The concentration brought a film of sweat to my forehead. At head height. At knee height. To the face. To the chest.

After an hour I was taking nine from ten clearly. After a few nights, nineteen from twenty. After a week, ninety-nine from a hundred.

I began sharpening my reactions by instinct. I would grab at insects in mid-air. I would tap Tibby's nose annoyingly and repeatedly, attempting to flick away my wrist before he could bring up his paw. I missed the flies, and the ageing tabby left the back of my hand looking as though it had been autographed in red Biro by the entire Southpool United first-team squad, but it was good practice.

I trained each night with a vision of Sharon on a trampoline before my eyes. From the left. From the right.

After two weeks I was taking anything the garden wall could throw at me. My hands were weapons. I carried them in front of me, splayed and poised, like a karate fighter. My father complained that I looked like some sort of priest. I liked that. It suggested worldly denial, pristine dedication to my art and skills. Jim asked why I was walking around as though I was carrying a brimful piss-pot.

I was ready.

33

It was a perfect evening for cricket, warm but windless and with the sun veiled and sinking into high thin cloud. It would rain later, but not yet.

We were gathered in front of the pavilion, stripping off jackets and pullovers before taking the field for practice.

'Think I'll move a bit closer to the action if it's all the same to you,' I said nonchalantly to Billy Bibby, making sure Sharon was within earshot. He wasn't really captain but acted as a sort of intermediary. 'OK if I take mid-on?'

'Fine by me. Stan? Jan?'

They flicked hair out of their eyes as if coming out of hiding and nodded.

'Peein' wi' t' big dogs,' was Sharon's comment.

Good. I had her attention. I gave her what I hoped was a meaningful glance.

Inevitably, the batsman was Jan. He cast a concerned look in my direction as I took up station towards the sillier side of mid-on. I bent my knees, raised my hands towards him like a messiah, then hooded my eyes in concentration. He made a couple of dry strokes on a line which extrapolated straight through my scrotum, but said nothing.

The first couple of overs passed without event. A timid block in my direction, which I suspected Jan had pulled. Was he concerned for my safety?

That would ruin everything. I was on a quest for the sensational. I knew it would be hazardous. It had to be, that was the point.

I moved closer. After another couple of balls, closer still. Now only a few bat lengths separated me from Jan. I could see his expression clearly. Puzzlement? Amusement? Concern for me? Concern for him? All of these?

No matter. I was trained. My hands were hungry. I was fired by a zeal which was nearly religious. Purposefully, I inched forward to a fielding position which could only be described as mindlessly reckless mid-on.

Suddenly, I began to hear voices. I know that, under conditions of extreme and prolonged concentration, such cases have been recorded, but, if the Supreme Being ever takes it into his head to go to the trouble of addressing himself to you personally, you'd expect him to have something a bit more profound to say than:

'Watcher Tim. You getting any?'

I tore my eyes from the end of Jan's bat and turned to see Benny Birtwhistle at my shoulder.

Frankly, Bertie, as we called him, wasn't a person whose company I actively sought. A couple of years older than me, he was one of those types, there were approximately two million of them in England at the time, who looked, dressed, and talked exactly like Roger Daltrey. Very natty he was too, with his lightly-curled blond hair combed forward and neatly sculptured around the front of his ears to create the impression of sideburns. He sported a white, roll-neck nylon sweater, narrow-lapel, buttoned-up jacket in beige under a fur-trimmed, khaki parka and wide-angle chocolate loons. This was a type of trouser which clung to your thighs and buttocks like panto tights, then flared like sawn-off egg-timers at the kneecap.

As if that wasn't enough to envy, Bertie was straddling his forty-horsepower, two-stroke Vespa scooter, festooned with aerials, glittering with chrome trim, adorned with the badges of all the trendier first-division football clubs, and complete with every possible manifestation of contemporary male sensuality, including a woolly seat cover. Girls adored him. What self-respecting healthy adolescent male could avoid hating him?

I'm pleased to say that with virtually no exceptions the Daltrey look-alikes went on to become gas-fitters and marry girls called Doris. But that was all in the future, and did nothing to allay the burning inferiority complex which seized possession of me whenever Benny Birtwhistle was around.

'Oh, hi Bertie,' I said unenthusiastically, immediately returning my gaze to the wicket. 'How's it hanging?' Bertie was one of those adolescents whose conversation is not merely spiced with, but burnt tasteless by, male chauvinist slang, macho puns, and pseudo-sexual play-boy innuendo. Being too immature to despise him for it, I tried to emulate it.

He had ridden his machine on a wide arc which had already taken in chatty visits to cover point and third man, something which would have been tolerated with mild irritation during a league fixture but didn't even raise an eyebrow during practice. He now proceeded to lock his hands under the handlebars, rest his chin on top of his speedo – he didn't have a windshield, being one of those who favoured fixing his Chelsea FC pennants to the aerials – and proceeded to discourse on love.

'Fine Tim, just fine. Know Jennifer Clough?' he asked, leadingly.

'Oh, yeah. Her dad owns the grocers on Rosedale Avenue.'

Not being the most sensitive of creatures, Bertie failed to notice the bugger-off-I'm-busy edge to my voice.

'That's the one. What a lass!' he said, with a rakish growl.

'Oh yeah?' I kept my eyes glued to Jan Pederewski's bat.

'You bet. Brmm brrm!' His right hand twisted the accelerator of his scooter as he said this.

'Goes a bit does she!' I said, trying not to sound encouraging.

He gave a low whistle.

'Tigress! Took her for a trip on the old Starship One the other night. Been begging me for ages. You know, just around the estate. With an innocent diversion in the direction of Common Edge fields. Know what I mean? Eh? Know what I mean Tim?'

'Know exactly what you mean Bertie.'

I smirked sideways, quickly.

From previous discussion, Bertie had gleaned that when it came to the opposite sex I was, so to speak, drifting alone on a wide, wide sea. He thus tended to lay this sort of thing on pretty thick. In fact, I seldom got away before the third or fourth coating.

My pose of rapt concentration on Jan's big toe did nothing to check his tirade.

'. . . can always tell when they're expecting a good seeing-to. Get their frock up and find their silkiest, laciest pair of knickers. Come prepared to impress, see. So I goes down to the honey-pot and what does I find. What does I find?'

'What does – what did you find Bertie?'

I never did find out what Bertie found.

Taking advantage of a loose delivery, Jan hopped a yard or so down the wicket and connected at full swing on the half volley, the ball going off with a crack like summer lightning splitting a dried-up oak. Instinctively, I raised my left hand six inches. I heard an acoustic compendium of a smartly spanked bottom, a fly swat hitting masonry, a whiplash, and a perfectly struck golf drive. Looking down, I saw the ball nestling neatly in the palm of my hand.

There was a shocked ripple of applause. Unusual in itself, because, on practice nights, applauding a feat as outstanding as a double century was a bit like celebrating VE day after a war in which the Germans hadn't bothered to turn up. But even Jan broke radio silence to offer a cursory 'Good caught'.

Somewhat preoccupied with the initial sharp stinging in my palm, it was a few seconds before I noticed Bertie.

Bleached white and pop-eyed, he was twitching like a lunatic and emitting curious inarticulate little grunts, whilst slowly elongating stalactites of spittle drooled from the corners of his mouth. My rapidly warming hand was positioned exactly at the end of his nose. To him, Jan's shot must have been like having his head thrust down the barrel of a howitzer, hearing the explosion, seeing the shell speed straight towards his face, then having the hand of Almighty God intercede at the very moment of impact.

Almost weeping, shivering in the extremities of trauma, he was pathetically attempting to kiss the back of my hand. I transferred the ball to my right and inspected my left, momentarily leaving a bleary-eyed Bertie blowing wet kisses at thin air.

The others gathered slowly round.

'Ehm, I think you're out Jan,' one said.

'Bit of a smack. You OK Tim?' from another.

Bertie, between wheezing gasps and shudders which racked his whole body, was muttering fragmentary, almost incoherent expressions of gratitude.

I was disconcerted to note that, even in the short interlude since impact, my hand had begun to glow crimson and take on proportions about double its normal size.

'Dunno,' I said, peering and pressing at my puffy palm. 'Doesn't hurt anyway.'

I peeped briefly between the milling figures and saw Sharon on the horizon. She was all attention, straining on tiptoe to get a glimpse of events. That was all right then. I wondered how much she'd seen.

Bertie's white-knuckled fists were prized away from his handle bars where they had seemingly frozen in terror, and he was helped from his scooter. Immediately, the more delinquent element of the team fell on it like bandits after an ambush and wheeled it away, chuckling darkly. He appeared not to notice.

'Life. Save life. Nearly die. Cannon-ball.'

There was something almost chilling about the

instantaneous transformation of the debonair mod-about-town to this gibbering wreck, wildly scanning the faces around him for signs of reassurance.

'Do you think you need a doctor? Do you think Bertie does?' Billy Bibby asked.

My hand had continued to expand in size and deepen in colour. I stiffened my shoulders.

'Nah,' I said dismissively.

Bertie began to look less like a post-operative frontal lobotomy and more like Roger Daltrey. Though, perhaps, Roger Daltrey after an accident with a badly-wired amplifier. Even so, he seemed oblivious as the louts from the tail-end of the batting roared up and down the street on his beloved Vespa, throwing it into screeching foot-sliding turns at either end. The rest of us huddled in a little group examining my almost visibly ballooning mitt. It began to rain very softly.

'Might as well kick it in the 'ed,' someone suggested.

'Chippie?'

There was a general murmur of assent.

We began to move *en masse* to the perimeter. Bertie seized my arm and began urgently trying to speak. But only random groups of letters were making it through, like a transmission in code.

'Nin. Dert. Ngnn. Yew.'

By the time we reached the boundary, he managed to stab me three times in the chest with an urgent finger and say, 'Your chips. On me.'

'Oh, ta Bertie,' I said distractedly, but my eyes were searching for Sharon. My pulse picked up as she came over and fell in beside me.

'Good catch, lad. Great reflex. You must be a natural close fielder.'

I blew modestly.

She slipped her arm through mine with a familiarity which was more than gratifying. Immediately, I began to try and shake Bertie off and steer Sharon towards the pavilion. But Bertie clutched at me like a devoted servant and Sharon gently but firmly steered us on a course veering right. I persisted. She yanked hard over, emitting an irritated clucking sound, and set us on a deliberate and unmistakable bearing for the Jolly Bloater.

'Does your hand hurt?' she asked, nodding downwards.

It was now a very nasty shade of purple, numb but aching dully, deep inside, suggesting multiple fractures and internal bleeding.

'Not a bit of it.'

I wrinkled my nose derisively.

She giggled. 'Looks like you're wearing one boxing glove.'

It wasn't so painless you could make bloody jokes about it, I thought. Still, may as well capitalize. I jerked my head towards Bertie who was still gazing at me in supplication on my left.

'Sharon, this is Bertie,' I began. 'I saved his—'

'Well, hi!' she said, real interest warming her voice, and looking across me as though I was something inanimate. Deftly, she nipped around to my left and slipped in between us.

'I'm Sharon,' she went on. 'Has anyone ever told you you look like Roger Daltrey?'

Bertie's recovery was astonishing. His cheeks took on colour as though someone had opened a valve in his neck. He removed his grip from my arm and began fussing at his hair and clothes. There couldn't have been a more rapid reversal of symptoms since Lazarus.

'Who?' he said, winking and giving her elbow a pinch.

'That's right!'

They laughed together, Sharon taking advantage of the moment to slip her arm through Bertie's, then, as an afterthought, through mine.

'Sharon, I saved Bertie's—'

'I think girls look great in cheesecloth blouses Sharon,' Bertie cut in.

'Well, it's nice to meet a lad as has some dress sense. I

like your loons. Go lovely wi' that jacket.'

'Sharon,' I tried once more. 'Sharon, you'll never guess what. I. Sharon . . .'

Bertie asked Sharon what music she liked. Sharon said 'Tamla – you know, baby-baby!' throwing a tremorous hand over each shoulder and rolling her eyes in a brief dance portrayal of the Supremes, but admitted The Who weren't bad. Sharon asked Bertie if he watched *Ready Steady Go* on Fridays. Bertie said 'Not half' and asked Sharon if she liked Kathy McGowan's gear, to which Sharon replied 'Brill'. Sharon asked Bertie if he played cricket. Bertie, who didn't, deflected it perfectly with a 'Not with this lot' and a deprecating snort at the accompanying bunch of no-hopers. Sharon had to laugh too and took advantage of the moment to remove her hand from my arm and place it along with the other one which had moved up to massage Bertie's armpit. Bertie asked Sharon if she'd seen *Dr Zhivago*. Sharon said no but she'd really like to.

All the time my hand was growing inexorably, like some sort of horrible mutation in a science-fiction film. It was now the size of a dinner plate. What was more, moving it hurt like hell, with the result that I was forced to grasp the wrist firmly with my other hand. The result gave me a sort of shuffling gait.

Out of the corner of my eye, I noticed Charles Vart was staring at me steadily. He smiled, not exactly sympathetically, and said something to Billy Bibby. They laughed together.

'Igor!' he suddenly barked in a vaguely Transylvanian accent. 'I heff tolded you, you shudd remain in ze crypt.' He pretended to be lashing out. 'Keep away from ze gerls. Back, Igor, back!'

The rest of them noticed for the first time I was loping like a primate. There was a general murmur of amusement. Then Billy began skipping ahead crablike, contorting his face in a parody of Charles Laughton and calling back, 'The bells! The hand!' in a sort of lunatic cross-take between Captain Hook and the Hunchback of Notre Dame.

Amid general laughter, Sharon and Bertie dropped back a pace or two to give me the limelight and let the others enjoy the spectacle unhindered. Sharon's piercing honk was the loudest of all. It was like a run of farting notes on a saxophone. I sought to join in the general merriment – what else can you do if a dozen people suddenly decide you're a joke except try to share it? – but found it difficult to conceal a fundamental prickliness.

'Igor, that's a gud 'un,' Bertie chortled, slipping an arm around Sharon's shoulder without any noticeable objection on her part. 'Get a load of the grave-robber's apprentice.'

Sharon gave vent to another hoarse salvo.

There was now quite severe pain in my hand and it was fast approaching the dimensions of a dustbin lid. At the sight of Sharon's remote, unattainable curvy loveliness receding, a destructive spirit began to take possession of me.

'Tell me Sharon,' I began in a tone of reasonable enquiry, 'any history of mating with seals in the family? Donkeys?' Then, through gritted teeth, 'Pneumatic drills?'

'Oooh!' she cooed, 'get him.'

There was a group mooing session of the sort that in England is used to indicate that someone can't take a joke, usually meaning they don't see the amusing side of mortal insult.

I released my hand with an agonized grimace which I made as public as possible.

By the time we reached the Jolly Bloater I was sullen and petulant. Injustice and inconsideration seethed and frothed inside me. My feelings had been only slightly relieved by the good hard surreptitious kick I had managed to land unseen on Bertie's scooter.

Since the local youth club was open one night each week and fulfilled the purpose of a discothèque, the forecourt of the local chip shop fulfilled the function of a youth club. Each weekday evening, half the under-eighteens in the neighbourhood met here to pursue twentieth-century youth's four favourite pastimes: eat something stodgy, drink something gassy, listen to loud music and talk about themselves; the night had a thousand eyes and they were all the first person singular. The noise was provided by transistor radios. Also, there was much parading of status symbols in the form of bicycles, scooters, and, though not many, motor bikes.

Silhouetted against the glaring light of the shop front, we lolled untidily across a low wall feeding hungrily to the sound of the Beach Boys. The team knew every word of every song, and sang and clapped along, hitting the choruses like yodelling castrati.

I was sitting slightly apart, attempting to take chips directly from the paper with my teeth, because by now my hand was so tender I couldn't even rest my food on it. I held it vertically beside my head, which seemed to provide some relief.

Removing my face from a savaged and mauled but defiantly uncapitulating cheese-and-onion pie, I caught Sharon and Bertie grinning at me from a few yards away. They were muttering secretively to each other, and then breaking into fits of giggling in that extremely annoying way that young couples have.

'Hands up anyone who wants an arm wrestle,' Sharon spluttered, choking on her own snorting laugher.

'No, I know, Statue of Liberty wearing a nosebag,' I heard Bertie chortle, not quite low enough.

Sharon's peal of laughter didn't so much split the night as rip it along a perforated edge.

Enough was enough. I slipped from the wall, put down the remains of my supper and kicked off my shoes. Bertie's face slowly lost its idiot grin and took on the shadows of concern, as he realized I was fixing him with a glare of pure hatred. I took one step towards him, then launched myself through the air, gliding like a javelin. The panic and terror in his eyes as he realized I was a master of martial arts was almost enough to inspire pity, but no, it was too late, he had had his chance. My foot took him squarely between the eyes and he somersaulted backwards with a hollow scream, colliding with his scooter and tumbling into the road in an avalanche of aerials, chrome trim, pennants, and woolly seat covers. I landed as gently as a snowflake and bowed reverently to Sharon . . .

'You look as though you're miles away,' Billy Bibby said, banging me on the shoulder.

'How!' Charles Vart chipped in.

'Oh, it's my friends!' I said in mock surprise to an imaginary person at my shoulder.

'Ah, sod off. Have a drink.'

Charlie proffered a large bottle of Shandyade. Cream soda and Tizer were also in evidence. I noticed Bony Baxter gulp down three-quarters of a bottle of Dandelion and Burdock at one pull. Someone turned up the music.

The effects of stodgy food and gassy liquids, both imbibed copiously and rapidly, on the gastric processes and digestive mechanisms of adolescent males, are well documented and therefore consistent and predictable. So is, from generation to generation, the unfailing comic hysteria induced by the sound resulting from the forceful ejection of abdominal gases through an artificially constricted larynx. In fact, this lot used deliberately to integrate it to the music. There are certain songs from that period which I can't hear even today without expecting the chorus to climax in a resounding belch.

The tranny was playing a lilting ballad. Bertie seemed inclined to seize the moment. He manoeuvred Sharon until they were nose-tip to nose-tip, clasped hands and brushed lips intimately. He began to mouth the words of the song, miming to Sharon with real meaning in his eyes that God only knew where he'd be without, God only knew what he'd do without, God only knew what he'd be without . . .

'Burp! Burrup-urp!'

A barrage of farmyard noises rasped and honked their way into the evening air.

Sharon threw across a 'queen of the frozen north' look. She shouldn't have. It could serve only to encourage. The vulgar counterpoint to the lovers at sunset was too poignant. Half the team began guzzling carbonated fluids as though they were the elixir of life.

She seemed to think I was the instigator. I was treated to the special narrowing of the eyes and hardening of the cheekbones that a woman reserves for 'a man who has behaved badly'. I couldn't call across, 'Sharon. It were not me, I swure. I have not belched wunce, honest.' It would have been ridiculous. And demeaning. I lowered my gaze, like a Galahad who has mocked his vows.

Seconds later she was disappearing down Newhouse Road on the back of Bertie's scooter.

The Pederewskis, Billy, Charles, and I, gathered in a cluster at the kerbside and gazed after them. We must have looked rather like the dying seconds of a Lone Ranger episode.

'I saved the ungrateful sod's life,' I said bitterly.

'Never scored a bleeding run,' Billy added.

'Nor took a wicket,' from Charlie.

The twins, of course, were grimly silent.

34

But if you'd think that crushing humiliation, scything criticism and overt betrayal would dampen my ardour, then you've never been seventeen and sexually infatuated. I had briefly nibbled at the pleasures of the flesh, and was determined to gorge. Increasingly, my waking hours, and a goodly percentage of what should have been my sleeping ones, were dominated by dreams and fantasies featuring gravelly cackles, square-leg drives and seersucker blouses in severe danger of bursting apart with a rasping tear to disgorge the largest, fullest, ripest, pertest, bounciest jugs my young mind could get its imagination around.

But always I came up against my limited prowess in the field of human activity closest to her heart.

'All hands to the pumps, Saturday,' Billy Bibby said, turning to me between lessons the following Monday. We were sitting patiently at our desks awaiting the Latin teacher. Nuclear physics had just finished. Organic chemistry was to follow. What rounded educations we were getting.

'How do you mean?' I asked, my mind definitely elsewhere.

'Half the team are down with flu.'

My interest sparked for the first time.

'Oh yeah?' I said slowly. 'Who's out then?'

'Well, Jan Pederewski for a start. Charlie Vart. Bony Baxter.' He named two or three others. 'For certain, four of the best five players won't be available. And to make matters worse, number two Pederewski has hurt his arm and can't bowl.'

Well, well. I couldn't escape the notion that that gave the rest of us a chance to show what we could do. Perhaps justice wasn't quite blind. 'Stand a little less between me and the sun,' Diogenes had said to Alexander when the latter asked if there was anything he could do for him. Just as I might to Jan Pederewski. And, all of a sudden, sunstroke drops him. I was probably smiling.

'Glad to see I've cheered you up,' Billy went on. 'I take it you've forgotten who we're playing.'

I hadn't. It did slightly mar the unalloyed pleasure of anticipation. Telford Park. The local Borstal.

'Oh, we can handle that,' I said through pursed lips. After all, I was about to turn in the performance of my life. As far as Sharon was concerned, I could see my One Big Chance shaping up. If I failed, it would be through a total and complete lack of any talent or aptitude. As a sexually-charged adolescent, I wasn't about to let trifles like that put me off.

Of course, I don't want you to think I was being overly carnal about all this. Of course, I was yearning for a like mind. I wanted to discuss literature and art with her. I wanted to share her tastes in music. I wanted to hear her dreams and have her hear mine. I wanted to bare my innermost thoughts and convictions to the searing heat of her intellect and tell her I saw my soul reflected in her eyes. Anything to get inside her pants.

35

As the scratch Clarence Street team rallied nervously around Stan Pederewski on the patch of faded grass before their dilapidated pavilion, a dark blue Bedford van with bars on the windows drew slowly to a stop on the nearby road. It swayed and bounced slightly on its suspension for a moment, and from within came a smack and muffled yelp which could only signal the conclusion of some furtive but violent altercation. The back doors flew open, but for a time no-one disembarked. Clarence Street shuffled and fidgeted and edged leeward of Stan.

At length, the first two clambered down from the van and made cautiously towards us. I had rarely laid eyes on a pair of such evidently disaffected backsliders. One was squat and thickset with a flat forehead, eyebrows like outcrops of moss and acres of open shirt-front matted with curly black wire and threaded with silver chains and medallions. When he paused in front of Stan you half expected him to hunch forward onto his knuckles and grin toothily sideways.

The other, tall and nimble-looking, was more the sharp, ferrety type. His cold eyes were everywhere but upon us, as if casing the pavilion for signs of an ambush or checking possible routes of rapid egress. His complexion had the grey sheen of one compelled to the indoors, and he kept glancing at the sun as if he suspected it of something.

They halted before us and stared. None of us dared look away. It was the nightclub-bouncer type who spoke.

'Hello. We're teachers from Telford Park Approved School. We're accompanying a juvenile cricket team. Who's in charge here?'

I was aware of one or two quickly-drawn breaths around me. As usual, Billy Bibby stepped into the breach.

'How do you do,' he said. 'Welcome to Clarence Street.'

'Thanks. This is Mr Clarke. I'm Mr Shepherd. Where do you want them?'

Billy turned to Stan and shrugged.

'It's customary to toss a coin.'

'Oh, we'll dispense with all that,' the other said. 'Which do you want them to do, bat or bowl?'

Again, Billy turned to Stan, who crouched and rubbed his hand on the grass. It was brittle and straw-like after days of sunshine, but still carrying a film of dew. He rose and sniffed the air. Then he whispered something to Billy.

'We'll put you in if that's all right. Er, sir.'

Mr Shepherd nodded and turned purposefully back to the van. You couldn't escape the notion that they were pulling on heavy gloves and extricating irons and crowbars, like deckhands setting about a cargo. One of them shouted to a driver, who leapt from the front, thumped hard on the side of the van and then attended the rear doors.

'Two only!' shouted Mr Shepherd as if there was an attempt at a mass break-out. 'You're batting. The rest of you sit where you bloody well are till you're needed.'

Two figures descended from the back of the van, blinked briefly in the sunlight and proceeded to amble forward like beasts being pronged into the arena. Their clothing made no gesture whatsoever towards cricketing whites. One was dressed in a checked shirt, jeans and walking boots. He was burly with a mop of unkempt hair and a scar over his right eye, which appeared almost to close it. And the other one was little Mickie from the dingy cellar of Tollivers restaurant.

Already shaken by the proceedings, I turned in dismay and let out a low moan. It had been almost a year since Guy and I had spent our day as waiters at Tollivers. The last time I had seen Mickie, he was arse over tip with his head in a bath full of cold water, emitting bubbles of rage. Guy had predicted an institutionalized future for him, I remembered. He remained in my memory as one unlikely to let old scores go unsettled.

'What's up wi' you?' Sharon's voice said disparagingly. 'You look as if you've seen a maggoty dead dog.'

I winced. She could be so – unfeminine. There were times when I wondered why I was going to all this trouble.

'Oh, I—'

'Tim?' a voice called, bursting with mock joviality. 'Tim Armstrong! Tim Armstrong from Tolly's restaurant!'

I closed my eyes, breathed deeply, opened them again and turned.

I heard Sharon whisper incredulously, 'You *know* one of these lads.'

Little Mickie had changed only in the sense that they'd scraped his face clean of that sparse irregular bumfluff and chopped four inches off his hair. His grin still revealed cheesy green molars and was as welcoming as a cavern full of Camembert.

'Hello Mickie,' I said laconically.

The rest of them looked on in amazement.

'Well Tim,' he chuckled. 'Wouldn't auld Jack be pleased. It's a small world, is it not?'

I agreed that it was.

'I'm willin' to bet you never expected to meet your old pal Mickie again?'

I smiled weakly.

'We'll settle a few old scores today then, eh?'

He laughed uproariously. 'Eh Tim?'

'Mm.'

His laughter peaked and then seemed to snap.

You couldn't exactly say he 'noticed' Sharon, because she was not so much a blot on the landscape as a bush-fire. She stood out as a blaze of colour, like a Hockney in a chapel of repose. On her head squatted something which you would normally only see decorating the altar at harvest festival. Over the inevitable cheesecloth, her cape was a sort of sou'wester in lime green, and she wore a black pleated miniskirt which was designed so that when she bent over she was mooning for England. Luminescent lace-up boots finished just above her knees, and matched her cape.

'This your tart?' Mickie asked perkily.

'Pff,' Sharon said, and stamped off towards her vantage point, like a one-man Chinese New Year parade.

'Got a couple of bats for us?' one of their minders asked.

Two were found. Mickie and the other lad took them. With his, Mickie playfully aimed a stroke at my head, winked, and jauntily strolled to the crease. He locked his bat across the back of his neck with both wrists, the way the Romans used to make condemned prisoners carry the cross-beam of their own crucifix. He seemed to have slotted well into the criminal fraternity.

Tossing the ball in one hand, Billy Bibby looked around the silent team. It was a measure of our weakened strength that his eyes rested on me.

'Fancy a bowl?' he asked.

I felt sick with apprehension.

'Get him arf!' Sharon barked in agonized annoyance from the boundary.

I was about to make my final delivery to Mickie in an over which had cost us eighteen runs. Their batting technique was highly individual. Standing with bat raised to shoulder-height after the baseball fashion, feet planted apart like a boxer, they would glare at you, eyes narrowed, teeth bared, practically daring you to get them out. Verbal discouragement would be offered. Intimidating suggestions would be made, to which feasible, if painful alternatives might be explored. Growling, hawking and spitting in mid run-up was designed to impair the bowler's concentration and break rhythm. In my case, it all worked like a dream.

After Mickie had cracked two off my last delivery, I tossed the ball to Billy and strolled, head as erect as I could hold it, to silly mid-on. There, determined to throw off the mantle of failure, I raised my hands like the High Priest of Close Fielding that I had become, and held Mickie's partner's one good eye in a cool stare. He sniggered dirtily to himself and arced the bat in a practice sweep which extrapolated directly between my legs. I dropped my hands six inches, slightly unnerved. He nodded, as if in answer to a question, sniggered again and repeated the gesture.

I licked dry lips. It was impossible, surely. He couldn't be that good. I raised my hands again, trying not to betray any want of – well, ballsiness.

As Billy obligingly dollied him a full toss, his bat swept with geometric precision for a third time through that precise arc, and, with a sound like the fly swat of God the Father Almighty, despatched the ball on a scrotum-seeking course for yours truly. I screamed in naked terror and arched my spinal column into a curve which would have put a boa constrictor into physiotherapy.

Two further attempts, one at homicide, the other at emasculation, left me sweating and twitchy. I decided to cede a bit of ground and field at a safer distance. There was a tut behind me. I turned to see the boundary at my heels and the retreating figure of Sharon, shoulders hunched in rejection, head shaking in disbelief.

In this fixture of substitutes and prodigies, Billy was opening batsman alongside Stan. Sacrificing all hope of Sharon and glory, I had requested to go in last in the vain hope of not having to bat at all.

The team gathered disconsolately around our openers as they padded-up outside the pavilion. Telford Park had made 160 for two declared, the highest score of the season against us. I knelt and helped Billy fasten buckles.

'Well, what a relief we had you today,' he said to me over his shoulder, with a serrated edge to his voice. 'The school XI's gain was certainly our loss.'

I went to speak, but pulled my lips into a tight line.

'I could almost think you were in cahoots with the little lout,' he goaded. 'Or else you're his bunny.'

'You don't know him,' I muttered. 'He's a homicidal maniac.' I sought to illustrate. 'He carries a . . . a toilet chain—'

'Wow!' Billy answered, voice indignant with sarcasm. 'You don't say. Well that's not something to be pooh-poohed. If he pulls that our chances are right down the pan.'

Put plainly like that I suppose it did sound a bit fantastic. Billy seemed determined to hype up the irony.

'Then there'll be flushes all round. Would that explain why you're his stool? I'll get—'

'OK. OK.' I jerked hard on his last leather strap and stood up. 'Quit making faeces and go shit a miracle.'

Telford Park's minders began to unload the van.

'Right, on you go and spread out,' Mr Shepherd shouted. 'Not too far. I don't want anyone within ten yards of the wire. I mean boundary.'

The team was remarkable principally for its variety. Dressed as if their clothes had been selected by touch at a bazaar, they represented every physical type from outright hoodlum to girlish effete. Languidly, they spread themselves around Carson's Field.

The first ball was unique in cricket. A good-lengthed medium pace, Stan took it squarely in the middle of the bat and sent it scudding along the ground through extra cover. The fielder turned and gave chase since it was evidently not going to make four. But, as the ball slowed down, he accelerated. Overtaking it some yards before the edge of the pitch, he ignored it completely, quickened his tempo, leapt the boundary, careered through the long grass, hopped over the small fence and disappeared around the corner of Rose Avenue, still going for all he was worth. The more athletic-looking of the minders, Mr Clarke, immediately set off in pursuit with a practised, economic stride. Head back, nose vertically upward and his tie streaming behind him like a ribbon of smoke from a funnel, you couldn't escape the imagery of a destroyer on convoy duty racing off after an errant merchantman.

'Anybody else tries that is on the monkey climb!' Mr Shepherd bawled, vehemently and mysteriously. It seemed to do the trick. The rest of them settled down to play.

As you might expect, Telford's bowling was characterized by a certain playful menace, with attention focused on the batsman's person as much as on his wicket. Stan seemed to handle it capably, but, from the first, Billy was plainly in trouble.

Some way through the third over, that stunning crack and animal scream which signal contact between a cricket ball moving with real pace and an exposed elbow, were hailed jubilantly by their fielders.

Billy looked frail and wan as we stripped the pads from him. He nursed his ballooning elbow, which was taking on the form and colour of an overripe passion fruit, and said with a faint tremble, 'Do you know, I consider that might be actionable.'

And as it began, so it continued.

Stan fought on, a Crockett at the Alamo, but the non-Pederewski half of the batting rapidly began to prove itself unequal to the challenge. As in any rout, there were pockets of resistance, isolated incidences of heroism, even moments of revived hope. But, one by one, the wickets fell. Even Sharon fell silent.

Pale with trepidation, last man in, I padded-up for the first time in my cricketing career and was called to the crease with fifty still needed on the board and a full three hours of light.

As I approached the wicket through a gauntlet of cat-calls and whispered jibes, Stanislav made clear with a wave of his glove that he wished to exchange a word. This was something I had seen at the professional level. The experienced man would offer the newcomer invaluable advice on peculiarities of the bowler's technique, the condition of the wicket, or weaknesses in the field worth exploiting. I was all ears. Every little could only help. Also, in Stan's case, since I was uncertain if I had ever heard him complete a coherent sentence, this must be an event worthy of a slight diversion.

We met in mid-wicket. He cast furtive glances at the opposition. Good. Presumably this was something important enough for him to ensure that none of their side was in a position to overhear. Crucial strategic exchanges. I might be peeing my box with fright, but perhaps, even now, he could offer me the vital piece of intelligence which might get us through.

He bent his lips until they almost brushed my earlobe, tickling me with a veil of blond hair.

'Keep-a-straight-bat-old-chap,' he whispered, in stilted Slavic.

I stared at him in frank astonishment. Had I been carrying anything less solid than a cricket bat, I probably would have clouted him with it. Lord knows what mistaken notion of the ethics of British spiritual endeavour that signified.

Shoulders slouched in dejection, dragging my bat disconsolately in a tiny furrow down the wicket, I trailed to the other end and asked for middle-and-leg.

The first ball spiralled through the air towards me.

With a sigh I breathed:

'Weight on the front foot
Angle the bat
Smother the bounce
Two to the garden fence,'

and pushed it eighteen inches towards the bowler.

Then again.

Then again.

Stan hit ten off the next over.

I tenaciously blocked my way through a maiden, all the time whispering as though in prayer.

Stan hit eight.

Slowly it began to dawn on me that all was not lost. It seemed that my sole talent as a batsman was exactly what the situation called for. As I have said, after years of garden cricket in front of the drainpipe, my repertoire lacked any stroke which could move the ball further than ten feet, but, as long as I didn't do anything dangerous, like try and score, I could happily stay at the crease all day. All I had to do was quite literally keep my end up, and, every alternate over, Stan would give the bowlers a lesson in advanced ballistics.

I parried, blocked, smothered, virtually hypnotizing myself with my personal litany:

> 'Weight on the front foot
> Angle the bat
> Smother the bounce
> Two to the garden fence.'

Stan swept, hooked, drove, glanced. The number we needed to win dropped from fifty to forty. Forty to thirty. Thirty to twenty.

The atmosphere around us stirred, heated, electrified.

Telford Park's playful lampooning and football-crowd ribaldry gradually subsided. In frustration, medium pace was replaced with speed, and, in desperation, speed with spin. Finally, spin gave way to mortar fire. Little Mickie was cautioned twice by Mr Shepherd for blatant throwing, and not at the wicket either.

Meanwhile, our little knot of brothers-in-arms grew vociferous. From the odd snippet of verbal encouragement grew timid applause, which became solid, then vigorous as the target we were chasing loomed attainably. With a dozen runs needed, each successfully survived delivery was hailed like a curtain call. The scoring of a run became a street party.

We needed four to win. I had strike to Mickie's bowling. I stonewalled my way through five balls. The sixth had more the characteristics of a capital offence than a sporting effort. A viciously spiteful bouncer sang towards my head. Thankfully, my logic circuit had an override. It was called self-preservation.

'Weight on the front foot.
Angle the—
FUCKING DUCK!'

'Brilliant lad! Well left! Battin' instinct. Born wi' it!'

It was Sharon, her voice just discernible above the team's cheers. Before I had recovered, Stanislav clipped the winning four off his toes. He was carried shoulder-high to the boundary. I was thumped, stroked, patted and squeezed. There was much mutual hugging.

'Tim!' squealed Sharon excitedly into my ear. 'You were marvellous darlin'.'

The imitation marrow she was wearing on her head had been knocked slightly askew and her cape was hanging off. Presumably, the result of over-exuberant hugging. Otherwise she looked like a five-foot-three-inch liquorice allsort. Edible.

'I could kiss you, you little hero,' she confided.

I smirked to myself. The very idea.

PART 4

Learning the Game

36

Lanchester University spread over some several square miles of the rural Midlands, and, whilst its research laboratories, advanced equipment, and scientific professionalism were respected throughout the academic world, its sports facilities were positively drooled over. Acres of football, rugby and hockey pitches, first-class tennis and squash courts, an athletics arena and even a full-sized golf course promised to provide ample balance to the intellectual exertions, when not downright open competition.

A letter had informed me I was allocated to Newton Hall of Residence, at Lanchester all Halls being named after a famous scientist or engineer. I secretly wished it had been Einstein, which would have looked good on the letters home, but then reflected that I had at least come off better than at school where, all houses being named after English Catholic martyrs, I'd ended up captain of Blessed Fulle House. Summoned a day or so before the start of term, I was to attend a gathering to introduce the 'Freshmen' to hall officials, students' committee and Members of the Senior Common Room, whatever one of those might be.

Speaking as someone who had done his homework on the kitchen table using a bottle of HP Sauce to prop up the textbook, I was pretty impressed by my room – G-plan furniture, desk and fitted bookshelves, pin-board, my own reading-lamp for goodness' sake – but slightly cowed to learn that the social event in question was to be a wine and cheese party – not the sort of bash that I'd had much experience with before. Or since, come to think about it, but our institutions of learning must have their traditions.

Informed that dress was 'optional preferred formal' I selected my purple brushed-velvet hipster flares, bottle-green 'budgie' jacket, pale lilac curly-collared shirt with a kipper tie patterned in a sort of floral tribute to the star-spangled banner, and slipped carefully into my maroon platform-soled boots. I say carefully, because one false step in the footwear of the day could land you in intensive care. Giving the faint down on my upper lip an encouraging tug – still what my father called a football-team moustache, meaning eleven-a-side, but a firm aspiration ever since first laying eyes on the cover of *Sergeant Pepper's Lonely Hearts Club Band* – I tottered off to learn what a Senior Common Room Member might be.

The room was a bit like a golf-club bar, all dark wooden panels with lists of names in stencilled gold lettering lauding historic winners of mysterious and obscure honours like the 'Curtiss E. Le Brun Award', but the first thing I noticed was that nearly all the men were in dinner-jackets while the women were in evening dresses. Fortunately there were exceptions. A half-dozen or so anxious youngsters milling around timidly were dressed exactly like me though perhaps with a touch less *vif.* All save one abject, sunken-headed poor wretch, wearing a grandad teeshirt and jeans, who was being highly conspicuously ostracized in a corner. These, it appeared, were the 'Freshmen'.

I was approached by an unhappy-looking oldish young man with a naval full set and very-dark-rimmed glasses, who introduced himself without smiling as 'Your chairman, Board' which I at first interpreted as a statement on his condition and, looking round, nodded solicitously.

'Warm up when everyone gets a drink perhaps,' I offered.

He looked at me acutely, as if I'd said something very sly and apropos, then turned abruptly to a sideboard.

'Have some wine,' he ordered, pouring out a glass. A trifle nervously for someone in his position, I thought. He gave off a shifty impression, as of one engaged in something not quite legit.

It may seem difficult to believe, but, social habits being somewhat different then, I had never tasted wine in my life. In our family we drank tea with our meals, water when we were thirsty, and beer to celebrate. Wine I had imagined as having a tremendously fruity and alluring taste, as being immediately intoxicating and, above all, erotically evocative.

I put the glass to my lips and sipped. I'm proud to say I didn't immediately spray it all over his snowy-white starched shirt-front. I merely nodded with a noncommittal sort of expression. It tasted exactly like warm silt.

'Like it?' he asked anxiously. All the time he had been watching me intently, like a scientist following a particularly tricky laboratory experiment on a white rat.

I nodded again and feigned taking another mouthful, but in fact cunningly emptied the contents of the first one back where it had come from, resolving not to let any more of that muck pass my lips for the rest of the evening.

He seemed to cheer up miraculously. Becoming suddenly very garrulous, he perkily explained that amongst his many duties was the selection and purchase of wine for all formal occasions. Whilst modestly disclaiming any conspicuous talent in that direction, he did admit that, in his opinion, particularly in view of the – and here he became noticeably resentful, setting his jaw and clamping his teeth together – financial constraints involved, it demanded a certain experience of life, a *savoir faire*, a sophistication of taste which could only be expected of a maturer student who had – eyes narrowing knowingly – 'knocked about a bit'.

Student? I had thought he was a lecturer in early middle age. It turned out he was in his final year, named

Nicholas, and only three years older than myself. Amazed, I checked myself just in time from taking a further sip at the glass which I continued to clutch for appearances' sake, and reflected ruefully what three years here might do to me. Perhaps it was the pressures of picking wine at six bob a bottle. Only later, when I got to know and love Nicholas, did I learn that he was one of those people who yearn to get into middle age from the moment they don their first pair of long trousers. The sort that spurn physical activity as unintellectual and disdain enthusiasm as 'juvenile'. At twenty-two, Nicholas had a cat and a tea cosy, and shuffled around his room in a cardigan and heather-mixture slippers. He even feigned short-sightedness. Speaking to fellow students as if they were children, and most lecturers as if they were promising adolescents, he always, uninvited, addressed professors by their Christian names.

He led me to a little circle of fresh-faced youngsters who were gazing, wide-eyed and open-mouthed, like the occupants of an aquarium, at a couple of very donnish senior-common-room members. Associated to the hall, I learned from Nicholas, as counsellors and advisers to pimply confused innocents away from the bosom of the family for the first time ('like you'), they were indulging in their favourite pastime of being intelligently insulting to them.

'And what are you doing?' asked one, motioning his full glass (I noted everyone had full glasses except Nicholas) at a tall, lean young man with beads, shoulder-length hair, the scrappy beginnings of a beard, and a stoop.

'Social Sciences,' he answered, stooping further.

They smiled broadly at each other.

'That's not a subject. It's the expression of an opinion. And you?'

This to a rosy-cheeked, slightly tubby type with very neatly trimmed hair.

'French and Russian.'

'A language every civilized person should speak already, and a language no civilized person should be bothered with.'

They chuckled together and turned to a small blushing young beauty, whose low-cut dress revealed the sensuous curve and swell of a proudly female bosom.

'American History,' she whispered apprehensively.

Neither her boobs nor her blushes were to spare her.

'Surely that's a weekend seminar,' they roared, leaning back and yo-ho-hoing like a pair of morally insensitive Father Christmases.

Nicholas drained his glass and, swaying slightly, whispered towards my ear.

'Taking the piss out of the idealism of youth. Buggers. When it comes to your turn tell 'em you're here to play rugger, get ratted, and fornicate like a stallion till your fetlocks frizzle.'

I didn't get the chance. To the accompaniment of short, sharp, attention-getting handclaps, a deep strident American voice with a sort of sinister gravelly edge to it, a bit like a Dalek from New Jersey, announced, 'If I could introdooce my self.'

The 'my' was accentuated, as if to say that anyone who had introduced themselves up to now was about to pale into insignificance.

'Norman Schulz, Noot'n Hall Warden . . .'

Mounting a little rostrum at one end of the room was a short but powerfully-built man of forty-five or so with grizzled hair, Churchillian jowls and a skin tanned by a climate kinder than Leicestershire's. He wore a dark suit which was expensive enough to nearly hide the fact that he spread out a lot around the middle, but a pair of bright scarlet braces, occasionally glimpsed under the jacket, were obviously under a lot more strain than that of just holding his pants up. His expression suggested he hadn't enjoyed lunch, his manner that he had an imminent more important engagement elsewhere, and his tone that it was about time someone cut the crap. All three were permanent.

'I am Visiting Professor of Business Administration from Columbia University Noo York, Youesseh,' he went on, 'assigned to this hall for a period of one year by the University Senate. As Warden, I am responsible to you for the optimized provision of accommodation, balanced nutrition, and a stable and secure environment in which to persoo your academic aspirations. You are responsible to me to conduct yourselves as diligent stoodents and mattora dults.

'I steer the boat, you shoot the ducks.'

Any suspicions that this was an attempt to strike a slightly light-hearted vein were quickly banished by the humourless glare with which the one or two nervous chuckles were mercilessly put down.

'I take up my doody,' he went on, lifting his chin heavenward, evidently a man with a mission, 'at a time which I would describe without fear of exaggeration as one of grave social crisis. A social crisis not only with regard to the Western society situation in general, but to the history of this great institootion in particular. A time when the existing standards and ethics of our great nay . . . mm . . . when existing standards and ethics are increasingly being questioned, even mocked, particularly by young stoodents. A time of permissiveness in behaviour and shifting emphasis in moral responsibility. A time of degradation in popular taste, in literature, the movies, music and dress. A time which scorns the virtues of self-discipline, whilst indulging the excesses of liberalism.

'Excessive liberalism, gentlemen, is an advanced stage of decadence.'

He dropped his head and fixed us firmly, one eye narrowed as if he were training a weapon on us.

'Oh Lord,' I whispered. 'He's pretty horrible isn't he?'

'Appalling,' Nicholas agreed miserably. 'I've had this

all afternoon. I'm sure he'd be happier commanding a penal battalion in Vietnam.'

As if on cue, Norman joined his hands behind his back and began rocking on his heels like a staff colonel at a military briefing.

'None of you, I think, would disagree.'

None of us even embraced the notion.

Warming to his theme, he raised his gravelly voice threateningly.

'At an advanced educational institootion,' he rasped on, 'this moral decline is characterized by a general lowering of standards, a lack of respect, an atmosphere in which stoodents feel observation and criticism to be ends in themselves.

'Moving among you tonight I have been subject to near pinko attitoods of stoodents indulging themselves in the persoot of studies of questionable practical relevance. I have observed insolent hippy costoom, part denim, part underwear. I have witnessed the emblems of great nations mocked and held up to ridicule.'

At this, the social-science student's stoop became a bow, and his head seemed to disappear between his shoulder-blades like a tortoise, whilst the wallflower in jeans and teeshirt actually fled the room whimpering, sandals flopping pathetically.

'Nowhere is this general demise more clearly reflected than in the recent fortoons of Noot'n Hall,' Norman ground out.

We cowered.

He went on to hit us with a sad litany of declining academic standards, defunct societies and dismal sporting achievements. Even our social functions were disdained by the rest of the university, it seemed.

I must admit, I had been forewarned that church was widely considered more of a pull than a Newton Hall disco. But it was daunting indeed to hear that our dining-club evening had all the careless joy of the Praesidium of the Central Committee of the Supreme Soviet celebrating the announcement of a five-year plan for the production of pig iron.

'My task, ladies and gentlemen,' Norman concluded, 'is to turn Noot'n around before it goes belly up.'

He stepped down smiling broadly as if to thunderous applause. In fact, the silence was so absolute I actually heard one of the donnish Senior Common Room gulp from five yards. The other was deathly pale, swaying slightly, and looking at his glass of undrinkable wine as if he dearly wished it were a stiff whisky. They were all Conservative to a man, but they'd never encountered this particular variety.

For the rest of the evening, Norman proceeded from group to group like an armoured car at a student sit-in, dispersing salvoes of right-wing rhetoric and grenades of gritty sarcasm.

'Sound stuff, very sound much of it,' Nicholas said to him as he joined us. 'Perhaps you could have made it clear that there are exceptions though.'

'You wanna light a fire, you burn a few asses Nickie boy,' Norman growled.

'Quite,' Nicholas agreed soberly, as though it were the sort of thing he might say. He saw he'd better change the subject and cleared his throat uncomfortably.

'You've met Bob and Frank,' he said, gesturing towards a stately Professor of English Literature and the Dean of the Mechanical Engineering faculty respectively. 'And this is young Timothy, one of our freshmen.'

There were handshakes all round.

'I see you're not a connoisseur of the grape,' Nicholas ventured, vintage Old Worlder to vigorous Brave New Worlder. Norman was clutching a glass of orange squash in his huge hand as if he had something by the throat.

'On the contrary Mr Chairman.' There was little humour in his grin. 'I truly enjoy a glass of good wine. I have sampled tonight's offering, and I can honestly say the last time I took a mouthful of something like that was when I went fly-fishing on Edmonton mud-flats and fell in.'

The effect on Nicholas was devastating. He threw back his head as if slapped, paused, and then took an enormous gulp of wine as if verifying the truth of what had been said. Suddenly, he became as joyless and silent as a Trappist. For the rest of the evening, he was plunged into a gloom which was virtually sepulchral. The poor chap was never more vulnerable than when he was having his *savoir faire* mauled.

'The theme of the evening, gentlemen,' Norman went on, serenely oblivious, 'as I hope I made clear, is, paraphrasing the words of our late great President, "Ask not what my Hall can do for me, but what I can do for my Hall."'

Bob and Frank became suddenly very animated, babbling about discussion groups, bridge evenings, ping-pong tables and 'a very interesting film I have about Isambard Kingdom Brunel'.

Norman glared at me.

'Well,' I began nervously, 'I've played a bit of sport.'

Hostile silence.

'Football.'

A noncommittal 'Mm'.

'Cricket.'

A slightly encouraging 'Mm?'

Well, no-one was talking about standards were they? Anyway, I've always had this fatal tendency to keep talking when I'm nervous.

'And I was first XV rugby captain for St Michael's in the Fylde.'

'Well were you now?' Norman said, a bit of true chumminess getting into his voice for the time. 'Weren't we saying, Nickie, we need a sports organizer on the stoodent committee. Someone to get it together. Get some results. Make it *go*.'

De profundis, Nicholas said we were.

Norman made decisions with alarming abruptness.

'Welcome Mr Sports Secretary,' he was pumping my hand, 'welcome.'

So, once again, sport appeared to be opening doors for me. This one creaked rather ominously.

37

I had pictured myself in a variety of roles once my life at university began. Earnestly serious at lectures, chin resting lightly on index finger, taking sparse notes and occasionally posing a succinct and pointed question which would cause the lecturer to start, reconsider his stuffy predigested attitude to his subject matter, and then offer me a sidelong, reluctantly admiring, glance. Discussing the meaning of life with silver-haired, soft-spoken old sages ensconced in the Chesterfield sofas of their firelit studies, leather-bound works of genius in first editions from floor to ceiling. Taking Jean-Paul Sartre and his existentialism apart in the Union bar over a couple of halves of bitter. And, of course, leaning forward by candlelight at a table for two in a little-frequented bohemian place where I was known as 'that brilliant young chap from the university' to slip the heavy-framed NHS glasses off a bookish young female, revealing (to her, me having realized it from the first) that she looked just like Julie Christie.

The timetable came as the first shock. I rapidly realized that the scheduling of lectures and tutorials for the average engineering student, coupled with the associated reading, preparation and lab work, was calculated to leave a precise amount of time for eating and sleeping, but not much for French philosophy. It seemed the average engineering course consisted of a vast heap of established knowledge which was to be force-fed to the student by the shovel-load. The first question I ever asked at a lecture, in front of two hundred fellow students, was greeted by the young Scottish doctor of fluid mechanics (why do so many Scots get into engineering?) with, 'Uf ye dunna know that b'now young laddie, ye shouldn'a be here.' Not the sort of response to encourage an enquiring young mind.

I did have to report to my personal tutor once each week during the first year, to make sure I managed the emotional transition – sort of like being on probation without having done anything wrong. Not in a study, but in his office which, being slightly smaller than the average Chesterfield sofa was, of necessity, Chesterfield sofa-less. Also, Dr Mountford had no silver hairs, he being bald as an egg. But he did give me tea, and then lean over, hands joined in front of him, to ask in an earnest, fatherly sort of way, 'You're sure everything is all right then, Thomas?'

As for the women – well, we're all products of our environment. The average Lanchester lady wasn't just bookish, she was a Thick Print *Encyclopedia Britannica*. Broad-bottomed (from too much sitting on hard chairs) spotty (from spending too much time indoors) huge spectacles (from all that reading) and greasy-haired (from having better things to do than get dolled up for the likes of the scruffy, pimply, podgy swats who constituted the male population of the university) the only chance most of them had of ever looking like Julie Christie was if Julie were to suddenly decide to give it all up to study for a degree in welding at Hartlepool Polytechnic.

But at least these were all recognizable parodies of my preconceptions. I had never reckoned with anything as terrible as Norman.

Norman's subject was Business Policy. To him, everything large and small was to be seen in terms of the planning and implementation of a strategy to achieve predefined goals. Having taken over, as one of his many goals, the rejuvenation of Newton Hall, he selected a committee of students to assist him and then proceeded to define their objectives for them and tell them, in his inimitable style, how to get there.

The vehicle for this was a Friday-evening council of war in his lounge. A dozen or so students would be scattered around him, almost literally at his feet, since he occupied the only hard chair and desk, and all the rest of the furniture seemed to hiss languidly or boiyoing elastically until your backside sank to within an inch of the floor. From his thus elevated position, Norman ran these meetings like the shark executive sent in by the US multi which had just bought out a piece of limping English Victoriana and was trying to break it to these people that the twentieth century had arrived.

Thus for example, to his admin secretary, brandishing a report on revised Hall registration procedures:

'Trees die to make paper, Derek. Happy little trees, bending gracefully and flicking their little leaves in the breeze,' he rippled his fingers in illustration, 'are brutally cut down and mashed to a pulp so that paper is available for people like you to write reports on. This, Derek,' shaking the report earnestly at shoulder height, 'this is a sad and terrible case of arboreal genocide.'

Or thus to his social secretary:

'Margaret, this is the programme of events for our people for the entire team. It should invigorate. It should enthral. It should make people excited about the time ahead. Margaret, I feel more excited about the future when I read my own testament.'

Or to Nicholas:

'Nick, what did we *drink* Friday? What did we offer our guests? Nicholas, my good friend, you are in the process of giving an entirely noo conceptual interpretation to the term alcohol abuse. The alcohol is no longer abused, it abuses. It is no longer wrongfully consoomed in large quantities, it is wisely consoomed by the dessertspoon.'

And of course to me, though with an imperfect knowledge of non-American sport:

'Tim, we lost at sockball to Faraday! I can't handle this. To Faraday! Do our guys call themselves a footsie team or do they! I mean do they?'

'Well no, Norman. I couldn't frankly imagine them calling themselves that. No.'

'Right!' Bemused but taking it as affirmation. Then, with less conviction, 'Right.'

The thing about Norman was that he was thick-skinned, pig-headed, single-minded and energetic enough to make a first-class leader and brilliant manager. He was teaching us things at least as important as those we were learning in the lecture hall and probably more apposite. What you could never, under any circumstances, imagine him saying was, 'OK. I give up. Forget it.' Failure was a concept he either didn't seem to grasp or felt himself totally above. Temporary setbacks were examined and analysed and the lessons learned incorporated into the strategy leading to ultimate victory. Subject no object, whatever he put his mind to, his involvement was all-embracing, his commitment absolute. Just as my mother used to invoke that most ancient yet vitally relevant of clichés, 'If a thing's worth doing, it's worth doing well', here was Norman demonstrating that, leader or follower, people will forgive you an awful lot if you're seen to be giving it everything you've got.

So Derek would go away and produce a computer program which provided a sort for every conceivable item of data which Norman might need relating to all the students under his control – no simple matter at a time when data was fed to computers via punched cards which, for a largish program, needed to be transported by heavy-duty crane and wheelbarrow, and, if minutely inaccurate or disordered, resulted in an output resembling a cross between errant binary and seventh-century Mandarin. Margaret would persuade a group of final-year commercial art students to design a set of stunningly original posters which were not only eye-catching, but which won acclaim even beyond the confines of the university. Nicholas would found a Senior Common Room Dining Club Steering Committee which not only provided him with what he called a 'discerning boozer's kitty' but enabled him to attract after-dinner speakers of true note.

And so on.

And me? Well, I set about trying to win the University Intramural Sports Championship for Newton Hall, for the first time in its history.

38

With the exception of those that involved cruelty to animals, the Lanchester University inter-hall sports competition embraced virtually every sport devised by man. Students were perfectly at liberty to spend their every waking hour swiping at, kicking, throwing, thumping or chasing the inanimate object of their heart's desire – be it big and round, egg-shaped and leather, little dimpled and white, bouncy fluffy and yellow, black squishy rubber, or one of those hard shiny red ones that hurt like hell when they crack you on the elbow. They could flex any muscle, sweat through every pore, and even burn up the odd brain cell or two. Each hall competed against the others in a league system far more complicated than any mere Olympiad. And the powers that be were so determined to get us exercising that points were even awarded for turning up.

Of course, the vast majority of students had just escaped from years of parental dictatorship and compulsory school games, so there was a fairly widely dispersed ethic of 'not bloody likely'. Added to that, this was a generation rapidly becoming noted for, if not paranoid about, anti-authoritarianism, and organization of any sort was regarded with suspicion, particularly if it conjured up images of Strength through Joy and formation gymnastics in elasticated underwear at a secluded camp in the Black Forest.

So image was the keynote.

I organized a display area outside the main dining-room which gave a comprehensive explanation of the competition, provided a potted history outlining Newton's pretty ordinary performance to date and declared a modest programme of improvement. This wasn't difficult because Newton's performance to date revealed itself to be more ordinary than a wet Wednesday in Wigan.

One night after hall dinner, I took my heart in my mouth, stood, banged at the table with a spoon and made a short impromptu speech. Perhaps concentrating too much on striking a chatty, informal note, I introduced myself as sports sec, admitted that previously their secs had put the accent on just getting a bit of exercise in a boring straightforward way, but hoped that in future secs would focus on variety, fun, and mutual encouragement to reach a satisfying outcome. I for one was determined to ensure everyone in hall had a bang before the end of the year.

It got an ovation. Even when it was explained to me why, I still felt elated, partly because enthusiastic cheering was a totally novel response to my powers of oration, and partly because, what the hell, I was on the map.

Next, I instituted a weekly meeting of all captains.

I sought advice from Norman on how best to impress upon them that my appointment constituted a complete break with our undistinguished past.

'Easy,' he said, as if stating the obvious. 'Fire 'em.'

I demurred. Determined at the first meeting to hit all the right notes – reconciliation, unification, dedication to a common purpose – and flaunt my new-found grandiloquence, I delivered a stirring discourse, climaxing in what I hoped was a rousing finale.

'I take it we will fight them in the fields and on the pitches and "nevah surrendah" then,' said one flatly, the moment I had finished.

Clearly, firing was an option.

I gently pushed the captain of the cross country team (which had been on a run-slow in protest against government education cuts) and the entire chess team (which was in the habit of channelling its funding to the PLO) in the direction of the Students' Union, made snap appointments as best I could and added photographs of them all to the display area, each accompanied by a few lines on their sporting credentials and talents rather after the style preferred by authorized biographers of First Secretaries of the Communist Party of the USSR.

I had an enormous magnetic leaderboard manufactured and mounted at the common-room entrance, from which the overall competition status could be assessed, with Newton's position highlighted in red. It got christened the Lifeboat Appeal, but it got noticed.

Thanks to Norman, I acquired the registration details of every student in hall, examined each for the sporting interests they had declared when initially applying to Lanchester and personally visited everyone who hadn't followed up a professed interest to ask why. Those who maintained they were just waiting to be asked, I encouraged warmly. Those who feared they didn't think they'd be good enough, I flattered extravagantly. Those who admitted they'd just thought it would look good on the application form, I blackmailed mercilessly.

I advertised fixtures, drummed up groups of supporters and attended matches. In response to the requests to recount what happened, I began taking along a camera and producing reports. This naturally led to a news-sheet and then a makeshift magazine, which gave me the fatal opportunity to scratch further, my long-held itch to be a feature-writer. As, for example, in:

SQUASHED!

After the five–nil drubbing Newton gave Halley at squash last Friday, our captain ACHIM BEN ASAAD took great exception at having his finesse with a squash ball called into question. Indeed, when the gauntlet was thrown down in the form of a bet, Asaad glowered at Halley's captain like a cobra that's had its tail trod on during an afternoon nap.

After wordlessly scratching at the curly black scrub that blurs his chin, Asaad reached out his long arm and rippled his fingers for a squash ball. Striding to the front of the court, he balanced a half-crown on the top of a tin can, then went to the back corner and began drumming the ball up and down the wall. On the tenth shot, he slashed downward on the turn, and struck the ball towards the coin five yards away. There was a muffled ping and the half-crown spun into the air like a fragment of shrapnel.

The last time your correspondent witnessed anything like that, he was nine years old. In order to rescue the nervously watching settlers, the Lone Ranger had struck a deal with the Mexican bandit chief. If Tonto spun a dollar into the air, and the Lone Ranger could draw and shoot a hole through it, they could go home. If not, well . . . The bandit chief eyed the settler's beautiful daughter and laughed darkly through bad teeth. He reckoned he was on to a sure thing.

Bang. Tinkle.

The Lone Ranger used silver bullets. Asaad uses little black ones. See him against Brunel, Tuesday at eight pee em.

Neat eh? Slightly exaggerated, of course, because the altercation in question took place after six pints of lager and frankly any of them would have had difficulty hitting the side of a building, never mind a coin of the realm, but I assumed that was what was meant by poetic licence.

Nicholas came forward to reveal a totally unsuspected theoretical and practical mastery of the art of archery. He unearthed, from his many sturdy leather trunks and cases, a bow of laminated willow, beautifully shaped and honed by fine craftsmen into a piece of magnificent precision weaponry. It was so intricately equipped with antennae-like projections, vernier screws and miscellaneous metal gadgetry that when he asserted straight-faced that it included forward-looking infra-red and radar-controlled track-while-scan, I was unsure whether or not to laugh. Accoutred with leather armlets, and guards and straps of obscure design and purpose, he toddled off to do battle, looking like a cross between Cupid on a space walk and an extra from a Reeperbahn S and M collage.

If Nicholas were offering his services, I could rightly claim to be getting somewhere.

I socialized. I took tea, for example, in the rooms of my tennis captain, Penny, a fresh-faced, sportingly buxom young lady of the superior social classes, surrounded by class photographs, silver cups, framed certificates and all the memorabilia of a distinguished girlhood.

'Believe me, Timothy, I enderstend your difficulties only too well. I was kepton of hoice at Rossingdale.'

'It's very much a question of generating the interest and enthusiasm.'

'Oh ebsolyootly, I simply couldn't agree more. Particularly with the gells. Sometimes, simply getting them to show up is an achievement. It can be so terribly difficult getting a gell excited enough to come.'

My face froze. I cleared my throat. My complexion rocketed through the entire spectrum, finishing up somewhere around ultraviolet. Her eyes widened, then understanding dawned, and her cheeks flushed scarlet. She suddenly became extremely active amongst the tea things, outwardly managing to maintain the pose of practised hostess, until the cake stand crashed to the floor and proceeded to roll around in uncontrolled circles, throwing off buns and éclairs in its wake like comet debris.

I solicited. I pleaded with the future Nigerian Deputy Minister of Railways as he pumped iron in the gymnasium, biceps ballooning like chocolate-flavoured condoms on a testing machine.

'Come on Ekasi, it says here you've done the hundred in ten point eight.'

He stopped, sat back and smiled, the totally fat-free skin on his stomach settling into a series of little parallel ripples. The enormously powerful body, the startling contrast of huge smiling ivory white teeth and purple-black face, the dispassionate bloodshot eyes, combined to give you an impression of toying menace. Ekasi frightened me a bit. Talking to him was like playing chess with a big black bear whom you quietly suspected of being a bad loser.

'Aw. Ah was bein' chased by a lyan man,' he drawled.

'C'mon. It's important. I need you.'

'Boxin',' he bellowed, and began feinting punches at me, his big fists like bunches of outsized, overripe bananas hissing to a stop an inch or so from the end of my nose. 'Boxin'. Now there's a sport.'

'We don't do it. Thumping your fellow students is frowned on.'

And I stood in whenever the ability to field a team was in jeopardy – a vitally important aspect of the job, considering the system of points allocation.

Thus, despite a lifelong dread of water, I even played in goal for the water-polo team, resulting in the following half-time conversation between myself and the captain, a no-nonsense highly practically-minded young engineer on an RAF scholarship.

Me: 'Do you think we could ask them not to bother with changing ends for the second half?'

Him: 'What on earth for?'

Me. 'I thought we were playing in the small pool.'

Him: 'So what?'

Me. 'It's an even depth – four foot.'

Him: (getting impatient) 'So what?'

Me. 'This isn't.'

Him: (definitely testy) 'I know that. It's eight foot at the other end. I still don't see the point.'

Me: (mumbling) 'I can't swim.'

Him: 'You bloody what!' (ripping off his swimming cap).

Me: 'I said I can't swim.'

Him: (exasperated-incredulous-furious) 'Then what the bloody hell did you offer to play in a bloody water-polo team for?'

Me: 'I've already explained. I didn't think swimming was a prerequisite.'

Him: (throwing his cap to the floor) 'You didn't think . . .' (lost for words) 'I suppose you think Graham Hill doesn't have a bloody driving licence. Or Neil Armstrong has a fear of flaming heights. My sainted bloody auntie! You probably think the equatorial rain forests are crawling with bloody polar bears!'

Me: 'OK. Calm down. I'll do it.'

I did, too. Not that I had a lot of choice. They would probably have thrown me in with a rubber ring around my neck. I clung to the posts when we were attacking, and doubled like a squaddie on jankers when we defended.

After a promising first half had ended all square at two all, we finally lost seventeen-two.

Or, despite my relatively diminutive five feet nine, I joined the arms-on-shoulders 'time-out' at a basketball match, linking my neighbours' buttocks and looking up at the captain, thinking, now I know how a rugby ball feels in a scrum.

'Tim, you take their big lad.'

'Jack, he's seven foot if he's an inch. And he's their best player.'

'I know, but I can't spare a proper player. With any luck,' reaching down to tousle my hair, 'he may keep tripping up over you.'

So I spend the next twenty minutes staring somebody in the kneecaps, leaping up in the air, arms raised totally ineffectively, every time he gets the ball, feeling exactly like a pygmy trying to put a giraffe out of action by fetching him a right hook.

Thankfully, not all my contributions were as demeaning.

A couple of years of Mr Adam had taught me all I needed to know about touch-line bawling in a north country accent. At first, the football team, Home Counties types to a man, looked not a little piqued to have 'BACK OFF FURST, KUM OFF WURST' foghorned at them if they flinched in the tackle. An Alpine-horn rendition of 'IF CAUGHT UNAWURR, GIVE IT SUM URR' would bring them to a stunned and bewildered standstill, even leaving the ball trickling innocently towards the opposition. But, after a couple of matches, they seemed to warm to it. They exchanged smiles and knowing looks, threw me little hand gestures of acknowledgement, and began repeating some of Mr Adam's more memorable exhortations, even if in girl's-blousey voices. Before a particularly crucial clash, I promised them a slap-up feed of babbies' 'edds and Accrington Kebabs if they pulled it off. It was a sensational success. Extra large steak and kidney puddings and three meat pies on a skewer became a sort of traditional victory feast.

Of course, as a batsman, I could claim to have extended the repertoire of conventional cricketing strokes, adding to the drive, sweep, cut and the rest, my very own 'two-to-the-garden-fence push'. My distinctive prowess as a close fielder was described wryly by the captain as like watching a hungry koala bear stalk lion, which seemed a compliment in a sort of way.

Then of course, there was rugby.

Scene: 10.30p.m. Saturday night, the union bar, a ghastly modern affair of glass and chrome with stone-paved floors. The air is a dense blue mist of cigarette smoke; people are packed in like a cup final crowd; the floor is awash with spilt beer; the row is tumultuous, the atmosphere saturnalian or Bacchanalian or both.

I am in the arms of Howard, a tall bearded Welshman with long blond locks, now plastered to his neck with sweat. We are the central figures in a group of twenty or so, all dressed in jeans and our spare blue-and-gold-hooped rugby jerseys. A thirty-six–nil victory in which I have figured prominently, six pints of Guinness and blackcurrant, and twelve bawdy verses of 'Who killed Cock Robin?' are all behind us.

'If you weren't bloody English, I'd kiss you boy,' he shouts beerily into my face.

'Je ne comprends pas mon capitain.'

'Oh fack it then.'

To the fuzzily co-ordinated cheers of the rest of the team, he throws me theatrically over his left knee and plants a slobbery kiss vaguely in the middle of my face, in the process sending fresh supplies of Guinness cascading all over the table and floor.

Tony the barman, white shirt transparent and clinging with sweat, black braces twisted and wig askew, shouts angrily towards us, counting us out like a boxing referee, his words of complaint totally drowned in the din.

Surfacing gingerly, swaying a little, I look straight into the eyes of Dr Mountford, my personal tutor. His expression is not one of approval. It occurs to me I missed our last appointment. I smile uncomfortably and essay a little wave.

39

Arriving back from lectures one evening about halfway into my first academic year, I dumped onto my desk a pile of mail retrieved from my pigeon-hole in the main hall, and began to scan through it. Most of it, as usual, was in the form of handwritten notes on folded plain paper.

Tim,

We murdered them eight–one.

(unsigned).

Tim,

George bust his squash racket last night. We

play Rutherford on Friday and he says he's broke.
Can we fund it – at least a loan?
You know how important this one is.

I'm in all evening.

Jack.

Timothy,

Tennis v. Pascal

Venue: Allweather centre.
Date: 2nd May
Result: Ladies w. 5–0
Men w. 4–1

Best regards,

Penelope

PS Super of you to have secured money for restringing!

Well done!

Tim,

No training tomorrow. Floodlights u/s. Piss-up as usual 8.00 p.m.

Howard

Dear Mr Armstrong,

Professor Williams has asked me to remind you that your Material Sciences laboratory reports are now two weeks overdue.

Alison Bell
Sec. to Prof D. Williams

Room 7 Block 6, Armstrong.

If you don't move your bloody bike out of our kitchen I'll dismantle the sodding thing and secrete bits of it all over the campus.

Room 9 Block 12, Warin.

Mr Sports Secretary,

Gravest developments in the indoor pentathlon team. Require your immediate assistance.

Phil Martin

Timothy,

Mr Rankin informs me you do not attend lectures or tutorials in applied mechanics any more and are behind with the coursework. Could we please discuss.

Dr C. Mountford

Mentally sorting them into priority, I decided to skip the evening meal and pop over to see Phil Martin. I'd paid very little attention to the indoor pentathlon team, mainly because they seemed to do quite nicely under their own steam. They were the only Newton team who had won their discipline the previous year, and they continued to turn in winning performances which Phil usually reported with a laconic 'Saw them off 5–0'.

Only once until now had they experienced what appeared to have been a close-run thing, and Phil's report had been both appropriately expanded and suitably admonishing.

'Won 3–2. Andy very poor time. Paul's throwing abysmal. Have instigated intensified training programme.'

Clearly a serious, dedicated captain with an iron grip on his team.

This surprised me a bit. Of the rest of the team I knew nothing, but Phil and I, being on courses which occasionally shared lectures, were casual acquaintances. He'd struck me as the sort of guy who would have difficulty taking even the prospect of death by disembowelment seriously.

With the obvious exception of being a gifted athlete, he was everything which Norman abhorred in modern youth. Sporting a mane of vivid carrot-coloured hair which was frizzed into the Afro look then popular, and which increased the diameter of his head by about a foot and a half, his sense of dress even by the colourful standards of the day was flamboyant. He favoured caftans in violent reds and noisy shades of yellow, extravagantly flared cord jeans which might be of regal purple or plum, and white baseball shoes which he adorned with personally designed motifs applied with a set of children's crayons.

Add to this the fact that he was a highly vocal and demonically irreverent Liverpudlian, and you begin to understand why Norman, unable at one of the weekly meetings to remember Phil's name, snapped his fingers. 'You know the guy I mean – evident stoodent subversive. Looks like a goddamm lion in a Mardi Gras costoom.'

Phil wasn't in. I enquired of his neighbour and was told, a little scathingly I thought, 'One of his training nights. You'll find him at the bar.'

Nothing wrong with that. I pondered at the derisive tone. If a man punishes his body to the limits of physical endurance, surely he's entitled to relax with a well-earned lime-and-lemon afterwards.

At this relatively early hour, the bar was virtually empty. Apart from someone buried behind a *Times* with a half of cider in front of him, the only customers were a little group in the corner, scattered around the dartboard. Phil's shock of red hair and blazing orange Cossack shirt were difficult to miss among them.

He saw me coming.

'Ah welcome Mr Sports Secretary, emissary of Lanchester's own Tricky Dicky – General "Norman Schulz" Sheridan – famed for that unforgettable quip, "The only good student is a dead one."'

He turned to his companions and chanted loudly.

'We love that man!'

There was a chorus of jeers and lip farts and a shout of 'Love him!' evidently a sort of group war cry.

'Hi guys,' I said slightly taken aback, proffering a sort of communal wave.

I must admit, I was rocked by the sight of them. Not just the fact that they were puffing out more smoke than the Ruhr Valley, or even the pints of Ansell's bitter which they clutched lovingly to their breasts in the practised drinking style favoured by folk-singers and real-ale freaks. It was their physical appearance that was the shock. They looked exactly like a coach party of sumo wrestlers on a pub crawl.

'Meet the team,' said Phil, clapping his hands like an impresario, and proceeded to introduce the group in the manner of a bandleader taking an audience through his soloists, encouraging each to blow a little fugue.

'On the javelins, Paul.'

From the neck up, Paul was a good-looking, dark-haired type with penetrating blue eyes. His belly was a mere sheep's bladder to the others' barrage balloons, but the buttons of his shirt still appeared to be under enough tension to convert them into dangerous missiles should he breathe out sharply. Taking three darts and addressing the board with an expression on his face anything other than frivolous, he arced his right arm in perfect rhythm three times, and landed them, each with a satisfying leaden thud, in a neat little cluster around treble twenty.

Phil smiled at me with a 'that's my boy' twinkle and moved on.

'Our speed drinker, Andy.'

Andy was mountainous. He was perched on a chair which he dwarfed as if it were a potty. It was hard-backed and seemingly specially positioned for him, because had he settled into one of the numerous low couches or armchairs scattered around, he would never have risen again without some form of mechanical assistance. His balding head appeared to be scaled wrongly, a bit like a cherry crowning a huge blancmange.

A pint of bitter was placed on the table before him. One of the team began rubbing his neck and shoulders from behind, another started to work his right forearm backwards and forwards as if playing a one-armed bandit, and a third went to work massaging his sprawling midriff with eager fingers.

'OK team,' said Phil, producing a stop watch, 'stand back.'

Andy's right arm took the pint and moved smoothly table-to-mouth in a perfect arc from nine o'clock to twelve o'clock. His Adam's apple jerked rapidly three times, and the beer disappeared down his throat in an unbroken extension of the same arc – twelve o'clock to three. The empty glass clattered to the table amid cheers.

'Two point nine,' Phil reported, clicking the watch. 'Better, much better.'

Demonstrations of a similarly arresting prowess were provided by Dennis, flicking, cleaving and then concertinaing a pack of playing cards, and then Arthur, clicking billiard balls in an impact sequence which brought Newton's laws of action and reaction into question.

I looked at Phil.

'You don't have anything to do with athletics,' I said flatly.

'Athletics.' He scratched at the patchy orange scrub which adorned his chin and neck. 'Now that's an interesting question m'boy. Not one I've pondered, mind, but now you come to ask, I suppose you could say,' he pursed his lips and folded his arms, looking upward and sideways in a sort of thoughtful pose, 'I suppose you could say, we have about as much to do with athletics as someone watching *Match of the Day* with a fish supper and eight cans of lager has to do with playing centre forward for Liverpool.

'Our sporting specializations are more in the direction of what might be termed the sedentary disciplines.'

I sighed. So one of the cornerstones of Newton's bid for the championship was a bunch of beer-bellied reprobates whose sporting prowess owed everything to the classic indications of misspent youth. If Norman found out he'd go thermonuclear.

'Oh well,' I said resignedly, 'I suppose the idea is meant to be sport for every man. You mentioned something about a problem.'

'The fifth discipline – table football.' I couldn't repress a slight rolling of the eyes. 'My defender was carried off in practice with a major injury. It's going to keep him out for months.'

'A major injury? How do you sustain major injuries playing table football, for Christ's sake?'

'Attempting to open a bottle of Newcastle Brown on the edge of the table with the flat of your hand. He broke a bone.'

I was beginning to find them faintly incredible.

We all walked, or waddled, our way over to a table-football machine in the opposite corner. It was the sort you see in amusement arcades, billiard saloons and second-class pubs, and I had noticed several, surprisingly, were dotted around the campus. It consisted of a table about five feet by two at waist height with eleven plastic men a few inches tall mounted on transverse metal rods in a one-three-four-three arrangement, the teams interspersed. The rods could be moved in or out via protruding handles, or spun to allow the men to propel the ping-pong-sized ball. Phil took one side with Andy in defence, and Paul and Arthur the other. Phil slipped in a shilling on the end of a piece of wire to release the balls, then deftly whipped his money out again.

I admit I was prepared to see all four commence feverishly windmilling their men to the accompaniment of childish yelps and animated growls, as the ball zigzagged randomly between the rows. I should have known better. These were gentlemen who took their frivolities very seriously. To the silence of intense concentration, Phil inserted the first ball.

'Well, what do you think?' he asked later as we took a breather, despatching Paul for a tray full of fresh pints. 'You've obviously got it in you, I can see that.'

'Why not one of the others – they're all pretty impressive, when not outright virtuosos like yourself.'

'Against the rules. No one person is allowed to take

part in two events. Teams of six. Incidentally, I shouldn't have to be telling you this.'

'Other disciplines have consumed my efforts,' was all I said.

I bit my lip. Time, time. I had virtually dispensed with eating. That left only the other.

'Strict training mind,' he said seriously. 'Mondays, Wednesdays and most weekends, here in the bar.'

'He means most *of* the weekend,' Paul interrupted, putting down the tray and dishing out pints suspended from spidery fingers like a miniature crane.

'Bloody hell! When do you guys work?'

'Skills like these aren't acquired without sacrifice,' said Phil earnestly. We laughed.

There was a pause. I took a deep breath.

'OK,' I said, 'what the hell – I'm in.' Then, loudly and gung-ho, 'Mondays, Wednesdays, Saturdays, Sundays. In the bar.'

During the D'Artagnan-and-the-merry-band sort of cheer and clash of beer mugs that followed, I was aware of someone standing next to me, silently watching like a spectre. I turned and looked up.

Dr Mountford had evidently sipped his cider and finished his *Times*, which was now tucked neatly under his arm. He was smiling, in a rather pinched sort of way, as if someone had given him his smile to wear and it didn't quite fit. He pushed his specs up his nose with his index finger. The light bounced blindingly off his bald head.

'You got my message, Timothy. I think I'd appreciate a little chat.'

'Er, yes. I'll be there, Friday.'

'Good.' He looked up and nodded curtly to the others. 'Good evening gentlemen.' Then he left.

In the silence that followed, I looked blankly across the table. By chance, I found myself staring straight into Andy's knowing squint. He produced a sinister little chuckle, chins wobbling mirthlessly.

40

Balancing at the top of the ladder beneath the leader board, I clipped Newton into second place behind Rankin, noted sporting fetishists and competition-winners of the previous year. Their programme had been completed, though, and we still had two fixtures in different events. Victory in either would be enough to take us past them. It was a tense finish, one which had generated a buzz of excitement throughout the hall community and was even managing to repress temporarily my 'examination gut' as the complaint was generally known. The symptoms were progressively worsening, and now included a doom-laden voice which woke me in the small hours with incantations in the imperative like 'NEGLIGENTLY PRESENTED AND SLOVENLY WORK WILL BE PENALIZED'. For the moment, they also appeared to involve hallucinations. Two penguins waddled towards me down the corridor. I blinked.

'Timothy my boy,' said Nicholas brightly. 'Ceaselessly at work directing our sporting contingent as always, I see.'

He beamed at me, with Guy Lavelle beside him. They were looking very dapper in dinner suits, hence the momentary illusion. Dashingly cavalier red velvet cummerbunds circled their waists. Guy was visiting me from Cambridge, a long-standing invitation issued before my current predicament had developed. Face-saving would not allow me to retract this gesture of friendship and returned generosity. Pleading pressure of work, I had dumped him on Nicholas and fortunately they seemed to be getting along famously. They were attending an end-of-term dinner, Guy having borrowed my recently acquired evening wear and guiltily accepted my thirty-bob ticket.

'We're just off for an aperitif. Why don't you join us in the common room for a glass of that excellent amontillado?' Nicholas was forever tippling the vintages now he was in funds.

'I won't bother with the sherry but you can get me a half of bitter,' I said not very enthusiastically. 'I'll just put these ladders away, then I'll be with you.'

Guy Lavelle had lost none of the puckishness which went with those shining cut-glass eyes. He had cultivated his sideburns into a straight luxuriant beard a shade darker than his reddish hair, but managed to maintain his overriding boyish demeanour. You could see that in a few years' time people would be refusing to believe that he wasn't ten years younger. Women loved him.

'I can't say he would have been my choice for after-dinner speaker,' Nicholas was saying as I joined them, feeling curiously artisan in my jeans and pullover to their DJs. He handed me my beer absently. 'Apparently, he recounts rather vulgar stories about his work as demolition contractor. Blowing up old buildings, tree stumps and that sort of thing.'

'More often cesspits and shithouses,' I interjected brutally. Nicholas scratched at his beard and ignored me.

'Now last week we had the left-wing Labour MP, Mrs Elizabeth Riley Hoare, you know, the CND woman. She was magnificent.' Nicholas's eyes glazed a bit. It occurred to me Elizabeth Riley Hoare was probably the sort of woman he wanted to marry. Middle-aged, intellectual, tweed two-piece, sensible shoes. Totally unfrivolous. 'She made a riveting case for the non-military state. The conversion of all that wealth and labour from the production of weapons of misery and destruction to the service of mankind, the improvement of the common man's lot. Art. Culture.'

'Yes – the same sort of person who considers modern art and culture to be vulgar fumbling compared to ancient Rome,' I broke in. 'But if you had suggested to Augustus Caesar that he disband his legions and use the bulging coffers to improve the working conditions of Rome's service industries – slaves comprised about ninety per cent of the population I seem to remember – you'd have probably found yourself sitting down to dinner with a great big liplicking pussy cat and saying, "Hey – what do we eat around here?"'

Christ! I was even starting to talk like Norman.

They both smiled, if a little wonderingly.

'Meaning?' asked Guy.

'I don't know. Probably that the money would go on Gay Rights and Equal Opportunity Tribunals anyway. Or that Augustan Rome wouldn't have lasted long without the legions. Both.'

'I think I detect the random bad temper of an overworked student,' Guy said sympathetically. 'Why don't you change your mind and come this evening. I could wear a lounge suit and pay for my own dinner. Come on.' He sounded genuinely concerned.

For one moment I was tempted. I had a brief tantalizing vision of the three of us sipping liqueurs, sucking huge cigars, chortling contentedly, a sumptuous dinner behind us, bawdy 'Blaster Bates' ahead.

'Nah,' I said finally. 'No can do. No time. I'm even compelled to adopt a policy of statistically selective revision.'

Guy's brow furrowed. 'Of what?'

'Statistically selective revision. I carry out an analysis of the last few years' exam papers, identify the topics which most regularly come up and map their frequency. Then I make a prediction of the most likely topics for this year's paper and concentrate my revision on those areas. With a bit of margin, of course.'

They were both silent.

'It's perfectly legitimate,' I said defensively. 'You could produce a mathematical model with a percentage probability and confidence limits for each major subject and each exam. It's a scientific approach.'

'I'm glad you're not studying medicine,' said Guy at length.

'Why?'

'Oh it's just that I wouldn't like to turn up in your

surgery covered in horrendous red blotches to be told, "Ah! Spots! Well, I didn't actually *do* spots if you see what I mean. They weren't due on the exam paper that year and I was a bit pushed for time. Sorry! Not flatulent are you by any chance? Breaking wind uncontrollably? Letting off is, so to speak, one of my fortes. Farting, I *did*."'

I had to smile. Nicholas snorted and choked as he knocked back the last of his sherry.

'Come on, young sir, we'll be late.' He motioned to Guy to finish his drink. 'Timothy, as you will no doubt know, has been under tremendous pressure in an extra-curricular sense. He has literally made sport to Newton Hall what warfare was to ancient Sparta.'

'Does that mean all these lusciously nubile young ladies I see around have amputated their right one so they can shoot arrows straighter?'

'That was the Amazons, as you well know. What it means is that Timothy here has totally enthused a body of modern British Youth. No mean achievement.'

Sentiments more or less echoed by Norman at the final committee meeting of term a few days later. Arriving late, I had been condemned to one of Norman's horribly modern, enormous, leather pouffes. Subsiding gently to rest, I attained a position in which my legs had actually ended up higher than my head, a sort of rub-my-tummy puppy-dog position, and my view of Norman was framed by my own ludicrously projecting feet.

'If I understand your brief correctly Tim,' he said, shuffling papers and looking up notes, presumably quite content to address the soles of my feet, 'a victory in the hockey tie Sunday morning or the indoor pentathlon Wednesday makes us University champs. That right?'

'That's correct,' I said evenly. I was bloody chuffed and I found it difficult to hide. I moved my feet wider apart and vainly attempted to sit up.

'Regardless of the outcome of those ties, I would like to place on record,' Norman said, nodding at the secretary, 'a most deserved vote of thanks to Mr Armstrong. His efforts in promoting sporting activities throughout Hall, and placing Newton amongst the athletic élite of this university, have been nothing less than,' he sought an appropriate word carefully, 'stoopendus.'

There was a general ripple of applause, a light banging on the arms of chairs and knocking on tables. These were the student leaders. They were paying me tribute. It was my moment and I was proud of it. I just wished I hadn't had to acknowledge it from a position of seemingly having my nappy changed.

'Well, those indoor pentathlon guys seem to know their stuff,' he mused. I remained prudently silent.

'This hockey captain,' Norman continued ruffling papers. 'Ah, Susan Blackwell. She knows how important this tie is?'

I nodded. 'I don't know her, funnily enough, she's just taken over, but I'm pretty sure everyone knows what's riding on this one.'

'Pay her a call. Put the fear of God into her. If that don't work, mention me.'

There was obedient laughter.

I would. I would call on Miss Blackwell. I would enthuse her. I would make her aware of the many long arduous hours of dedication and sweat which several hundred young people had expended in order to bring Newton Hall to this propitious possibility. It would be my last act as sports secretary. I would then spend two undivided, totally concentrated, absolutely undiverted weeks in complete sacrificial dedication on the altar of my Part A examinations. Nothing, I told myself, nothing on God's beautiful earth would under any circumstances prevent me.

We shouldn't talk like that. We really shouldn't. We should know better.

41

'Oh hullo, you're the Sports Man aren't you?' she said, only her head visible around the door. 'Come to give me a pep talk?'

It was a clear, mellow, extremely feminine voice with a little bit of childlike innocent enquiry about it. The sort of voice that has men buckling on their armour. She seemed to have the face to go with it too. Short, honey-coloured hair that curled around her ears and temples, eyes as big and brown as a fawn's and cheeks like two ripening peaches, even down to the soft dusting of faint golden hair.

'I've, er. I've come to wish you luck.'

'Oh goody.' Her smile seemed to say that would be the biggest treat she could imagine. 'In that case, come in and have a cuppa.'

I followed her in, closing the door behind me.

I had noticed that there was a marked difference between the rooms of the male and female occupants of the university. With few exceptions, the men lived in places where they studied, slept, and stored one or two books, a few clothes and an amazing amount of stereo equipment. The women lived in homes. Discussing the phenomenon with Phil Martin, something he callously referred to as the 'nesting instinct', he had told me in all seriousness of a former girlfriend who crocheted covers for desk lamps 'so you didn't burn your fingers on them'. Susan hadn't quite gone to those extremes, but the personalizing touches were very evident: an extremely green and healthy fig plant filtered the window light; there was a large pointillist print of a Provence picnic scene over the desk, an attempt to convert the bed into a couch with a cover and a scattering of cushions, a cane occasional table with a tray and tea things.

The hockey stick and boots were plainly visible between bed and desk.

The room only had one chair. She motioned towards the bed. I plonked myself amongst the cushions, kicking off my shoes, and watched her busily clatter about amongst cups and saucers.

'I must say, I'm terrified about Sunday,' she said, as if explaining the nervous clatter. This was Friday evening. 'I wish this hadn't all fallen on us. We're not that good now we've lost Sissy and Mike. Mike was our real star. I wish they hadn't asked me to take over from him as captain. He has to keep giving me pep talks. I feel . . .'

'Honoured?'

'Petrified. Will there be a lot of people there?'

'Well yes, I expect so. Certainly a hundred or more. It is a decider for the championships. We need you to win. Or the indoor pentathlon team.'

'Golly!' She froze for a moment while spooning in tea and stared straight ahead. Then she plugged in the kettle with very much more determination than you'd have thought it warranted.

Now that I could see her clearly, I had time to note the contours of what fashion editors call the 'fuller figure', though without a hint of flabbiness – ample, youthful, firm. She was wearing jeans and a terrain-following teeshirt which brought out the nature of the curves beautifully. I saw her hair was actually a shade lighter than honey, and it bobbed in a playful echo whenever she moved her head; pixie-like, boyish, very sexy. I found myself reflecting on things only tenuously connected to her hockey-playing. Then my mind cast its moorings and glided away on a pleasant little sea of speculation, until she yanked on one of the guy ropes.

'And I suppose horrid Norman Schulz will be there too?'

'I'd be very surprised if he weren't,' I answered, recovering.

'Ugh! He scares the living daylights out of me.' She grimaced. I had a mental image of myself interposing my body between Susan and a fire-breathing Norman, hand on the hilt of my sword, eyes narrowing, jaw set in determination.

'He has our best interests at heart,' I assured her, 'he just doesn't empathize well with modern youth.'

'He's horrid,' she said with female finality. I couldn't help wondering if she expressed herself as lucidly in examination papers.

She bent to a little cupboard with sliding doors at the far end of the room and began emptying biscuits from a tin onto a plate. A tautly denim-clad expanse of Rubenesque bottom and upper thigh presented itself to me and bobbed seductively. I clenched my teeth in an effort to prevent a prolonged sigh from developing into a lecherous moan.

Where do we get our notions of sexuality? Are they hidden deep in the subconscious, product of precognitive experience in childhood, or even inherited at the breast? My mother was on the cuddly side, I remember. Are they written in our genes? Or simply an aspect of our appreciation of form and geometry? At any rate, I found myself looking forward very much to Sunday, when I would have the chance to see Susan Blackwell in a hockey skirt.

She poured tea and handed me a cup and saucer which I gratefully accepted and immediately strategically positioned in order to conceal my brief, but now thankfully subsiding appreciation of her figure, then she sank into the armchair, and began sipping tea. She sipped and smiled. Smiled again. Crossed her legs and began to bounce her foot. Sip. Sip. Bounce. Bounce.

She threw me a puzzled and vaguely concerned look, as if wondering what on earth I was staring at. Her pensive face disappeared briefly behind her tea cup.

There was a pause, during which I was deciding whether she wasn't the loveliest thing I'd ever laid eyes on. It lengthened. It became uncomfortable, then embarrassing. It declared its firm intention to see out the millennium.

Then we both began talking at the same moment.
'Sorry?'
'No – please.'
'No – you.'
'Oh, I wasn't going to say anything important – please go ahead.'
'I was just wondering,' I said, totally unaware but interested, in a curiously detached way, to see what my brain was going to come up with, 'which position you like best.' I nodded towards the hockey stick, winking intimately, sportsman to sportsman, realizing a mortifying fraction of a second later that this could be construed as a lurid gesture towards the pillow.
She coloured deeply and gulped. Oh no!
'Hockey. Which position. Not . . .' Oh damn and blast and hell. From the moment I had discovered I liked her I had begun behaving exactly like a fumbling, youthful virgin. It would never have occurred to me to consider that this might be because I *was* a fumbling, youthful virgin.
She looked like a frightened animal about to bolt. Then she began gabbling nervously.
'Centre forward! I had a spell at inside forward which is where I used to play for the school, well actually I began at full back but Miss Cochrain, our teacher, said I'm a little bit squeamish in the tackle so I've moved gradually forward in fact I've played nearly every position except goalkeeper but I must say I do feel happier in the forward line it's just that when Mike got injured and had to pack in, well not permanently but he won't play for us again this season, although he does spend an awful lot of time helping me, he's always telling me I need supporting, giving a boost bringing on, well after Mike it was really a straight choice between Sissy and me but then lo and behold Sissy went and got herself injured, falling off a bicycle for goodness' sake, so you see there really wasn't any choice because we don't really have another shooter in the team except Jasib Kahn and he's such a gentleman he insisted on me taking it on, captain and all.'

She stopped abruptly, panting and exhausted.

Well, that certainly filled a gap old girl, I thought to myself. Shame you couldn't have rationed it a bit. Spread it out – over the next six months for example. Just because I'm so socially inept as to create a conversational drought doesn't mean I have to be deluged in a verbal monsoon.

'Oh I see,' I said.

There was a pause. Alarmingly, we felt it expanding again, like resurgent flood water. She moved to dam it.

'Would you like to hear some music?'

This was slowly becoming a nightmare. We'd be discussing the weather next.

'Oh. Yes. Why not?'

Blowing slightly, she selected a record and switched on the stereo. Simon and Garfunkel's voices flooded the room with the story of the boy from humble origins who learned that taking on the world is a very one-sided contest.

We listened in silence until the acoustic guitar tripped off its final little flourish.

'That song reminds me of my father,' I said.

'Your father's a boxer!' she asked incredulously.

'No, no. He's a lorry driver.'

'Oh, I *see*.' She hurriedly stressed her understanding, like someone attempting to humour an unpredictable idiot.

That was it. Finito. I had a momentary image of Sissy and Mike screeching with laughter as she recounted the whole episode, twirling a pointed figure at her temple. 'Well he seemed all right at first – you know, very practical and businesslike – but after a while he seemed to get a bit vacant and disconnected, as if he'd forgotten why he came, and then towards the end, well, it was like playing for time until the police arrived. Really, you know these sporting types. I mean *odd*.'

My social graces seemed to have deserted me under pressure. I thought I'd better at least establish my sanity.

I took a deep breath and began speaking very slowly and deliberately, determined not to be interrupted or put off.

'No Susan, you don't see. You can't see because I haven't explained it yet.'

She went very quiet, then said softly, 'I see – I mean . . .'

'The song has certain themes. These themes seem to me to be reflected in my father's life.' She nodded obediently.

'First of all there's the running away from home at a very early age. It's not explained why this happens, but you're given to understand the boy is in some kind of trouble. This running away leaves him almost destitute. Desperately searching for work. Any work. Also yearning for home and very lonely. Er . . .' I looked quickly into her eyes, then away, 'sexually lonely. He's obviously obliged to lower his expectations and survive in a world in which life is never easy and at times bitterly hard. He becomes one of life's survivors. And grateful for that. Asking no more than to get through. A fighter.'

She stared at me without speaking, but her eyes were gradually losing that flittering, threatened quality. My voice mellowed a bit.

'My father was an Irish immigrant in the Thirties. His family were reasonably wealthy – farm people – but he was disinherited by his father after a quarrel. He never talked about it a great deal. He won't discuss anything much unless he's pushed. He never opens up. Pride, I suppose.

'He came to England virtually with what he stood up in, and took what work he could get, mostly casual labouring. You know about those times. Walking to work to save bus fares. Humans toiling like horses, but determined to give a good day's work for a day's pay because that was what was right. Earning just enough to keep going, with your luxuries limited to a couple of pints and ten Woodbines. There was a whole generation of them. Asking little and expecting less. The generation that stopped Hitler.

'And yearning for home. You know what Irishmen are. You should hear him sing in the bath. We tell him there aren't any Irishmen left in Ireland, they're all over here singing about how good it is over there.'

I smiled. She smiled back.

'He had a lousy war as a prisoner to the Japanese. They were treated like very inferior oxen. And he lost his wife early, leaving him to bring up three boys on his own. It wouldn't have occurred to him to complain any more than it would occur to him to worry about succeeding or failing. It was simply a question of getting on with it. Taking it day by day and fighting through. No big victories. No big defeats.

'He's hard, my old man, as hard as nails. But like the person in the song, he's a born survivor. He takes everything life throws at him, leading with his chin. And at the end of it, he won't come out on top, he probably won't even come out smiling, but he'll be on his feet.'

I gave her the lyrics of the last verse, line by line – the image of the boxer with his feet planted firmly and his fists raised, flinching and wincing at each new cut, but never dropping his head.

There was a slightly embarrassed silence. I smiled, sheepishly. Carried away a bit. Well, she'd asked for it. I'd sooner she remembered me as studious than stupid.

'That's really interesting, Tim,' she said.

'Is it?' Try as I might, I couldn't keep the surprised squeak out of my voice.

'You must love your father very much.'

I snorted. 'You don't get near enough for that. I'm not even sure my mother did. Respect. Yes, I suppose I respect him.'

'And what about your parents?' I asked after a while.

Her face lit up. Whatever they did, she obviously thought a great deal of them.

'Daddy's a detective chief superintendent of police in Hemel Hempstead,' she beamed.

'Is he now?' I couldn't help raising my eyebrows.

'Oh, don't look like that. Daddy's very sweet. He's so serious and deliberate.' She squared her shoulders, tucked in her chin and deepened her voice to a half-growl like a child trying to be fierce. 'Now Susan. Certain evidence has come to my notice which suggests that you've adopted the habit of smoking cigarettes. I don't wish you to make any statement on the subject at this point in time, but I would request you to register the fact that I don't entirely approve.'

I chuckled.

'Mummy calls him Plod. She has done since they were engaged.'

'Any more at home like you?'

There were. Two sisters whom she referred to by their initials as Jay and Gee. They seemed nice people. I told her about the rest of my family. We traded views on the university. We exchanged experiences of the subjects we were studying. Hers was English. Suddenly, quite effortlessly, we were talking.

'Engineering,' she said admiringly. 'How tremendously practical and sensible and capable you must be. Do you like it?'

'Oh, well enough.' I couldn't hide the traces of – of what? Disappointment? Disillusionment? A suspicion of wanting in aptitude? I hardly knew myself. Whatever it was, she noticed.

'You don't exactly sound raring to design and build your first bridge.'

'I suppose not. It's just . . . I don't know. Somehow I expected it to be – well, *exciting*. Was that silly of me?'

'Gracious, no,' she said, seeing immediately what I meant. 'I took English because I love poetry. The gift of transcribing beauty and emotion and experience perfectly into words which multiply the beauty by virtue of their coming together.

"Kissing with golden face the meadows green,
Gilding pale streams with heavenly alchemy."

Bill Shakespeare, that. Gowers asks if you can imagine a more perfect or lovelier couplet, describing what the rising sun does to dew-covered grass and a sleepy river on a summer morning. I expected to spend three enchanted years bathing my mind, embalming my soul and armouring my intelligence with the distilled philosophy of the last four centuries ennobled into words of beauty. Most of the time I find myself poking about in poems as if they were dead frogs staked out on a biologist's dissection slab, and scrawling pages of drivel defining a piece of accentual verse as Anglo-Saxon or sprung rhythm, or explaining whether variation in metre has been achieved by elision or substitution, and if substitution, was it a pyrrhic or an anapaest or a . . .' She bunched her fists and shook her head in mock exasperation, making a sound which came out something like 'kkkrrr'.

I found myself nervously eager to keep up the contact.

'I'm fond of poetry too,' I told her.

'Oh, yes? What sort?'

'Mm, mainly modern.'

'Who in particular?'

I thought quickly. The names of the current England back row tripped lightly off my tongue.

'Never heard of them,' she said, but in a tone quite prepared to concede ignorance. 'Not really my period, though. Funny, they all have namesakes in the England rugby team.'

Any embarrassment I'd felt was suffused in the glow of elation at discovering how much we had in common.

'You could always write your own,' I suggested.

'Poems? God knows, I try.'

'You'll have to let me read some of them.'

'Not yet. When I know you better.'

A lovely warmth began to spread through me as the implications of that slowly sank in. I stood up.

'Brethren, we shall all now stand and sing hymn number 123 in your prayer-books, "Praise the Lord, the lady likes me".'

She paused, a bit taken aback, then this time really laughed, delightfully melodically, diving forward into her open hands to smother her smiles.

Sitting down again would have been somehow inappropriate. Besides, I wanted to quit while I was ahead.

'Must be off,' I said casually. Wishful thinking, or did her sweet little mouth droop a bit at the corners? An idea began forming slowly and my heart started pumping. Thumpety. Thumpety. We moved towards the door.

'I suppose you have your Part A's coming up too?'

'Rather.' Her voice sobered dramatically, as if confirming an impending leg amputation or a posting to Soligorsk in the remoter Urals.

'Been working hard?'

'You bet.'

'Me too.' Lying through your teeth is the easiest thing in the world if you want something badly enough.

I gave the impression of spontaneous inspiration.

'What say we take tomorrow off? Forget the exams for a day. Discover Leicestershire by bus.'

Thumpety . . . thumpety . . . thumpety . . .

She appeared to be thinking.

'It's a Saturday anyway. Relax you for the big match the day after.'

Thumpety . . . Thumpety . . . Thumpety . . .

Her eyes lowered. She suddenly became very serious. Of course, I'd been far too quick. Blown it. Embarrassing misunderstanding. Just because a girl's nice to you and pretends to laugh at a couple of silly quips, you have to take it a stage too far and ruin everything.

Apologize. Make light of it. Say 'Of course, you must be very busy.' Go on. Now.

'Of course—'

'Thank you, Tim. I think I'd like that very much.'

'You would?' My voice pitched like a rusty hinge.

'The weather forecast is very good.' She raised her eyes again. 'Do you have a bicycle? I know some lovely runs.'

I bit my lip.

'A bike? Well, I do – sort of. It's just, I don't know where some of the bits are just now.' Room 9 Block 12 had been making no idle threat.

A touch of anxiety clouded her face again as if a promisingly convalescent mental patient had just answered a perfectly sane question with 'Chirrup'.

'No, it's all right Susan, really. I'm pretty sure that the front wheel is hanging on that oak tree outside the library, and someone told me the saddle has been placed in the arms of a plaster gnome in the Vice Chancellor's back garden.'

That didn't help. She appeared to be doing some fast thinking.

'I'll borrow one,' I said quickly. 'Pick you up. Nine o'clock. Sleep tight.' I closed the door on her somewhat bemused face.

Halfway down the corridor, I had a really bad attack of examination gut. 'Answer FIVE questions, at least ONE from each section but not more than TWO from Section B. Use a SEPARATE ANSWER BOOK for each section,' the voice inside my head boomed. I clutched my stomach and leaned against the wall for support. Gradually, the sweating subsided and the booming quietened.

I started whistling, like you do as a child in the dark when you want to frighten off the willies, and I broke into a trot. Cross-country running, now there was something I hadn't done for goodness knows how long. I wondered if I might squeeze in a quickie this evening. Thinking about the next day, I gave a slight hop and clicked my heels in mid-air.

42

Standing behind Susan, I watched the last of the rain drip onto her hair, matting and caking it to the consistency of sodden straw, then running in little rivulets down the back of her neck.

Suddenly she said, 'Wheeee!'

Another duck zoomed in to land on the lake in front of us, very imperfectly skidding and splashing, flailing its wings as if it were frightened of drowning. Apparently surprised that it floated, it drew in its wings with exactly the same gesture as an indignant mother-in-law folding her arms, then cast darting little glances around the lake, an overt cover-up job, daring anyone to laugh at its undignified arrival.

It was now late afternoon. We had left the university in early morning, just as the clouds broke.

Both of us felt something of the exhilaration of being let out. I hadn't been off the campus for weeks. Susan only occasionally to shop for essentials. We had spent an ecstatically soggy day, freewheeling between the surrounding market towns and villages, doing everything the townsman does when let loose on the countryside. Riding two abreast down leafy dripping lanes too narrow to let cars past and making faces at the irate motorists; waving like happy children at the hard-pressed drivers of tractors, sunk up to their rims in mud, and being totally ignored; mocking the earnest expressions of masticating cows; being given sage advice by farm-hands; treading in cowpats, leaving gates open and having walking sticks brandished at us from two hundred yards; acclaiming the aroma of silage in West Country accents; lunching off cheese and pickles and barley wine in a thatched and gabled pub called the Eagle and Child; reprimanding anglers for cruelty to worms, being amazed at the sight of something wild and free like a pheasant or a hare, throwing stones into streams, waving red rags at bulls (with absolutely no effect), and picking (and later discarding) bunches of wild flowers.

Now we were back in Lanchester, watching the ducks on the small ornamental lake in the middle of the Alderman Hyde Park, not to be confused with the slightly bigger and grandioser affair in London which was possibly named after a completely different Mr Hyde. The rain had laid off, but the place was deserted. Only Susan was around to listen to my exposition on the aerodynamics of the duck.

'Wheeee!' she interrupted again. 'Don't they fly fast.'

'They have to. Being fat, round and heavy, they need a huge thrust-to-weight ratio just to avoid dropping out of the sky. Watch them when they're about to land. They spread their wings and angle them like landing flaps, rapidly trading speed for lift. That gives them that little upward glide. Then they spread their webbed feet desperately to act as an air brake, hope for the best and go for the splashdown. Rather unstable and very empirical. They couldn't get away with it on dry land.'

We watched and listened as they honked contentedly. Susan still had her back to me. On impulse, I slipped my hands around her waist and joined them in front of her, letting her damp warmth rest against my cheek.

'They're still awfully sweet,' she said, keeping very still.

A shaft of sunlight, the only one of the day, suddenly broke cloud and turned the sulky olive water to dancing silver. The ripples flashed like emeralds.

I turned Susan around, bent forward and brushed a very gentle kiss onto her lips.

She returned it, tender as a child, first on my throat and then just below my ear.

I put my hands behind her head to steady it and make sure I didn't miss, then dived tongue first into her mouth.

Surfacing a minute or so later to breathe, I opened my eyes briefly and noticed that, as often happens when strong sunshine follows rain, vapour was rising like fog from the footpaths and lake. I looked down and our damp clothes were beginning to steam. We were smouldering as if on fire.

It was a tender moment, but that was too good to miss.

'Lord, no-one ever had that effect before,' I said, pretending to dab out flames, but not very energetically.

I'd expected her to laugh, but she didn't.

'No,' she said simply.

Her lovely big brown eyes gazed frankly and intently into mine. Accepting. Trusting. Wanting.

I suddenly realized, with a thrill that was part yearning to give, part urgency to take, and undeniably part something close to fear, that tonight my long years of innocence, punctuated but not concluded by Sharon, would finally be ended.

Like a herd of elephants with indigestion, a hundred voices groaned in unison. Susan, with a balletic swing of her pleated skirt, cracked loose a shot which showed a lot of panache, and a lot of her knickers, but not much accuracy. The ball sped wide of a virtually open goal. It was the third sitter she had missed, in a match in which she had featured primarily by not featuring at all. Always in the wrong place, always a yard too slow, always second best in the tackle, always wide of the mark. Only I knew why because only I was in the same condition. My heart ached for her.

'Say, who's payin ya, honey?' Ever tactful, that was Norman from about ten yards down the line of supporters which bordered both sides of the pitch, two deep. I glanced at him. His breath clouded in the cold air, his jowls sank sullenly into the upturned collar of a leather coat. He snorted like a bull.

On my left, Howard's Welsh singsong chimed up.

'Lousy shot.' He paused reflectively, then added in a much lower voice, 'Nice arse though.'

I couldn't resist a penetrating stare and a high-minded, deprecating tut.

From behind came Phil Martin's scouse drawl.

'She doesn't know what day it is, does she? She spent last night either gett'n' bladdered or havin' some gentleman show her heaven.'

I ground my teeth and breathed out slowly without turning round.

'Nonsense.' This was Nicholas on my right, uncomfortable in, for him, unfamiliar surroundings, banging leather-gloved hands together and stamping thick boots into the mud, prolific enough after yesterday's rain. 'I know that young lady well. A charming girl. She's probably just suffering from overwork prior to the examinations.'

Christ, how could all of them be right!

'Knock it off fellahs,' I said testily, 'she happens to be a very nice, intelligent, sensitive person.'

I was aware of a turning of heads and a raising of eyebrows, without actually observing them. Phil cleared his throat conspicuously.

'Well, ehm, we won't be so indiscreet as to pose the obvious question, like.'

There was a pause.

'Or why change the habits of a lifetime,' he went on. 'How the hell do you know?'

How did I know?

. . . Sometimes people say things that stay with you for the rest of your life. It may be because they're very right, or very wrong, or very interesting or very appropriate. It may be the words they use or the tone of voice or the expression on their face. It may simply be the circumstances.

Susan and I were to have a deep and lasting relationship. We were to share a thousand experiences. We were to remain lovers throughout the rest of our university careers and part as friends thereafter, richer and happier, thankful for having met.

But the words that would remain with me the longest were those she said to me shortly after we had made love for the first time.

'Oh well, at least I'm not a virgin any more.'

Words like those leave a lasting impression on a man.

Our bicycle excursion had ended thus. Getting back from Alderman Hyde Park to Susan's room, with a minor detour to pick up a bottle of wine from the off-licence and a major detour at the university hamburger bar, had taken approximately three and a half hours. That made it the longest sustained erection of my life. Unfortunately, only the final six seconds of it were put to productive use.

Susan naked was every bit as beautiful as Susan clothed had promised she would be. Skin the colour of milk and the texture of satin, full arabesque curves, ample but as firm as an apple. Her deep trusting eyes flickered seductively beneath me, and her hair turned from honey to gold in the half-light. It was glorious. It was wonderful. It was mind-blowing.

But it was very brief.

Afterwards, I felt only slightly less subdued than she. Premature ejaculation hadn't entered my vocabulary yet, mainly because ejaculation only just had. But my poor willy, this being the first time he'd been subjected to this sort of treatment, felt as if he'd been clamped in a vice and then had his foreskin forcibly regressed with the aid of a nick from a razor blade, followed by a quick yank and sharp tear down one side.

Susan's less than euphoric comment on our first love-making was only really confirming what I'd suspected.

'I'll put some music on. Do you like Baroque?'

Susan turned to music like a mum to the kettle.

'Never heard of him,' I answered. As Billy Bibby had once pointed out to me, my education had been so purely technical.

She rose without switching on the light. Haunted strings bathed the room in rich melancholy. I caught sight of her naked outline. The purest, most intense form of beauty on earth. I gazed in wonder and admiration which soon, with the rampant wantonness of youth, turned to desire. To my astonishment, my little member started to rise again like a wounded and battle-weary soldier to the national anthem.

'Uh-uh,' she whispered as she settled into bed. 'No rushing.'

So we talked.

Through Vivaldi. Through Albinoni. Through Corelli.

And talked.

Through Bach. Through Telemann. Through Tomasini.

We must have talked for slightly longer than we intended.

Grey dawn was filtering through the curtains before our caresses became less friendly and more purposeful. This time she held me off, made me wait until she was ready, guided me. Despite her whispered encouragement to slow down, take it easy, make it gentle, I felt like I was struggling to prevent the inevitable, supporting the insupportable, stemming the unstoppable. It was too exciting, too new, too gorgeous. I began threshing again like an uncontrollable machine. Things drew irrevocably towards their conclusion.

Suddenly, that Judgement Day voice which had been plaguing me for weeks finally came to my aid.

'Demonstrate from first principles,' it bellowed, 'when a sheet of metal is deformed in uniform bending conditions, such that its width remains constant as the sheet progressively proceeds from the plastic to the elastic condition, that the ratio between the values, as predicted by the Huber Von Mises and Tresca criteria, for the maximum principal stress in the surface where yielding begins, is the reciprocal of the square root of one minus gamma plus gamma squared, where gamma is Poisson's ratio.'

And I did, losing sigma in the third line but miraculously regaining it in the fifth. It cancels out in the seventh anyway.

My concentration was extreme, but not on the physical act I was performing. For fifteen minutes, my movements became rhythmical and mechanical. Time enough for Susan to know she'd been to bed with someone, at least. Robotic, yes, but an improvement on six seconds. Sex between teenagers has been aptly described as a vigorous physical activity in which one party is trying desperately to come whilst the other is trying desperately not to. Or, as Oscar Wilde had it – no, that's not a recommendation, I mean as Oscar Wilde said – 'If youth knew. If age could.' Only he wasn't talking about sex. Or was he?

I put the square root sign around the one minus gamma plus gamma squared. Susan moaned from far back in her throat.

All of a sudden, we were sharing something wonderful. She had the sleepiest, dreamiest of smiles on her lovely face, her breath came in sighs that halted and shivered and her forehead and cheeks were dappled with warm salty dew. I kissed it away drop by drop, bit her neck with the gentleness of a lion carrying a cub, buried my face in her damp shining hair.

'Now!' she whispered urgently.

I cradled her head like a baby and pushed hard. Again. Again.

Right at the very end, she hissed my name into my ear three times. Harshly, urgently, as if it had been forced from her under torture.

Drowsily, I wondered whether Susan Blackwell or the course in Applied Strength of Materials had figured more prominently in my first tentative steps in sexuality. I drew her to me. We lay dreamily folded up in each other.

We had just drifted into that semi-real world of warmth and contentment and abandon that precedes deep sleep, when two of the hockey team came to pick her up, thumping rudely on the door.

'Because I know her quite well,' I said to Phil, casting my eyes around the hockey field.

'Since when?'

'Since Friday.'

Nobody said anything. I could feel them exchanging surprised glances

'Nice gerl,' he muttered, vaguely searching the horizon.

The final whistle blew. Against all conceivable form,

we had lost one–nil. The supporters, almost exclusively ours, began to drift away, picking a haphazard route across the muddy fields back to Hall, slow, subdued, like a routed army.

I moved along the touch-line to intercept Susan. She was dragging her stick, head down, looking very miserable. I decided it was time we went public. I waved to Howard and Charles.

'Up to you now whack,' I said to Phil, breaking into a trot, and, running backwards for a few paces, pointed straight at him. 'Noot'n expects . . .' I shouted, Normanizing Nelson.

I put my arms around her, kissed her like a brother, told her to forget it, it was my stupid fault. She gave me a very tired smile.

I touched her cheek with the back of my hand. A lot of people were staring at us.

She motioned towards her team-mates. 'Want to bet the news reaches the bar before we do?'

'A half of shandy with me and the team, then sleep.'

She seemed to like the idea of that.

'I say Susan,' said a strident male voice from a few yards behind me, 'judging by the effect it has on your admirers, you'll have to play like that more often.' The accent was cut-glass.

I turned. A thin-faced young man with a very straight nose and high cheek-bones smiled at me, more than a little sarcastically. With his nose and plastered-down hair parted in the middle, he looked a bit like an Afghan hound. On his feet were a pair of green wellingtons which had seen a lot of wear, at fêtes and agricultural shows, and his sheepskin car coat was meant to put him in the MGBGT set.

'Mike?' I said to Susan.

'How on earth did you know?'

'Call it male intuition.'

I put my arm around her shoulders and walked her

towards him. He ignored me and addressed Susan, taking a set of car keys from his pocket. I was spot on. There was the MG key-ring.

'Still OK for our pub lunch, Suzie?'

Things were in a bad way. I was physically knackered. I was in emotional turmoil, possibly, God help us, in love. The sports championship now rested on the shoulders of the most errant bunch of wasters since the Hole-in-the-Wall Gang. My Part A's were one more lost weekend nearer. This guy must have been pussyfooting around Susan for months.

Having your back to the wall makes you wonderfully direct.

'Shove off, creep,' I said, steering Susan past him.

43

The fifth member of the indoor pentathlon team had long since recovered from his Newcastle Brown incident, meaning I was no longer a permanent member of the gang. The following Wednesday evening found me in my room, hunched over an Aluminium-Silicon Eutectic diagram, vainly attempting to concentrate on making sketches of the microstructures of a fast-cooled 1.5% silicon alloy, a slow-cooled 1.5% silicon alloy, and a fast-cooled 11% silicon alloy. Stuff you can always use.

About nine o'clock, there was a shuffling outside in the corridor, and I turned to see a sheet of paper slide under the door. Feeling my pulse start to quicken, I put down my pen, stood up very slowly and deliberately, and walked towards it like someone approaching a prostrate man-eating tiger which might be dead or only sleeping. My heart was beating so fast the blood started singing in my ears. It was only at this moment I realized how much it mattered. Standing in front of the paper, I bent forward, looked down and read:

WE LOST.
I'M MOST AWFULLY SORRY.
PHIL.

I breathed in deeply and then let the air out in a long slow sigh. Well, that was that. Silly damn thing to get so worked up about anyway. As if there weren't more important things to worry about. And how! It was still worth it. Winning isn't everything, second from fifteen was still a pretty creditable performance wasn't it?

I was interested and somewhat disconcerted to note that my hands were shaking violently.

As I stood there, deflated, empty, somehow glad to be alone but wondering how on earth I would be able to concentrate now on the solid solubility of silicon in aluminium, a second piece of paper slid smoothly under the door and perfectly covered the first one.

On it was written:

ONLY KIDDING
CONGRATULATIONS CHAMP

I opened the door. There stood Phil. His frizzy orange mane was even more disordered than usual and his eyes appeared to be a bit glazed. The pentathlon team frequently went in to bat with a pint or two under their belts to 'steady the hand' and evidently the post-match celebrations were in full swing. Phil had a bar towel around his shoulders after the manner of a cloak, and a huge pewter ashtray on his head.

'You bastard,' I said slowly.

'Hail Caesar,' he shrieked, ignoring me completely. His right fist banged his left shoulder in salutation. 'I am come from the capitol, where many citizens, senators and handmaidens, who do love you dearly, are gathered in your honour to feast at your triumph and, with a bit of luck, orgy afterwards.'

Patiently, still recovering from a very nasty shock, I

rubbed the corners of my eyes with thumb and forefinger, folded my arms and looked at him, head askew. 'Phil, I am pleased. I am grateful. I am, as they say, over the moon. But nothing, nothing, nothing, would entice me to come to the bar tonight.'

'Good!' he shouted. 'Because that is *exactly* what I am offering you. Nothing!' He displayed empty hands in illustration.

My old friend's authoritarian, resonant tones rang forth: 'SILENT and CORDLESS calculators are permitted, but candidates are reminded that to obtain FULL credit, ALL WORKINGS should be shown in the margin.'

'In that case I'll get my jacket,' I told him.

44

I hadn't been to the Admin block since the day I registered. It was nearly new and typically 1960s. Polystyrene-ceilings, light aluminium frames, hardboard walls. The floor creaked as you walked like in a Portakabin. Some of the university buildings had been standing for a hundred and twenty years. This one was built to last all of ten.

This time I was here as the result of a summons, a curt one-liner instructing me to present myself at room E111 on the last Monday of term, for what was termed Post Examination Counselling. In some student circles the PEC was referred to as a Pre-Expulsion Court of Enquiry.

It certainly didn't look like any picnic. As I entered the room, three of them were ranged around an empty chair. There was a grey-haired portly chap I didn't know behind a desk and, flanking him, on his left, my tutor Dr Mountford, and on his right the kindly professor with the pince-nez who had first interviewed me and my dad all that time ago – more than a year – and of whom I had since caught very occasional glimpses in corridors here and there.

None of them smiled a welcome.

The portly chap introduced himself as chairman of something–something board and a member of Senate. None of it meant much to me. I missed his name and was too cowed to ask him to repeat it. 'Dr Mountford and Professor Callaghan, you know,' he said. I said I did. He indicated the chair and I sat down. The atmosphere was such that I had half expected to be made to stand.

'I presume you know why you've been asked to appear here?' he began. He was a Lancastrian like myself, but years of living elsewhere had softened his accent. He still said 'ah' instead of 'I' when he was talking about himself, and his vowels remained a bit guttural, but it was very much a case of taking one to know one.

'I imagine so,' I answered clearly.

Judging by the rather cold stare he gave me, he didn't seem to like the sound of that. Too defiant, perhaps. It was unintentional. I wasn't being defiant, I was just facing the music.

'Well, perhaps I ought to clarify,' he went on. 'Taken of themselves, the results of your recent examinations would not be sufficient to allow you to remain on the course. They are,' he held out his right hand, palm down, and shook it slightly, 'marginal – but tending towards being just under the line rather than just over.'

'Yes.'

'Now, let's be perfectly clear. In such cases, the University has every right to have your grant terminated and compel you to relinquish your place on the course. I needn't remind you, there are several candidates for each position here, and we often have to turn away good students simply because courses are fully subscribed.'

'No.'

'Pardon?'

'No. You don't need to remind me. I understand that.'

Again he seemed slightly put out by my answer.

He arranged his notebook so its sides were at a precise

right angle to the edges of the desk, then positioned his pen perfectly parallel to the top edge of the notebook. Finicky. Evident fusspot. Probably spent his life on committees. I didn't like him. Unfortunately, it seemed to be mutual.

'However, there are often extenuating circumstances. For that reason, we interview the student in question in order to get a feel for the background to each particular case.'

He seemed to expect me to say something. I didn't. It wasn't that I intended to be sullen, it was just that I felt so damned miserable. I looked at the professor and Dr Mountford. They kept their eyes on the notebooks that were resting on their knees. They seemed a little embarrassed by the whole affair, unlike the chap behind the desk, who was revelling in it. He leaned back and surveyed me over the top of his swelling midriff, rubbing his fingertips together. He had that air of pedantic gentility that one associates with eighteenth-century courtiers. I half expected him to produce a snuffbox.

'Now in our experience, there are several factors which often influence a candidate's examination performance adversely, assuming of course that he's considered academically equal to the task. He might have suffered protracted or intermittent illness, for example. He may have found difficulty in making the emotional adjustment from a home or school environment to life on a campus. He may get sidetracked into one or more of the many extracurricular interests which abound at any university. Or he may,' here he looked down, this one was plainly a bit distasteful, 'get mixed up with a member of the opposite sex.' His voice made clear that this last factor was the least forgivable. He produced a large handkerchief, shook it extravagantly, blew his nose and then enquired over the top of it, 'Would you say any of these circumstances applied in your case?'

I breathed deeply. Making excuses is belittling. Discussing your personal life is embarrassing. Combine the two and you have a situation which is more than a little unpleasant.

I raised my head to a corner of the room. One of the cheap polystyrene tiles was already stained and warped by a slow leak from the pipe which obviously ran above it. Warm water? Central heating? Bloody Sixties architecture.

'Well?' he prompted.

I shifted uneasily in my chair.

'I er, I got perhaps a bit carried away with Hall committee business.'

'Yes,' he agreed. 'We've already heard something about that from Dr Mountford.' He bowed and made a flowery 'my learned colleague' gesture with his left hand. 'And it's a matter we shall follow up further.'

His pen appeared to be lying one degree out of horizontal. He corrected it swiftly, delicately, pinkie up.

'Anything else?'

I looked down. Silence.

His voice took on a hint of agitation.

'You came to us with the highest possible recommendations from your school. A very good school. Your previous academic record indicates that you should have no intellectual difficulties with the course whatsoever.' For the first time I thought that perhaps he wasn't out to hatchet me. 'There must be some reason for such a poor showing. Frankly, we thought you were capable of more. Much more.'

Oh, you bet, sunshine, I said to myself. A thousand times more. Intellectually I could eat the course for breakfast and that's not being arrogant. But what was I supposed to say? That science and a dream got mixed up inside me? That I had expected to be stimulated, not bored rigid? That I had been so buried and engulfed in the sheer volume of the product of other people's brains that I was given no time nor chance to produce something with my own? That Norman Schulz lifted me by providing me with a challenge I wasn't sure I was equal to? And that at a critical stage in the examination preparation process, every time I opened a book or a file, a pair of brown eyes as deep as the universe looked back at me, and an urgent voice inside my ear whispered 'Now!'

It was hopeless. Yet the whole thing was so damned unnecessary. I thought of the pride in my father's voice every time he introduced me to a friend in the pub, or a chance encounter in the street. 'You know my son. Our Tim. He's home from university for a day or two.' What would this do to him? I could have wept. I realized abruptly, with a horrified start, that I might. I was close to tears. Oh dear God, not that. Anything but that. I didn't trust myself to speak any more.

'You have nothing further to add,' he said, statement not question, leaden in its finality.

I could hardly hear my own voice. It sounded light-years away.

'No.'

I almost expected him to produce a little black cap and pronounce sentence. But he merely picked up his pen and began scratching away on the pad in front of him. Slowly, neatly – you could almost imagine a great feather quill in his hand. Eventually he looked up.

'The outcome will be conveyed to you by your tutor before the end of term. Thank you Mr Armstrong,' he concluded, looking at me without the hint of an expression.

I stood up slowly. I was aware it hadn't gone well. It wasn't easy to explain, but I hadn't even tried. I had packed in without a fight. Again, I thought of my old man. Would he have gone down without throwing a punch? I stood behind the chair and put my hands on its back.

'Perhaps—'

'Thank you Mr Armstrong,' he broke in firmly.

I looked at each of them in turn. Dr Mountford and the professor kept their eyes on their notebooks, scribbling furiously. I nodded them good day and left the room without looking back.

45

The last night of term, the last night of the academic year, was the occasion in Newton Hall for a huge ball, called, appropriately enough, the Last Night Ball. A student committee, specially convened for the purpose, had been at work for weeks organizing the affair – developing a theme, designing, making and installing decorations, arranging music, putting together a programme and so forth. People were co-opted to assist with all the finesse shown by the Vikings to the virgins of Northumbria in the eighth century, but the result was the high point of the social calendar. A sumptuous meal, a little gentle banter in the form of a couple of topical speeches, a cabaret which usually involved thinly-disguised, highly libellous caricatures of prominent university personalities, and dancing until the early hours.

Each student was allowed to invite one guest from outside Hall. Out of politeness, a lot of people invited their personal tutors. I did too, but for pragmatic reasons. Today was the day I got the verdict.

There was a reception in the small ante-room to the dining-hall. I stood nervously clutching a sherry, waiting for him to arrive. The endless stream of pats on the back, handshakes, squeezed upper arms, thumbs-ups, girly waves, tweaked cheeks and feinted blows to the abdomen to which I had been subjected, led me to believe people were pretty pleased about the Intramural Sports Championship. The trophy, a two-and-a-half-foot art deco torch-bearing youth, circa 1930, formed an imposing centre-piece to the reception area.

Few people seemed inclined to dwell in my company, though. Most of them were probably put off by an inattentiveness, nervous fidgeting, uncharacteristic quiet, without knowing the cause. Official exam results were only published after the end of term.

The light glanced briefly off something by the door, and I saw that it was Mountford's bald head. As he looked around for me, it flashed again off his thick spectacles. I'd never considered before what a perfect parody he made of the mad scientist figure. Give him a white coat and a hunchback assistant, surround him with dials, sparking electrodes and irritating buzzing noises and he'd be perfectly at home in any science fiction B movie.

As I noticed him enter, I found myself momentarily alone with the large-breasted student of American History whom I had met on my very first night at Lanchester almost a year before. More talkative and confident, she had certainly flourished under Norman's dispensation.

In more ways than one. I knew little of these things, but I couldn't help wondering when they were supposed to stop growing. Surely by now? In her place I'd be starting to get worried.

'Yes, you did absolutely splendidly, Tim,' she was saying as Dr Mountford came and stood quietly beside us. 'I must say, I almost offered my services myself, several times. I just love archery. A superb sport. The concentration. The control. But unfortunately, I'm naturally somewhat handicapped.' She laughed nervously.

'Well, yes of course,' I had to agree, struggling to concentrate. 'I suppose it must be virtually impossible.' I suppressed an urge to point with my glass but couldn't divert my eyes in time.

'Oh, it's not so bad with contact lenses,' she ran on. 'But twenty-twenty vision is a must if you wish to take the sport seriously.'

I cleared my throat and quickly averted my gaze.

'Good evening Dr Mountford. Can I get you a drink?'

I was amazed at my own calm. I left them together and went to fetch a couple of sherries from a table in the corner. Perhaps not so calm. Noticing a whisky bottle, I poured myself a neat belt and downed it in one. It bit the back of my throat and then went glowing to work on my jitters like acid on alkali.

I returned with the sherries. As people do on these occasions, Miss Mammaries tripped pleasantly on, determined to attempt artificial respiration on every inane topic of conversation as soon as it expired. Whenever I clubbed something on the head, she would try massaging a little warmth back into it. If I drop-kicked anything into touch, she would obediently retrieve it. Eventually, the expression on my face must have been equivalent to a huge scarlet banner with 'BUGGER OFF!' emblazoned across it in gold.

She left.

We looked directly at one another.

'Well,' he said, pausing about a half-century before continuing, 'you're in. By the skin of your bloody teeth.'

Dr Mountford wasn't given to swearing.

I put down the sherry glass, because I was frightened it was going to shatter in my hand. I looked across at Susan, and gave her an almost imperceptible nod. She closed her eyes and began massaging the bridge of her nose between finger and thumb.

46

Plainly, things wouldn't simply rest there. Throughout the meal, Dr Mountford sat beside me at one of the long tables which, with the exception of the transverse head table where Norman entertained his invited dignitaries, were arranged lengthways, banqueting-hall style, each seating forty or more. Our conversation was desultory. Somehow I couldn't feel elated, simply numbed.

Norman made a bitingly witty speech in which he reaffirmed his lack of any faith in modern youth, but continued to hope. Nicholas replied for the student body, concluding with the presentation to Norman of a bottle of

Château Mouton-Rothschild Premier Cru, the sort of plonk he could only have dreamed of a year earlier. A speech was made by one of the final year on behalf of those who were leaving Lanchester for ever, full of cliquey asides and parochial witticisms, but, in the after-dinner glow, still taken in good part.

'There are of course conditions,' began Dr Mountford in a low voice. I had thought there might be.

'You have to get your priorities sorted out, Tim. We all understand that when you first leave home it can be a bit like a dam bursting. The controls go. You want to spread out in all directions at once. But you have to replace parental discipline with your own. That's what maturity is all about. Planning and controlling your own life. Not just doing whatever takes your interest.'

Well, it wasn't quite as bad as that, but I could see why he should think it might be. And it hadn't occurred to me before, but perhaps I'd lost him a bit of credibility too. The cost might not be all mine, then.

At the top table, Norman slowly got to his feet again and began speaking. 'Ladies and gentlemen,' he announced, 'I do have one further matter to conclude and I think this is an appropriate point in the proceedings . . .' I had counterpoint between the two of them, Norman in my left ear and Dr Mountford to my right. The one held forth in the loud, considered tones of public speech, the other whispered confidentially.

'Fortunately for you, the referees who were contacted stood by you to a man. You've also obviously made your mark here in Hall with your work on the committee, that's plain. And several of the department were prepared to acknowledge notable potential in some of your course-work, though not much of it recent, I hasten to add. I suppose you may as well know, the contribution of your Hall Warden was both crucial and decisive.'

I looked at Norman. 'You bloody lovely Yank,' I said to myself. I was only now beginning to acknowledge the depth of my respect for him.

'. . . Many of you here will recall a former stoodent of Noot'n Hall, Mark Lewis. Mark, a gifted and promising physicist, was tragically killed in a climbing accident last year, shortly before he was due to graduate . . .'

'You aren't being allowed to continue out of sympathy. No-one feels sorry for you, although, being perfectly candid, we thought we saw signs at the PEC that you were feeling a bit sorry for yourself. That's not on. Youthful misjudgement is only human, but you've been given allowance for it in no small measure, don't forget that.'

'. . . Mark's parents, in the midst of the agony of their bereavement, sought in some way to lend sense to this meaningless tragedy. They considered this might be possible via some form of gesture which would not only consecrate Mark's life, but celebrate the youth and love of life of the stoodent body of which he had been so vibrant and happy a member . . .'

Norman's voice was reverent to a degree almost religious. People began to sit up and take notice.

'You've shown capabilities in one direction and potential in others. Now it's up to you to work damned hard and convert that potential into achievement. You owe it to a lot of people and you owe it to this University. As I said before, there have to be conditions.'

'. . . As a result, in what I consider to be a fine and admirable gesture, they have placed in trust a sum of money, from which the interest is to be drawn annually in order to finance the purchase of a small silver goblet, like the one I have in front of me here,' heads strained right and left to get a view, 'as an award to be made to a stoodent member of Noot'n Hall. They have further requested that this award take the name of the "Grace Dieu" award. You will all be aware, of course, of the derivation. "There but for the grace of God . . ." How very appropriate . . .'

I had never seen Norman so sombre. He could have been giving us the Gettysburg address. But Dr Mountford had his piece to say. He was forced to drop his voice to a whisper and turn sideways in his chair to bring his mouth virtually next to my ear. Still, it had to be said and it had to be said now. I tried to feel less like a whipped dog and more appreciative of his discretion.

'As of the first day of next term . . .'

'Ssh!'

That was big Paul from the indoor pentathlon team sitting opposite. It was just for devilment, tweaking the noise of authority. I grimaced at him.

'. . . Mark's parents have stipulated that the award is to be made annually, and here I quote—' Norman picked up a separate piece of paper and blinked towards it, refocusing his eyes, '"To the stoodent who, in the opinion of his fellows, has contributed most to life in Noot'n Hall throughout the current academic year." Each person among you would probably have their own opinion, and their own idea of the best way to ascertain the most deserving member of Hall. In my capacity as Hall Warden, I decided to assemble a committee of twelve stoodents whom I considered to be broadly representative of you as a body, and to instruct them to reach a unanimous decision. You will appreciate, the model is a tried and tested one . . .'

'As of the first day of next term, and for a period of three months reviewable thereafter, you are to sign in at all lectures and tutorials except where absence is certified by a doctor's sick note.'

Back to school then. I nodded.

'. . . Ladies and gentlemen, the esteem and regard of your contemporaries cannot be valued too highly. It is not tainted by bias, it cannot be subject to favouritism, it contains no trace of desire for personal gain. It is praise which is given selflessly. It is praise hard-won. Fully earned. Something to be valued for the rest of your life . . .'

'You will deliver all written coursework and laboratory reports personally, on their due date, to the office of the

Head of Department. Again, written explanation for any deviation.'

I nodded again.

'. . . It affords me therefore a certain degree of personal satisfaction, to note that the committee's decision is in favour of one among you whose nomination I, personally, most wholeheartedly endorse . . .'

'And you will of course continue your weekly appointments with me beyond the normal one-year period.'

I nodded a third time.

'. . . Ladies and gentlemen, it is with the greatest of pleasure that I present the inaugural 1970 Noot'n Hall Grace Dieu Award . . .'

'I know it may sound a bit like being on probation, but—'

'. . . to Mr Timothy Armstrong.'

Dr Mountford sprang back as though I had slapped him. For a split second, there was sudden silence as if someone had fired a gun. I experienced that eerie nightmare sensation of having forty faces all turn towards me at once. Then the applause broke like a thunderclap.

My immediate reaction, typical for such occasions, was to imagine it was some sort of hoax. But, all around, people were turning the palms of both hands upward and gesturing for me to stand. Hands seized my arms and urged me to my feet. As I stood, the applause surged in intensity and was reinforced by some good-natured cheering.

Totally dazed, I half staggered towards Norman. As I passed the table which seated most of the rugby team, they began a deafening footstomping which was taken up from table to table until bottles of wine began to shudder and glasses tinkled as if in an earthquake.

At last, bewildered and shaken like the survivor of an accident, I stood before a beaming Norman. He squeezed my hand and passed over the award.

'No speeches,' he said, 'it's not that sort of a pot.'

The noises behind me continued on tickover.

'Thank you Norman.' I began to recover a bit of composure. 'I mean thank *you*.'

'The follies of men's youth,' he quoted, 'are in retrospect glorious, compared to the follies of their old age.'

I had never taken him for the literary sort. How full of surprises he was.

'Does that mean I'll laugh about all this one day?' I asked.

'Hell no. It means things just get worse.'

I grinned.

'Do me a favour,' he added. 'Throw in a little engineering study next semester. You may get to like it.'

I turned and faced the hall. The applause surged again. I drank in the moment, then walked quickly back to my seat.

EPILOGUE

Traditionally, the Last Night Ball would continue throughout the night – all part of the undergraduate urge to excess. Long after the dignitaries had left, when the music had softened, movement became lazy, and conversation a murmur spiked with occasional peals of desperate laughter, I wandered out of the hall, gulped air and slipped off my tie. Flown with wine but made drunk by something far more potent and lasting than alcohol, I stumbled halfway down the hill which overlooked the golf course, and, with all the nonchalance of youth, plonked my besuited backside into the soft earth. Spreading my legs, I took the small, shiny silver trophy from my inside pocket and placed it between my feet. Then I lay back and cradled my head in the palms of my hands. I felt as proud and happy as I had ever felt.

Something about the silent black gulf in front of me, and the twinkling lights of Middle England beyond, set me musing about my past and my future. I reflected with an inward smile how my urge to play had drawn a thread through my nigh-on twenty years, even if one which unravelled in a tangle of knots and twists. Mr Adam had sought to teach me to play football, and had given me a goodly measure of adulthood. Oxo had wanted to make a rugby player of me, and had saved my self-respect. Norman told me to win a trophy, and had inspired me to an altogether different prize. And Sharon? Sharon's search for the perfect all-rounder had inspired me as well, though, if I'm honest, predominantly to an erection which, if you'd slipped a nut over the end, could have supported a couple of girders on the Firth of Forth suspension bridge.

There were better reasons for playing games than merely winning or being good. And perhaps the worst reason for setting out on a voyage was to get somewhere.

If you thought about it, it was awesome where that playful spirit might lead you. My bachelor uncle Frank had once told me that given the choice between landing a ten-pound salmon, and any woman he had ever known in his life, the woman wouldn't get a look-in. I hadn't known whether to feel pity or admiration. That urge could lead you to passion, popularity or permanent disability. It might get you nowhere. If you were lucky, it might get you a moment like this, like me, tonight.

I reached forward and picked up the tiny trophy, breathed out slowly onto the silver bowl and polished it gently on my sleeve. It was that moment when late night becomes early morning, and, in the half light, I could just make out, in proud angular capitals, my own name.

'The simple difference between life and fiction, mate,' I told myself quietly, 'is that life always has to carry on after the happy ending.'

So, the future? There would have to be, as Norman had put it, a little more engineering study next year. And lately, I had found myself frequently looking forward to the next time I would see Susan Blackwell. That gave cause for thought. Beyond that, for the time being, I didn't give a damn. The future was a bright silver lake with the surface of a mirror. I couldn't wait to muddy the waters and make ripples. No, damn it, bloody big waves.

'Clearly, he would go on to never play at Wembley, Lords or Twickenham,' I said, again out loud, a slight chuckle marring the BBC commentator's voice I had assumed. No. But there was always going to be some game to be played. That was in my make-up.

The black gulf below was slowly resolving itself into the dog-leg seventeenth with the sand trap, and, beyond, the dreamy blue, green and yellow points of light now picked out the grim contours of the Didsbury Park council estate.

'What next? Where to now?' I whispered at the future.

There was a soft noise behind me, and I turned to see Susan, shoes in hand, slowly negotiating her way down the slope. Off-the-shoulder velvet in the middle of a golf course lent her an exotic beauty which quickened my pulse. As she came close, I could see that her eyes were wild and shining. She placed a kiss on top of my head, raising suspicion that a more precise target might be beyond her.

I rose and turned, tucking the little goblet securely back inside my jacket.

'Well, what next? Where to now?' she asked breathlessly, echoing precisely my own words of a few moments earlier, if with somewhat different intent.

I hadn't quite shaken off my train of thought.

'Anyone for tennis?' I asked, smiling.

Ignoring her bewilderment, I placed my arm around her shoulders, and guided her up the hill towards the brightening day.

THE END

Portofino

Frank Schaeffer

'Some kids I met told lies to be special. I told lies to be normal . . .'

For young Calvin Becker, the son of embarrassingly over-zealous American missionaries, the family holiday on the Italian Riviera resort of Portofino is the highlight of the year. The trouble is the remaining members of his family seem incapable of ever really relaxing. His father always seems to be slipping into one of his Bad Moods, while his mother will insist on trying to convert the 'pagans' on the beach. As for his sister Janet, *she* keeps a ski sweater and a miniature bible in her suitcase because you never know when the Russians might invade and send them to Siberia before they can escape.

Calvin's Dad says everything is part of God's Plan. But this particular summer, Calvin has a few plans of his own . . . plans that involve such exuberantly pagan locals as Gino the whisky-drinking painter and the *Banini* and his boats, the very sensible and very English Bazlintons and – above all – their very lovely daughter Jennifer.

Deliciously observed and often deliriously funny, *Portofino* is a wry, affectionate and wonderfully sustained evocation of a time, a place and a particular point in a young person's life.

'A RICH BREW OF CROSS-CULTURAL COMEDY . . . SCHAEFFER, BY TURNS, IS SENTIMENTAL, CELEBRATORY, EVOCATIVE AND VERY FUNNY . . . IMMENSELY APPEALING'
Los Angeles Times

'BEAUTIFULLY WRITTEN . . . SCHAEFFER CAPTURES THE EXPERIENCE OF BOYHOOD WITH GREAT INSIGHT AND UNSELFCONSCIOUS HUMOUR . . . A CONVINCING AND OFTEN TOUCHING NOVEL'
Publishers Weekly

0 552 99749 8

BLACK SWAN

The Cuckoo's Parting Cry

Anthea Halliwell

'AN INVOLVING AND ENJOYABLE READ'
Shena Mackay

For Fidgie, a child of the pre-war Years, the long school holiday stretched blissfully ahead. With her new friend Chaz as companion for idyllic summer days by the sea, she was able frequently to escape her edgy mother and her malicious older sister, Cly. Her father, mercifully, was away from home . . .

Through Fidgie's clear eyes the events of a brief hot spell in August unfold: her family and neighbours become involved in adultery, deception, and other, darker, misdemeanours. The eight-year-old is an engaging and lively narrator; swept along in her extraordinarily compelling tale, the reader will realize that underlying Fidgie's innocent accounts of family meals, fishing trips round the bay, tree-climbing and playing at May Queens, a very adult sub-text is developing. Its conclusion is both tragic and inevitable.

Anthea Halliwell's novel marks the emergence of a delightfully individual voice and a most original storytelling talent.

0 552 99774 9

BLACK SWAN